TOMPKIN'S SCHOOL

FOR THE DEARLY DEPARTED

TABI SLICK

Copyright © 2021 by Tabi Slick
Illustrations by Kody Haskins

Edited by Sarah Burton:
AnAvidReader.com

5th Anniversary Edition, 2021.

ISBN: 978-1544695402 (First Edition, 2017)
ISBN: 978-1-7345568-1-0 (Second Edition, 2020)
ISBN: 978-1-7345568-4-1

Printed in the United States of America

www.TabiSlick.com

TRANSITIONED UNIVERSE BOOKS
BY TABI SLICK

Tompkin's School: For The Extraordinarily Talented
Tompkin's School: For The Dearly Departed
Tompkin's School: For The Resurrected

~

The Unforgivable Act
The Detective's Nightmare
The Yuletide Killer

~

Timur's Escape

~

Join the Transitioned Universe reader's group to stay in the
know about upcoming series: www.tabislick.com/join

To Wanett Carbaugh,

the most loving grandmother a girl could ask for,

your memory will live on in my heart.

We're the villains you root for in the story.

—Melissa de la Cruz, *Return to the Isle of the Lost*

A SUPERNATURAL TRILOGY
BOOK 2

I

ΛND SO IT BEGINS

- Kain -

"Thought you'd get away, did ya?" A man taunted, waving the pitchfork in hand. *"You demon!"*

I tossed in my sleep, unable to rest as the events we'd witnessed last year tormented me in my dreams. After using Mr. Valkyrien's key to unlock the library door, Izzy and I had somehow stepped into the year 1911, where we'd witnessed the nightwalkers murder Edwin. We couldn't stop it. Our powers only worked when it was close to the full moon.

"He's using his magic." The nightwalker's voice echoed in my nightmare. *"Stop him!"*

A gun sounded through the air, and the forest burst into flames. Suddenly my dream changed, and a cloaked stranger appeared in the distance, floating towards me. Taking a step closer to the figure, my body twisted in pain, and I fell to my knees.

A dark voice hissed in my head, We will fight you. We will devour you. And we will triumph over you.

I cried out, the words stinging my body like a thousand knives were thrown at my head. I was acutely aware that this was a dream because I was sure that the black-cloaked figure hadn't been there when we time traveled.

"Who are you?" I manage to gasp.

The figure hidden behind the black cloak didn't respond.

"NO!" Izzy's voice cried in the distance.

This wasn't right. Wasn't she right beside me? And this cloaked figure hadn't been there last year, so why was he showing up in my dreams? The pain subsided, and I was able to pick myself up. Pushing off the ground, I wanted to see who was underneath the cloak, but Izzy's heart pulled me in the opposite direction.

Before I had a chance to pull the hood back on the figure, the world around me rippled, as it had before, and soon the darkness was replaced by the setting sun. The cloaked figure vanished as the world changed.

"He's gone." I heard myself say, but my lips hadn't

11

moved.

Suddenly, a fire ignited in my hands as a falling sensation took over me. This was definitely not my power. Only Iz could conjure and manipulate fire. My heart skipped a beat. Finally, the free-fall sensation subsided. The flames dissipated, smoke rising from the palms of my hands. Was it even safe to touch my face?

I chuckled at the thought. What a weird thing to be concerned about.

"Lawrence," I gasped, but it wasn't my voice at all. It was my sister's.

"What do you want?" My voice came from beside me, and I looked over to see myself.

"What the hell?" I cried.

Glancing down, I saw my sister's body. Gross.

Her voice growled in my thoughts, Get out of my head!

How? I didn't even know how I had transferred my consciousness to hers in the first place. Another thought crept in, and I shivered. Was this only in my dream? Or was I actually communicating to my sister in my sleep? I didn't know which was worse.

Shaking my head, my heart flip-flopped as the falling sensation returned, and soon I was back in my own body.

Sorry, *I sent my thoughts to her.*

Izzy rolled her eyes and returned her attention back to Lawrence or Choyce. Something like that.

12

"How are you here?" Izzy asked.

"I felt your pull," Choyce replied, shoving his hands in his jeans. "I've felt your heartbeat before, but it wasn't as strong as it is now. I had to come and see if it was true."

"If what's true?" I asked.

I knew for sure that this part wasn't part of the conversation. I remembered talking about this before the winter break.

"You and your sister are the most powerful shifters I've ever sensed." Choyce paused, leaning against a tree trunk.

"Wait, you've sensed others out there?" Izzy asked.

"Some, yes. But their heartbeats are different, weaker. Yours and your brothers' are undeniably powerful."

"But how are you not, like, a hundred years old?" I asked.

"He must've followed us from the past." Izzy shrugged.

Choyce shook his head. "I didn't follow you, and I am well over a hundred."

"You don't look it." Izzy folded her arms.

Choyce laughed. "You two have a lot to learn about us."

"So, what do you want?" I asked.

"You and your sister are going to use that nifty little 'time traveling to the past' power to save my brother." These were the last words I heard as fire engulfed my entire body.

Twisting in agony, everything around me dissolved into

nothingness. The dark figure flew by me, and I tried to grab the hem of his cloak, but my world spun, and then he was gone. I closed my eyes. Shaking my head in an attempt to wake myself up. I needed to wake up, but it was like I was captive to this dream state.

The pain subsided, and I carefully opened my eyes. I wasn't in the forest anymore but on a sidewalk. I scanned my surroundings. A green sign with white letters that read 1st street combined with a waft of something rotten made me realize I could only be in one place—Sulphur. But why?

Across the street, a building lay in shambles as fresh smoke emanated from the ground around it. A swoosh of air moved just above me, and, looking up to the blue sky, a man and a woman with giant black wings like my own flew away. How was that possible? It wasn't even the full moon yet. Their heartbeats pounded in my chest, and I longed to be with them, but they disappeared before I could call out to them. The ground shook below me, and suddenly everything vanished as I fell into the darkness.

***

I woke up with a start, my entire body covered in sweat. What a messed-up dream. Ever since Iz and I'd met Lawrence last school year, we'd been having the exact same nightmare of his brother. Over and over again, we'd witness

Edwin die at the hands of the nightwalkers. Then we would travel back to our present-day only to find Lawrence there, now calling himself Choyce, demanding that we help him save his brother. I also kept dreaming about this mansion on 1st street that I knew didn't exist in Sulphur. It also seemed like Izzy, and I could communicate with each other in our dreams. As if we were living a second life while asleep. It was exhausting, to say the least.

I swung my legs over the side of the bed, pressing the little button on my nightstand as the drapes opened. Gazing out the window, I blinked as the bright sun shone through the bustling streets of New York, cascading into my bedroom.

I'd been in the city all summer, staying with my aunt and uncle in their townhouse while working a student internship as a music journalist. It wasn't anything fancy, but it kept me busy. The best part about it was that it allowed me to discover a variety of new bands to add to my playlist while getting paid for it. Not that the pay was anything to brag about, and there were a few tasks that weren't fun, like coffee runs and picking up dry cleaning for the VIPs. But I figured that was why a business would hire an intern in the first place. At any rate, it was better than staying at my dad's house with his slut wife.

Izzy had decided to stay in Oklahoma instead of coming back to the city. She wanted to stay with Lee. At first, I thought it would be awesome because I'd get a break from all the mind jumping and telepathy, but the distance had proven to not hinder our abilities around the full moon. We had to learn how to control our powers somehow. Unfortunately, the local bookstore didn't sell the latest copy of '*how not to jump into your twin sister's brain for dummies.*'

Grabbing some clothes, I headed downstairs.

"Morning!" My aunt called as she ran for the front door. "There's some money on the table for your breakfast."

"Thanks." I waved as she left.

Sometimes I had a hard time believing she was related to my dad. She was friendly, and dad was such a jerk. I still remembered when my mom was diagnosed with cancer, dad wasn't there. He didn't even call. Later on, we found out he was with his new wife. Smashing my fist on the table, I tried to remove this memory from the forefront of my mind. I had to get to work. I was already a slave to the full moon; I couldn't be a slave to the past, too.

I headed to the closest bagel shop on 22nd street and 8th avenue. It was my day to bring breakfast to the office. When out of the corner of my eye, as I crossed the busy street, a FedEx truck speed towards me. Its tires squealed as it tried to break before hitting me. The full moon flashed before my eyes, my instincts taking over as my free hand shot out, slamming against the front of the hood. My feet slid a bit as I brought the truck to a complete stop. The metal bent around my fingers, and I panicked. What if someone saw me?

16

Shaking my head, I removed my hand to find an outline left on the hood of the truck. The driver laid on his horn as he shouted obscenities at me. I couldn't get out of there fast enough, crossing the road and disappearing into the crowd. I didn't need any trouble. How was it even possible I could do that? My nerves on high alert, I counted the days of the month and realized the full moon was closer than I'd thought.

Arriving at the bagel shop, I grabbed the food and extra coffee for my boss before heading to 24th. I glanced at my watch, picking up the pace as I realized I was going to barely make it on time.

I didn't bother waiting for the crosswalk sign to light up. No one was coming. Not that it would matter because everyone in this city crossed the street like there wasn't any oncoming traffic anyway.

"Do you have a spirit full of diamonds today?" Someone called out to me.

Looking over my shoulder, a homeless man sat on the corner. His eyes locked on mine, and he smiled a partially toothless grin. For some reason, I couldn't look away. There was something familiar about his eyes, but what was it?

Someone pushed by me, knocking me out of my trance as hot coffee spilled all over my jacket.

"Crap!" I brushed the liquid off my clothes and ran the rest of the way to the office, throwing the wasted coffee into a recycling bin before entering the building.

I took the nearest elevator to my floor and prepared myself for the worst. Being late wasn't acceptable, especially not for an intern.

"Morning, Kain." The other intern, Josh, greeted.

"Morning," I replied, setting my things at the workstation across from his. "Have you seen Patrick yet?"

He shook his head. "But his assistant already dropped off our to-do list. Here."

He tossed a pile of papers over onto my desk, some falling to the floor.

"Dick." I rolled my eyes, sifting through the documents.

"Love you too, man." He laughed, grabbing a taffy and popping it in his mouth. "That's half, FYI."

"You should really think about cutting the habit." I nodded to the half-eaten bag on his cluttered desk.

"Nah." He smacked his lips, his eyes suddenly distracted by one of the reporters walking by. "Hey, Nancy!"

She barely glanced in his direction before heading to the breakroom.

"She wants me," Josh sighed.

"Yeah, whatever." I rolled my eyes, chuckling to myself as I got back to work.

"Hey, did you hear about that shadow someone saw in the subway?" Josh asked. "It was holding some guy in the air. They said this thing killed him, ripping his heart right out of his chest."

My heart raced as I remembered my last transition. It was only bits and pieces, but I remembered the subway's dingy tunnels, and the man's screams were unforgettable. The darkness took over me, and every fiber of my being begged me to take the heart. I hated myself for it. For this curse, my sister and I had to endure. My blood ran hot as my muscles tensed. I needed to calm down. To act natural.

"Yeah." I shook my head. "That's why I don't sleep on the subway."

I hoped that was believable enough.

"With all those slashings and shit? You have to stay alert." He agreed.

Desperately wanting to change the subject, I finished organizing my assignments. "Look what I got in my stack. The Fruit Bats are playing tonight."

"Folk-rock? No, thank you, that's all yours." Josh shook his head.

I probably would've said the same thing before moving to Oklahoma. Country music was still horrible, but folk was growing on me.

"Your loss." I shrugged. "Great music with Nancy. It'll almost be like a date."

"Wait, what?" Josh nearly fell out of his desk.

I smirked. "That's what it says."

"Give me that!" He snatched the paper from my hand.

His face fell, and I snickered.

"Liar." He threw the paper back at me.

"Worth it." I laughed, turning back to my computer. I didn't understand why he was so into Nancy. Sure, she was hot, but she was too into herself. The way she checked herself out in every shiny surface made that clear.

Another heartbeat erupted in my own out of nowhere, and I grabbed my chest as it fluttered. It wasn't Izzy's, I was familiar with her rhythm. A woman's shriek echoed from the front of the office. I looked up in time to see papers flying everywhere and a guy stumble back like something had run into him, but nothing was there. A stack of files fell to the ground, seemingly on their own, scattering all over the floor.

"What the—?" I stopped mid-sentence when my keyboard started typing on its own.

A word document appeared on my screen as the keyboard continued to type.

"*This isn't you.*" I read the text underneath my breath.

The ghost continued to type. *Being so professional. You need to come out and play. Meet me outside, or I'll turn this office into my own playground.*

The typing stopped, and I shook my head, realizing who it was. I stood up, locking my assignments in my desk drawer before excusing myself. Racing towards the elevators, I was determined to give that dude a piece of my mind. I wasn't going to tolerate being bullied.

"Lawrence!" I hissed once I was outside. It was insane that this guy could use his powers at any point in time, but I wasn't about to ask him how he did it. I didn't need to owe him twice.

"Please, call me Choyce." A familiar voice chuckled behind me.

I whirled around and grabbed his throat, pushing him against the nearby building. I didn't care that we were surrounded by a ton of people.

"Not cool." For once, I was glad the full moon was close, so I could use my strength.

"Relax." Choyce gasped, the veins in his neck protruding as he fought for air.

I dropped him, shaking off the rage as he coughed.

"I only meant to get your attention."

"Well, you've got it," I growled.

"Come on!" He laughed. "You need to lighten up. I thought you were the fun one."

I waved towards the building. "I'm at work."

"Yes, but you're like me. Like my brother Edwin was. You're a shifter. Practicing your gift needs to be your top priority."

"I think I'm doing just fine." I shrugged.

"Oh really?" He raised an eyebrow. "Are you truly happy only being able to use your gifts near the full moon? Randomly smashing FedEx trucks without any control?"

I frowned. "Are you stalking me?"

"Merely watching."

I laughed. "Yeah, 'cause that's less creepy."

"You could have more." He stretched his arms out wide. With a gust of wind, a dumpster on the corner suddenly shook, sending debris flying, and a magazine from a nearby newsstand flew into Choyce's hand. "You could have more. Yet, here you are. Being the *responsible* twin while your sister flutters off the deep end."

"I don't think she flutters." I waved him off, turning away.

"That's not the point." He sighed before following me. "You need to let go. Trust me. This next full moon, I'll show you how to reach your true potential. You have to stop resisting your power."

"I haven't been resisting anything. What if I don't want it?"

He grabbed my shoulder, and I glared at him.

"What you want is control. I can show you how." His brown eyes met mine with desperation.

"Then where's the journal?" I asked. I cocked my eyebrow when he looked away. "You've got it, right?"

He suddenly let go of my arm, his mouth dropping open like he was about to say something he shouldn't. "It's in a safe place."

"Can I have it, then?" I taunted.

He ran a bony hand through his ridiculously long hair. "All in due time, mate," he laughed. "But before I can give you that, I'm going to need you to do something for me."

"What's that?"

"I already told you, I need you and your twin sister to save my brother."

I shrugged. "Okay, done. How do we do that? We can't just time travel again."

"Not yet, you can't," Choyce said, tucking his hands in his pockets. "But once you break the ties between you and the full moon, you'll be transcendent."

I didn't know what that meant, but I was reasonably confident, trusting him would be the worst decision of my life. But did I have any other choice?

2
INTO THE WOODS

- Izara -

Fire. That's all I could think about these days. How the smoke twisted and curled in my hand. I looked upon it as if it were an old friend, soft and comforting. The pain it once caused me had dissipated since my last transition, and it mesmerized me.

The darkness of my potential had continuously been knocking at my door, following me. At first, I'd tried to ignore it by not using the full moon's power, but it was too enticing.

While the others weren't looking, I brought the flame that used my fingertips as kindling to my lips, breathing it in.

The burn turned to liquid as it crawled in my mouth, its sweetness too much to bear.

"You okay?" Lee asked, bringing more firewood.

I coughed as the smoke-filled my lungs.

"Yeah," I choked, curling my fingers into a fist to extinguish the flames before he could notice. "I'm fine."

Lee smiled, joining us around the campfire his dad, Shane, had lit. Staying with the Walkers had proven to be as slow and sad as I'd imagined since the passing of Lee's mom. Shane wasn't himself these days, and Lee did everything he could to distract his dad. He suggested lighting a bonfire and inviting some friends over, but as soon as Lee's dad set everything up for us, he locked himself up in his office.

"Is your dad okay?" Leslie asked, snuggled up next to Amadeus.

I still had to avoid looking him in the eye. As much as it pained me, if he was one of the students with a special ability, then it was my duty to protect him from the nightwalkers.

"He should be." Lee shrugged, sitting in the camp chair next to me.

The fire crackled as he roasted a marshmallow in its flame. What was it about the fire that attracted me so much? My hands began to heat up, and I knew a fireball was about to form in my bare hands. I clamped my hands shut, trying to prevent it from developing. What was wrong with me? Why

25

couldn't I control my power as the full moon neared?

"You cold?" Lee asked.

I shook my head, feeling my hands ignite once again. "Did you hear that noise just now?"

"What? Where?" He asked, looking behind him.

Everyone followed Lee's example, and I quickly opened my hands, throwing the fireball that ignited in my palm towards the fire, which hissed and sizzled as soon as they met.

"I didn't hear anything," Laurent said, leaning back in his chair.

I sighed with relief, glad no one noticed what I'd just done.

"Hey, so who's up for a game?" Duran asked.

"Depends on what you had in mind." Leslie laughed, nudging Tiffany, who sat next to her.

She grimaced in reply, partially listening. The look in her eyes told me she couldn't get over what happened last year, and I didn't blame her. She almost died. But would knowing what I was be too much for her? Would she go to Principal Chomsky or blab to someone else connected with the nightwalkers? It was better for all of us if she remained in the dark.

"And don't say spin the bottle." Leslie scolded him.

Duran held his hands up in defense. "Alright, alright. I was going to say flashlight tag, but if you all want spin the bottle, then I'll have to oblige, cause ya know, you can't get enough of this." He popped his collar, laughing as Leslie playfully punched his shoulder.

"Seriously, bro?" Laurent raised an eyebrow.

"Let's play a real game," Leslie said. "Who's up for flashlight tag?"

"I am." Amadeus's voice sent a shudder down my spine.

What was it about him that could have that much power over me? Why did I see images flashing before my eyes when I met his gaze? There were so many questions I had about him that I wanted answers to but couldn't ask.

"Flashlight tag could be fun if we were five." Laurent laughed.

"Come on, are we all too cool now to play flashlight tag?" Leslie groaned. "Izzy, would you like to play?"

"I'm in." I stood up. I needed to distract myself anyway.

"Me too," Lee said, slipping his hand around my waist. "I've got two flashlights in my bag."

The others stood up as Lee handed out the flashlights. We divided into two teams, agreeing that anything beyond the Walker's property was out of bounds.

"So, who wants to be—" Lee began.

"Not it!" We all shouted at once.

Lee rolled his eyes. "Fine, I'll go first, but y'all don't stand a chance. I know this property like the back of my hand."

"I'll take that as a challenge." I winked, giving him a peck on the cheek before running off into the darkness.

My heart raced as I ran as fast as I could. The calming air rushed against my ears, my breath smooth and even. Although I hadn't run this much in my life, my endurance was heightened these days. I was less sluggish, more alert, and each full moon brought me closer to this perfection. I was invincible.

I made it all the way to the woods at the edge of the property before I stopped. I shouldn't have been able to get here so quickly. Turning around, a light in the distance indicated Lee wasn't even close to finding me. A painful lump formed in my throat as I watched Duran, his brother Laurent, Tiffany, and Leslie all laughing, running around trying not to be caught by Lee. I was never going to be like them. No matter how hard I tried, I would always have this secret that would keep me from getting close to anyone.

Suddenly, the whole world flashed yellow, and I was no longer surrounded by woods in the dark. The sun was high and the air smelled of hot dogs and asphalt. Another heart beat inside of me, and I grabbed my chest. There was something familiar about the feeling. A twig snapped, jolting me back into the darkness of the woods.

"Stop playing games!" I shouted, remembering why this heartbeat was so familiar.

It was the same one I'd felt right after the event with

Lee's mother. Something had followed me out of the Walker's house that night, nearly killing me.

"Show yourself!" I called again, allowing the anger inside of me to surge.

My hands ignited into flames, and I stood, waiting for him to reveal himself. His warm breath hit my cheek. I spun around, but he was gone. I threw the fireball from my right hand and saw it form into a human shape.

"Ow!" He exclaimed. "Ouch, that's hot!"

His body shimmered into sight as he ripped off his flaming shirt, exposing an extremely pale and thin torso. He had a round scar in the center of his chest, and I wondered where he could've gotten something like that. It looked like it had been painful.

"What was that for?" Choyce asked, his brown leather eyes wide, feigning innocence.

"You know what." I glared.

"My lady." He took my hand to kiss it, but I pulled it away before he could do so.

"What do you want?" I asked, crossing my arms.

"Can't a man simply stop by and say hello?"

"Not you."

"How did you know it was me?" His eyebrows rose.

"Well, for starters, I know you're the only one who can make themselves invisible. It also had to be you because of your annoying way of getting too close to people's personal

29

space."

"My apologies." He swung his arm across his body at the waist, bowing low.

"Would you stop with all that already?" I hissed. "It's not like we're in—like—1752."

"Oh, fun fact. Did you know that in 1752, eleven days went missing"—he snapped his fingers—"just like that? You see—"

Would he ever shut *up*?

I spun on my heel and sprinted in the other direction, determined to get as far away from him as possible. But it was pointless. The air wooshed next to me, and he was running effortlessly by my side, his long, messy blond hair flying in tangles behind him.

"You think this is running?" He taunted.

Shaking my head, I pressed myself forward, gaining the lead. He chuckled behind me, and I ground my teeth. Throwing care to the world, I leaped over the fence, forgetting about flashlight tag and everything else. The only thing that remained was the strong desire to beat Choyce. Nothing would give me greater pleasure than ignoring him altogether, but easier said than done. Besides my brother, he was the only other person I knew who was like us.

He whooshed past me, striking my competitive nerve, and I urged my legs to move faster.

Don't hurt yourself, his voice slithered into my

thoughts.

"Get out of my head!" I spat, grabbing a loose branch and throwing it at him, but he leaped out of the way at the last second.

"You forget that I'm your match." He raced back to my side.

"What do you mean by that?"

"You can communicate with the past, as I can with the future. I knew you would do that."

I stopped in my tracks so fast it took him a second to come to a halt.

"Then how come you didn't see that coming?"

He ran back through the trees to stand next to me. "It's complicated."

"I've got time." I shrugged.

Looking away, he balled his spindly fingers into fists, cracking his knuckles.

"No," he finally replied. "You don't get to know that."

"I don't *get* to know?" I exclaimed.

He swallowed hard, his eyes glazed over, reminding me of when he was just Lawrence, an older brother looking to protect Edwin. I liked it better when that was all he was—someone from my dreams.

"It's personal." He stepped in close, his warm cinnamon breath on my ear. "And, love, we're not that close."

"You know my secret. How much closer could we

possibly get?"

He stepped away, his hands running through his hair in frustration.

"I know you want me to help you save your brother," I said, "but it's been a long time since 1911, and I don't trust you."

A line appeared between his brows, and he growled. "You want to talk about trust? You and your brother promised to warn us if something bad happened as a result of us going after the journal. You *used* us! And I lost my brother for it."

I swallowed hard. He wasn't wrong, but it wasn't like we did it on purpose or didn't try to save Edwin. With the school's nightwalkers working against us, we never stood a chance.

"I'm sorry," I replied.

"Save it. If you want to try to make it up, you can help me. So, will?"

I paused.

"If I told you why my powers aren't reliable, would you help me or not?" He repeated.

I folded my arms. "Maybe."

He cocked his brow, and I faltered. He knew I was bluffing. He knew what I really wanted was the journal, but that was his leverage over me. I was sure he'd withhold that until he'd gotten everything he wanted out of us.

"Do you know what happened to my brother?"

I nodded. "I saw him get shot."

"How?"

"I was there. But how did you know?

"After it happened, I felt your heartbeats. I tried to find you, but then you vanished. You can go back there. We can go together and change it. To save Edwin."

I shook my head. "The key is what took us back in time."

"The key was just a mechanism that activated your time traveling power."

I frowned. "You know about the key?"

He paused, glancing away as tears threatened to spill. The emotion of losing his brother must've still hurt him as I knew it would be if it was Kain.

"I've only heard rumors." He confessed. "But there's enough truth attached to them that I'm certain these keys are tied to our powers somehow."

Pausing, he looked into my eyes with desperation. "You can time travel again."

"I wouldn't know where to begin."

He smiled. "I can show you how to tap into your power."

I shook my head in disbelief. "How can you be so sure?"

"It's just a theory, but I believe I know why I can't communicate actively with the future." He folded his arms.

"Many of our powers are tied to our siblings somehow. You still have your brother, so that makes you significantly more powerful than I. But I have more years and knowledge. I can show you how to tap into your powers whenever you want and travel to the past. We need each other."

I considered his words carefully. The thought of learning how to control my powers outside of the full moon excited me. It would also make the fight against the nightwalkers and the school a lot easier. But something told me trusting Choyce was a bad idea. What had he been doing for over a hundred years? Why did he choose now to come back? Why wouldn't he give us the journal? This school killed his brother. Wouldn't he be just as determined to bring them down as we were? It didn't seem like he cared about that at all, though. Trying to figure out the reason behind Choyce's... choices was like trying to find logic in a sea of madness.

"Think about it," Choyce said, and with that, he vanished, leaving me alone in the night.

3

TIME TRAVELER

- Kain -

I tossed and turned in my sleep as strange images flooded my mind. I was acutely aware of Izzy's heart beating within my own, and somehow, I was seeing her dreams. Stars twinkled above as Choyce strolled towards a large building with a sign reading The Artesian Hotel. With top hat in hand, he looked like he'd just stepped out of The Great Gatsby.

He followed the throngs of people all piling into the hotel dressed for a party. Glancing around at the street, I immediately recognized it as 1st Street in Sulphur, Oklahoma. It was the same spot I'd dreamt about before, except this time instead of a building in shambles, it was of a grand four-story brick covered hotel.

Suddenly, it was as if I could hear Choyce's thoughts, see his memories as if I was reliving his past. It was the summer of 1919 and boy, it had been a good one. Lawrence, calling himself Bart these days, was much closer to finding the others he sensed were like him. He could feel their pull and taste their thirst for blood. It was as strong as his own. Whenever he passed by The Artesian, their presence was strong, and he knew that this was where he would find them. But he couldn't just storm through all the rooms he had waited. He'd foreseen this event and bided his time until he could negotiate himself onto the guest list of the annual party the faculty of the Tompkin's Academy put on.

It was lucky that he was even able to foresee this event in the first place. Something had been wrong with his powers ever since the nightwalkers killed his brother, Edwin. He couldn't actively communicate with the future as he'd been able to before, and his abilities weren't progressing anymore. He could feel that he hadn't reached his true potential yet, but something prevented this from happening, and he suspected it had everything to do with his brother's death.

"Name?" The man at the lobby entrance asked.

"Bart Bessler," Lawrence replied, handing him his invitation.

"Excellent, sir," the man said, ushering him inside.

A band played a lively tune as dancers did the shimmy,

and champagne was passed about in excess.

"Bart!" A familiar voice called.

Lawrence turned just as a man dressed in his best danced his way through the crowd towards him. A slender woman in a silk evening gown and pinned up hair wrapped in a band followed behind him.

"Robert," Lawrence greeted, shaking the man's hand.

"You remember the little misses," Robert said, after shaking Lawrence's hand, enthusiastically.

"Of course." Lawrence was sure he'd never met her in his life. "It's nice to see you."

"Listen, Bart." Robert clapped a hand on his shoulder. "Helen and I've got someone we'd like you to meet."

"Oh, now I don't want any setups," he said.

"Truly, Bart, you really must meet her!" Helen exclaimed.

"Well, if the lady says so." Lawrence chuckled.

"Attaboy!" Robert cheered, slapping him on the back and leading the way.

"But first, I'm going to need to see a man about a dog," Lawrence replied.

"Oh, but of course." Robert's composure turned severe. "First things first. That's important business."

They all laughed as they headed towards the bar. Lawrence didn't know why, but his heart skipped a beat when he saw her. Leaning against the bar, her back was turned away from him, and all he could see was her vibrant red hair that lay in neat waves. Her deep blue dress clung to her physique, accentuating her lustful shape and pale complexion. Who was she?

"Three of your finest, sir," Robert called to the bartender.

"Well, hello," Helen greeted a blond woman who made her way to the group. "Bart, this is Mary."

"Oh, how do you do," Lawrence said.

"Just swell," the lady named Mary swooned. "Robert and Helen have told me so much about you."

"Indeed, I'm sorry about that." He joked, eyeing the redheaded woman who was making her way farther and farther away.

He swallowed his drink whole, determined to meet this mysterious woman.

"Excuse me." Lawrence nodded to the lady.

"Well, won't you ask me to dance?" She asked as Lawrence walked away. "Where are you going?"

Robert called for him, but he ignored their attempts. He was already distracted by the weight of the other beating heart that threatened to burst through his chest. It was her. It had to be her he was feeling. It was the only thing that made sense.

He followed her across the dance floor before she turned down a narrow doorway and disappeared. A hand on his arm halted his advances.

"There you are!" Robert exclaimed, a slur in his words.

Helen and Mary giggled at his side.

"Let's dance!" Helen suggested.

"That sounds marvelous." Mary's bright eyes widened as she stared at Lawrence in a sort of dazed way.

Lawrence had no quick response to get out of the situation, and all of a sudden was dancing. Dancing and women were the last things on his mind. Well, except for one woman. He looked all around the room for the luscious redhead, but she was nowhere to be seen. He glanced down at the lady in his arms and immediately regretted it. Her eyes were as wide as a kitten, and she looked as though she'd never seen a man in her life.

"Don't you just love jazz?" Mary asked.

"Eh, sure." He smiled. "It's swell."

All of a sudden, he saw something glisten brightly. The intensity of the light made him squint.

"What's wrong?" Mary's high-pitched voice asked, but Lawrence chose to ignore it.

Once the light subsided, he couldn't believe what his eyes were seeing.

***

I was getting pretty tired of seeing Izara's dreams and knowing that they were all about Choyce. I just wanted to get back to school. But then I remembered what school we were headed to, and I cringed.

It was all too much to think about. First, a guy who should've been dead showed up looking as though he hadn't aged a day to tell me he needed my sister and me to save his brother. The brother whose murder I witnessed in 1911 by the employees of the Academy called nightwalkers. This was the same school I was *currently* enrolled in now. And apparently, Izara was only able to actively time travel because I was around. Otherwise, something caused her power not to function correctly, like Choyce's ability. What did that make me? The freaking sidekick? Why did Izzy get to have all the cool powers?

Thinking about Choyce's offer, it felt a little manipulative to dangle the promise of receiving the journal in exchange for teaching us to control our powers and save his brother. I didn't trust him. Hell, I didn't even really like him, but it would be irresponsible not to have full control over our powers when bringing down an influential school like Tompkin's Academy. I'd witnessed firsthand what the nightwalkers could do, and I wasn't about to let them carry on. I just wished he'd give me all the facts straight off the bat. Everything he said was all too secretive for my liking.

Choyce and I arrived at the school, and as we gathered

40

our things from the taxi, I noticed many new faces. Hopefully, this meant that we'd have a pretty good basketball team this year to keep our winning record.

"Do you play basketball?" I asked.

Choyce snickered. "Not at all."

I shrugged. It was worth a shot. "You should stop by Chomsky's office."

"Oh, good old Chomsky. How is she? Still the librarian?"

"No, she's the Principal."

"Tsk-tsk. Have we no standards?" He shook his head, grabbing his bags and heading for the front office.

I chuckled to myself as I headed for the dorms. I entered the old familiar building to be welcomed by first-year students' sounds asking for directions and the RA shouting at a group of seniors for one reason or another.

"Hey, Joe," I called to the RA. "Can I get my key?"

"I don't want to see that in here again." He warned the laughing teens. "Hate seniors during the first week."

"Sorry?" I asked.

"Nothing." He sighed. "Room key, you said?"

"Yeah."

"Okay, follow me." We headed back to his office as he hopped on his computer. "Huh, looks like your last roommate requested a change, so you'll be roomed with the new junior."

"Who's that?" I asked.

"Choyce Barton, it looks like."

"Sounds good." I was pretty sure this would be a lot better than rooming with Amadeus. Anything was better than that.

"Here's your key," Joe said, handing it to me. "Need me to show you where it's at?"

"Nah, I'll manage."

Leaving the office, I headed for the second floor that housed the juniors and looked for my door number. I was definitely glad that I had a new roommate. I wouldn't have to deal with the rage that bubbled within me whenever Amadeus was around. He always had some way of making me want to punch him in the face. I wasn't sure why, but I wouldn't hold back if I ever did find out.

Once I found my room, I threw my bag on the floor, crashing on a nearby bed.

"Roomie!" Choyce called from the doorway as he entered.

"Don't call me that." I groaned.

"Whatever, love," Choyce said in the creepiest high-pitched voice ever. "Don't mind me I'll just be taking the window bed. I never got to have the window bed when I last came here."

"And when was that again, old man?" I asked sarcastically.

"Ah, those were the days," he said, throwing his

42

suitcase in the closet without bothering to unpack.

"So, did Principal Chomsky recognize you?" I asked, knowing it was the million-dollar question.

"Absolutely not. And, come to think of it, I'm rather offended because I used to spend so much time in the library. I mean *literally* days. There's just no appreciation nowadays."

He waved his hand, and suddenly is suitcase unzipped itself, sending his clothes flying onto hangers and folding themselves into drawers.

"Whoa, that's pretty cool." I sat up. "How did you manage to untie yourself from the full moon, anyway?"

"All things in due time." He avoided my question as he sat down in his desk chair, spinning around.

"So, what else can you do? Besides your failed power of predicting the future."

His foot landed on the desk, bringing his chair to a halt. "Communicating. I communicate with the future and still can. Sometimes. I just can't time travel."

"Yeah, okay." I shrugged. "What else?"

"I can also see everything."

"I get it. You can see into the future."

"No." He turned to me. "Not just that, I can literally see everything. It's a bit overwhelming at first, but when I focus, I can see even the smallest piece of lint or count the dust floating about."

"That must be a headache."

"You've no idea. I can also make myself invisible, although you know that."

"That one's got to come in handy," I said.

"Well, I've been known to sneak a peek in the gals' dormitory."

I laughed. That wasn't what I meant, but whatever.

"Want a whiskey?" He asked, motioning for his backpack, and suddenly a bottle flew out, landing on his desk with two glasses.

"Um, sure." I shrugged. "How'd you get that, anyway?"

"Come on, your new roommate is over a hundred years old. I've had to go through my fair share of IDs."

He poured a small amount of the brown liquid into the glasses, handing me one.

"Cheers," I said, taking a sip.

I nearly choked as the hot liquid made its way down, but I kept my composure. I'd tried worse things.

"Smooth," Choyce whispered.

"So, you seem to have this whole thing figured out. When are you going to help me?"

"What thing?" He asked.

"You know, this whole magic business."

He coughed on his drink as the room filled with his laughter.

"Sorry?" He managed to say in between bouts of

snickering. "You think this is magic?"

I shrugged. "What else could it be?"

"No," he said, setting his glass aside. "This is so much more than that. Don't you get it?"

I didn't have a better answer for him. What else could this be?

"My parents didn't even know," Choyce said. "They obviously never had abilities like we do, so we didn't get these powers from them. So, where'd they come from?"

"Do you know?" I asked, taking another sip. "'Cause I sure don't."

"Well, not really." He caved. "I haven't quite put that one together yet, but I can tell you that this is so much darker than your so-called magic."

"And how are Mr. Valkyrien and Principal Chomsky still alive?" I wondered.

"Beats me." He shrugged. "I figured they'd be long gone by now. If they were shifters like us, then we'd be able to feel their heartbeats, or I'd at least be able to sense them."

"Then are they human?" I asked.

Choyce shook his head. "That's the only thing I'm certain of. Like us, they're not mere mortals."

The room went quiet as we sipped our drinks, both deep in thought. If they weren't human, then what could they be?

"So,"—I put my drink down on my desk—"Will you

help me control my powers? Show me how you can access your power whenever you want?"

"Sure. I'll help you. We must all have full use of our powers if we're to save my brother."

"Cool," I said, standing up to clean my glass.

"Catch!" He said, suddenly throwing his glass in the air.

Eyes widening, my reflexes kicked in as I stretched my hand out, catching the glass in the air as whiskey spilled on the floor and the glass shattered in my grasp.

"What the hell?" I exclaimed.

"Oh, guess that's not your power."

"Are you insane?"

"Possibly, but I thought you could freeze things."

"No, that's Izzy's," I said, grabbing something to clean up the mess. "But you knew that already."

"Oh, that's right. It was worth a try."

"It's not even the full moon. It wouldn't have worked even if it was my power."

"Have you checked the calendar recently? It's soon, and the more you practice having your ability now, the easier it will be to master once you're unleashed from the full moon."

"And how might one do that?" I asked.

"You'll see soon enough. For now, you just need to challenge yourself. Put yourself in situations where you're forced to use the instincts that could only come from your power."

"Like jumping off a cliff?" I joked.

"Exactly."

My jaw dropped. "I think I'll be calling in sick that day."

"How else do you suppose you'll gain control over your ability to fly?"

"I take it you've tried this?" I asked in return.

"Something like that." His eye contact was unwavering, and I knew he was serious.

"You'd have to be suicidal." I shook my head.

"Maybe so." He shrugged, standing up from his chair. "It all depends on how much the journal's worth to you."

With that, he headed out of the room, leaving me with a lot to think about.

4

GONNA BE A NIGHTMARE

- Izara -

Stepping onto the familiar green grass of the quad, gazing out at the old campus around me, I couldn't believe how ordinary it all was. A masked monster, a wolf, hiding behind a plain red cape. On the outside, it hadn't changed, the same brick buildings standing strong upon the manicured lawn, but it was built upon innocent blood.

Students greeted each other after the long break like nothing had happened. Like the Academy hadn't changed. I didn't know what I was expecting. Maybe for everything to be less cheerful, to look more doom and gloom. The students walked about the path I'd followed Lawrence and Edwin in 1911 as if it was nothing. It was the same path that had led to Edwin's death, and everyone was acting as if nothing had happened at all.

To them, nothing had, but I knew better. This school was not as pleasant as it presented itself to be. It had secrets. Every single person around me could be one of the nightwalkers. It was ridiculous to think Chuck had been working alone. But who could it be? Who could've been working with Chuck?

"Hey, look who I found," Lee said, interrupting my thoughts.

"Izzy!" A familiar voice squealed as I got pulled into a hug.

"Hi," I said, realizing it was Kia. "How was your summer?"

"It was spectacular," Kia replied, stepping back as she did a twirl.

Her hair was chopped into an asymmetrical bob, and her black and maroon highlights were gone, replaced with rose gold. "What do you think?"

"Wow! That's definitely a change. It's beautiful." It was definitely something to get used to.

She gushed. "Come on, let's drop off our stuff at the dorms. We need to catch up."

"Wait one second," Lee said, grabbing my free hand just as I was about to leave, pulling me in close. "Are you forgetting something?"

"Um, I can't imagine what." I playfully pondered for a moment. "I've got my bags, my phone... nope, I think I've got everything."

He chuckled, leaning in for a kiss. Our lips barely touched when Kia whistled, causing me to blush.

"I'll see you later," he said before handing me my bags and heading back to his truck.

"Come on." Kia grinned, linking arms with me.

"See you later, Lee!" Kia waved over her shoulder as we walked towards the bridge to the dorms. "It seems like you two had a good summer together, huh?"

"Yeah," I said, trying to forget about the awkward silence that had crept into our conversations whenever Lee's mom came up.

Lying to Lee was the hardest thing I had to do, which made me sick to think about. I tried to push the memory of it out of my thoughts. I needed to react the way any other girlfriend would in these situations, but it wasn't normal. Usually, girlfriends didn't turn into monsters each full moon or kill their boyfriend's mom.

"It's been great." I lied.

"You two are the cutest. We'll have to make a celebrity super-couple nickname for you two like Izarlee or Lezar."

"Ha! Please no." I shook my head, entering the girls'
dorm.

After checking in, getting our keys, and being
reminded of orientation, we made our way up to the second
floor.

Kia groaned. "If Principal Chomsky's speech is as long
and dull as it was last year, I swear—"

"Don't worry, I'm sure it will be." We laughed, pulling
our luggage up the stairs. "And I'm sure Mr. Valkyrien with the
long neck will be just as weird."

"The biology teacher? I think I could live my entire life
happily without seeing his beady eyes again."

Osbel Valkyrien was in charge of teaching the sciences,
and he also worked in the library. He was definitely a strange
sight to behold, with his foggy eyes, the longest neck I'd ever
seen, and the attention span of a goldfish. Oh, and apparently,
he used to be the Principal of Tompkin's Academy back in
1911, but that was something Kain and I couldn't tell anyone.
There was also the gold key both he and Principal Chomsky
wore around their necks. What was it? Who were they talking
to on the other side? And how had I been able to use this to
activate my time traveling power?

"I really wish this school would invest in some
elevators." Kia huffed as we finally made it to the second-floor
landing. "I mean, what would they do if they got a student that
couldn't take the stairs?"

I shrugged. "Maybe they'd hire people to carry them up. Or just put them on the first floor."

Kia laughed. "I think that last one's probably what they'd do."

I nodded as we rolled our luggage down the long hall.

"Here's room seven." Kia motioned to the door on our right, and we entered the dorm room.

I noticed that it was pretty much identical to our room from last year, from the spacious closet on one side to the gigantic window that spanned the entire space of the far wall.

"Okay, this room is amazing!" Kia exclaimed.

I shrugged. "It looks the same to me."

"Uh, no, it's *way* better. Look, we even have our own bathroom."

"What?" I spun around to see what she was talking about.

Sure enough, to the left of the doorway, there was another door that opened up to a bathroom.

"No more community showers." I sighed, entering the large bathroom. A giant mirror hung above a double sink vanity, and a shower bathtub combo was installed on the opposite side. A linen closet and a door closed off the toilet, which completed the bathroom in the far corner.

"This is awesome," I said, genuinely excited about not having to wait for hours for a shower.

"Now I know exactly where we can lay our makeup

out." She spread her hands across the vanity, a huge smile plastered on her face.

We heard a door open behind us and jumped.

"Did you see her?" A girl's voice came from the other side of the bathroom. "It's like she totally gained fifty pounds over the summer."

The two girls came around the corner of the bathroom and stopped when they saw us.

"Uh, what are you two doing in our bathroom?" The girl asked.

"Your bathroom?" Kia's eyebrows shot up. "What are you doing in *our* bathroom?"

"I don't think so." She shook her head, causing her blond curls to fall over her bare shoulder. "This is our bathroom. Our room connects right there."

"Well, it looks like we'll be sharing. I'm Izzy and this—" I stretched my hand out to greet her, but she crossed her arms.

"That's not happening." The girl scoffed. "I'm calling daddy. Uncle Theodore was supposed to give us our own suite."

My jaw fell, unsure if I'd heard her correctly. Was her uncle the president of the school? If that was true, then that could only mean one thing. That she was related to Chuck, the guy who'd kidnapped and tortured Kain and me for weeks last year. He wanted us to prove we were monsters. He'd nearly buried Tiffany in the quarry. What sort of family was the Tompkins?

"Come on." The girl ordered her friend to follow her.

"Wow." Kia rolled her eyes. "What a brat."

"Seriously."

"Cute shirt, though." She shrugged, referring to the girls off the shoulder floral blouse. "But that attitude? She needs to take it down a notch."

"Just a notch?" I asked skeptically.

"At least."

We were both a little disappointed about having to share the bathroom, mostly since our neighbors were so rude. I was also worried because she was someone who could be a potential danger. What if her uncle put her in the room next door on purpose? What if she found out about what I was and turned me into the nightwalkers? Could she be one of them? Would she come into our room at night and slit my throat?

5

THE RESISTANCE

- Kain -

Her skin glistened in a way no ordinary human should, and Lawrence knew she had to be like him. Was she the one he'd been sensing this whole time? If so, why was she here?

"Is everything alright, Bart?" Mary asked as the song they were dancing to came to an end.

"Of course," Lawrence replied.

"Aren't you two darling!" Helen exclaimed.

"You've done it again, baby, matching Bart up here with Mary." Robert chuckled, kissing his wife on the cheek.

"Oh, you two." Mary blushed.

Lawrence tapped his foot impatiently. He didn't know how long he could keep up the polite conversation. He had to get away and find the red-haired girl.

"Oh, I think I just saw an old colleague of mine. It'd be rude not to say hello." He said as the song changed, swearing he wouldn't get roped into another dance. "Excuse me."

He scanned the room again for the mysterious woman. Suddenly, he spotted her on the opposite side of the room, chatting near one of the few black men in the room. Lawrence was taken aback by the dynamic between them, as if they were the only two people in the room. The man whispered something in her ear, and the most blindingly white smile spread across her face.

Lawrence's eyes locked on hers from where he stood and could've sworn he heard his own jaw drop. Her eyes were as yellow as the sun. At that moment, a strange sensation ran through him like a stampede was galloping through his heart. He grabbed his chest as another swarm of heartbeats flooded him, and he thought for sure it would burst. What was she doing to him?

Blinking away the tears that threatened to spill from the pain, he noticed that her glowing face was ever so subtly tense, and her eyes darkened for a second before going back to their vibrant shade of gold. She wasn't happy to see him; he was sure of that. Did she even know who he was? Did she also have the ability to sense that he was like her? If so, he'd think she'd be happy to see him.

The man that accompanied her glanced over, glaring at him as another swarm of beating hearts erupted inside of him. Was it possible that this man with her was also a shifter?

"Hey!" a voice exclaimed, and I shot up from my desk, leaving behind a puddle of drool.

Blinking, I realized I was still sitting in my dorm room. I must've fallen asleep hereafter Choyce had left.

"Are you okay?"

I knew I'd slept but didn't feel rested at all. That dream was so real, it had to be more of a vision. This must've been what Izzy had been trying to describe to me when she first had dreams of the brothers, Edwin and Lawrence. Although, Lawrence was now Choyce who, in my current dream, called himself Bart. Choyce had a lot of explaining to do.

"Kain," Choyce nudged his shoulder.

"Yeah, I'm fine," I finally said, rubbing the sleep from my eye. "Why did you decide to come back now?"

"I told you, I sensed your power." He sat down on the bed. "You and your sister have what's necessary to go back in time and save Edwin."

"And why were you there in 1919?"

A grave look spread across his face, and I could tell that he knew exactly what I was talking about.

"Why do you want to know?" He shrugged, heading over to his desk and picking up his room key.

I stood up, my jaw clenched as the anger boiled inside of me. "You're not going anywhere until I get some answers. All last year my sister and I searched for answers. We needed the journal, and we almost *died* trying to get it. The one thing that could finally take down this school, and you're withholding it so that we can just risk our lives again without anything upfront? You've got to give me something."

He turned and shrugged.

"We need to know *something*." I blocked his path on his way out. "Please answer the question. Give me anything. You're the one who told my sister that the truth lies in the history of this place."

"It does." He interrupted, pausing as he met my gaze straight on. "This school was made to take out shifters like us.

"Yeah, well, after the president's nephew kidnapped me and tortured Iz and me for weeks, I kinda figured." I rolled my eyes. "But what are we? Why are we like this?"

"The journal won't answer those questions," he said.

"Can you, then?" I asked, knowing it was a long shot.

Choyce took a deep breath, hesitating, and a chill ran through me. He knew something. He had to. His eyes shifted to one side, and he seemed to be struggling with something.

He shook his head. "I don't have a clue."

My heart sank as I realized that we were right back to square one.

"What we can do is be stronger. Bringing my brother

back will increase our collective power, and we'll be able to take out the ones who did this to us and all the other innocent students. But only if we're all together."

"I'd hardly call us innocent."

I was sure he was as guilty as my sister and I. What with him transitioning for over a century now, he'd had to of left a good deal of bodies behind him.

"My brother didn't kill a soul!" Choyce cried, his eyes pleading. "He'd only transitioned once, and he was so frightened of himself that he chained himself to a tree. He died without any blood on his hands."

I didn't know what to say to that. I definitely had blood on my hands. Remembering the first time I'd taken a life, the look in his eyes as the millionaire took his last ragged breath. I shivered at the memory, reliving the darkness that had taken over me. I didn't want to feel like that again, and yet, with each full moon, the darkness threatened. But somehow, I was able to get myself to Collings Castle before the darkness tempted me. That is, until my internship in New York. I squeezed my eyes shut, not wanting to think about it.

"You can have the journal," Choyce finally said, and I looked up at him in shock. "It won't give you the answers you want, though."

"What do you mean?"

He ran a frustrated hand through his long hair that passed his shoulders. "I've read through the whole journal; it

59

says nothing about putting a stop to this school."

I shook my head. "That's impossible. Theodore Tompkin said it had a way of getting rid of what he called '*angels,*' which I'm sure actually means Principal Chomsky and whoever the Assembly are."

"He was misinformed. The only thing that journal does is reveal how sick and twisted the founder of this school truly was," Choyce replied. "True, that would ruin the school, but that's not enough. This school murdered my brother. They have to pay the ultimate price."

I paused, hoping he didn't mean death by his use of ultimate price. The school needed to be stopped, and we needed proof to end it, but couldn't we just leave it at that? I didn't like that he was just so quick to kill, just like Izzy was turning out to be. How could we keep what little humanity remained if we just went off the rails with revenge?

Despite all this, I couldn't, in all good conscience, be the one to turn him away. How many lives had the nightwalkers taken over the last century? How could I not want the school to pay for all the rotten things they did to those students? To me? How could I not be furious? No, if what Choyce was saying was true, then I wasn't the only party here who needed to agree to help him. If Choyce was going to get my help, he would have to persuade Izzy. If he couldn't convince her to help, then the whole thing wouldn't work.

"Okay," I finally replied. "I'll help you get your

brother back and with your revenge against this school, but no one innocent can be harmed in the process."

He sighed with relief. "Of course."

"And you've got to get my sister on board."

"No problem." His five o'clock shadow-chin lifted, confidently.

It amazed me that he could grow a full beard, but then I remembered, despite his looks, how old he actually was.

"I'll get right on that," he said. "Coming to the cafeteria?"

"Sure," I said, smiling to myself as we left the room. It would definitely be harder to convince my sister than Choyce seemed to think.

We made our way down the path leading to the main campus when, suddenly, my muscles shook, and a surge of anger rose from the center of my body. The pain of it nearly brought me to my knees.

"What's going on?" Choyce asked.

"Careful," I growled, grabbing his shoulder for support as my muscles twitched. "Amadeus."

"Who?" he asked.

There was no need for me to answer as the brown, curly-haired guy knocked his shoulder into me. He glanced back at me, and my bones shook in rage. It was like every bone in my body wanted to break.

"I see," Choyce said, his eyes widening.

61

"Why isn't he affecting you?" I asked when Amadeus was finally out of earshot, and my muscles relaxed.

He shrugged. "No idea."

"Can't you sense if he's one of us? If he's a shifter?" I asked.

"I can't sense a heartbeat from him," he replied.

"Isn't that strange? Shouldn't there be one?"

Choyce made a face. "Human hearts are a little harder to sense. There are so many of them."

I shook my head, not really knowing what to make of that. Amadeus couldn't be human, but if he wasn't a shifter, then what was he?

Choyce glanced back, a look of interest spreading across his face before we continued our trek down the path.

I wondered why Choyce seemed unaffected by Amadeus. Something strange was going on. I couldn't put my finger on precisely what it was, but I knew it couldn't be good.

We got to the section of the trail where the two paths met leading to the dorms, one to the girls' the other to ours. Izzy and Kia's chatter met my ears, and I knew we were getting close to the bridge to the main campus.

"Oh, that must be Izzy," Choyce said. "I'll catch up with you in a minute."

"You're going to ask her now?"

"Why not?" He turned towards the corner and spotted the girls heading our way. "No time like the present, I say."

I waved towards them and kept walking. When I stepped onto the bridge, my hand firmly planted on the handrail, I was suddenly free falling. Even though my feet were still on the bridge, my heart dropped as I fell. The air grew cold around me, and my vision blurred.

6

I CHOOSE YOU

- Kain -

The full moon flashed before my eyes, and I was no longer standing on the bridge but back in the woods staring at Choyce walking in my direction. I must've been in Izzy's mind. I hated how my powers had a life of their own when the full moon neared, and it seemed to be getting worse.

"What do you want?" My mouth moved, but it was Izzy's voice and not my own.

"Just coming to say hello." Choyce grinned a crooked smile.

"Fine, hi," Izzy replied, dripping with disgust as she crossed her arms.

"Okay," Kia said beside us. "This is getting awkward, so I'm going to go. Catch you over there?"

"No, I'll go with you." It was a dizzying sensation as I moved against my will, a passenger in Izzy's mind.

"Izzy." Choyce stepped closer, blocking our path.

"It's Izara to you." I could feel her annoyance as if it were my own, and I chuckled to myself. She really didn't like Choyce.

"Izara," he corrected, holding his hands up in defense. "I need to talk to you for a second."

"Seriously?" Izzy exclaimed.

"It's about the full—er—research you were asking about."

Izzy heaved a sigh. "Fine. Kia, I'll meet you over there."

"Cool." Kia waved, shooting a curious yet worried glance at Choyce before heading down the path.

Something pushed against my temples. *I know you're there, Kain.* Izzy sent her thoughts to me. *Do you mind hopping out of my head?*

I'll try, I chuckled.

Ouch! Jeez, volume, please? she replied.

The pinching sensation returned. I shook my head, trying to return to my own body. My stomach flip-flopped as the sense of the ground being ripped out from underneath me returned. The full moon flashed around me, instantly returning

65

me to my body standing on the bridge. I must've looked insane while in Izzy's head.

"Hey!" Kia greeted, her eyes narrowing when I came into view. "Are you feeling okay? You look like you've been standing too long."

"Er, yeah." I coughed. "Just a bit of a headache."

"Want to join me for an early dinner?" Kia asked. "Izzy and this blond guy have issues to work out."

"Sure." I followed her across the quad, a bit disappointed that I wouldn't be able to witness Izzy's reaction to Choyce's proposal.

But maybe it was better to leave them alone. At least I didn't feel like my brain was being squeezed out like the last bit of ketchup.

Upon entering the cafeteria, the familiar scent of freshly cooked barbecue flooded my senses. It was one of the only things that made this school bearable. There were many things this school failed at, like not murdering their students for one thing, but the food was one thing they got right. They could've skimped on anything, like choosing laminate over the gray tiles. Or opting for cheap fluorescents rather than the chandeliers that hung from the vaulted ceilings. But the school had gone all out both on the decor and the food, which I appreciated. After we got our food, we found a table in the corner and waited for Izzy to join us while wondering how the meeting was going.

***

- Izara -

I didn't know how, but Kain was able to jump out of my mind. At least now, I could focus more on the task at hand, which was to get rid of Choyce.

"So?" I raised an eyebrow. "You're here to convince me to help you time travel to save your brother so Kain will join you?"

Choyce's gave an incredulous stare. I could tell he had no idea that Kain and I had the power to head-hop and that I'd witnessed the entire conversation he'd just had with my brother.

"How did you know?"

"The full moon is nearing. You've no idea the kind of power we have. Despite all of your *sensing*." I put the last word in air quotes.

His blond brows drew together.

I chuckled. "So, you never saw through your brother's eyes?"

"No. That must just be you two."

"Ha!" I gave a smug smile. "Guess you're not as powerful as you thought."

"Anyway." He shrugged, moving on and intentionally ignoring my taunt. "How about it, then?"

67

"How about what?"

"Help me," he said with a hint of an edge. "Go back in time, save my brother from the nightwalkers. If you heard your brother and me, then you know that's the only way we'll be strong enough to bring this school down once and for all."

"Oh, right. I don't think so."

"Would you just think about it for a second, please?"

"No. I've only done it once, and it was on accident. Even if I wanted to help you, I couldn't because I don't have the key."

"We'll get one." Choyce insisted. "From Chomsky or Valkyrien."

"And what about the bit about my not being able to choose what time period we wind up in? We could land anywhere and never be able to get back."

"We'll figure something out. Come on," he pleaded, "I've been alive for over a century now. I think I can help you get control of your powers."

"You can't travel back in time." I pointed out. "So, how do you know that you can help me?"

"You're being really daft right now, you know that, right?" He shook his head, and I seethed at his condescending comment. He pressed on. "I told you already. You and I, we're each other's match. The perfect pair. Two peas in a pod. Whatever phrase you want to use, that means that we're *equals*."

I huffed. "Insulting me is a great way to get what you want."

Storming past him, I continued down the path.

He grabbed my shoulder gently, stopping me, and I glared up into his leather brown eyes. He quickly removed his hand, his expression softening. I scoffed, storming down the path.

"Look, I'm sorry," he called.

I whirled around. "What happened to you? What happened to the Lawrence in you? The one I knew from my dreams? You used to be a pleasant person, but whatever—or whoever the hell you've become, I don't even care to know."

"I know," he whispered, his brow pinched together.

He took a step forward, carefully examining my reaction. When I didn't run off, he walked the rest of the way, removing the distance between us.

"You're right." His voice was hushed as tears welled in his eyes. "I've changed. I'm cynical, sarcastic—"

"And rude," I added.

"Yes, and rude." His thin lips formed into a crooked smile as his long fingers grasped both of my hands in his. "I'm most definitely the rudest person I've ever met. I've been living the worst version of myself for the past century without my brother."

I blinked, wondering where this emotion was coming from. The tears in his eyes, the desperation in his voice, it all seemed so sincere.

"But you can change that." He grasped my fingers like they were his only lifeline.

"But." I gulped. "You're a liar. The only person you care about is yourself and—"

He shook his head. "I choose you. I'll change, just please—"

He suddenly lowered to one knee, still holding my hands in his. "Izara Torvik," his voice shook as he whispered. "Will you make me the happiest man in the world and travel in time with me? Help me bring my brother back from the dead, and I swear to you, I will reveal all of my secrets. I'll hold nothing back. This, I promise you."

I really didn't know what to say. In only four days, he'd accused me of using him, insulted my intelligence, and annoyed every fiber of my being. But here he was, practically begging me to save his brother's life. I'd watched Edwin get shot, and I knew it was a fate he never deserved. A part of me pitied Choyce. If the situation was reversed, I would do anything to bring Kain back.

I sighed. "If this works—if you can help me get control of time traveling to the past, then we'll try to save your brother."

Choyce smiled slowly, his eyes looking upward. He leaped from the ground, his long arms squashing me in an enormous hug.

"Thank you," he whispered in my ear.

"But I won't help you with your revenge," I added, my chin against his knobby shoulder. "We'll go there, grab your brother, and come right back so we can work together and bring down this school in our time. Okay?"

"Of course," he agreed, still holding me.

"Ahem." A cough sounded from behind Choyce, and I glanced over to see Lee standing there with a horrified look on his face.

"Lee!" I called, pushing Choyce away from me.

"Hey," he said, coming to stand next to me, protectively placing his arm around my waist and pulling me close to him. "What's going on?"

Lee sized up Choyce, and I wished he hadn't hugged me just then. Or ever, for that matter.

"My apologies," Choyce said, his annoyingly formal attitude returning. "You must be the boyfriend, I presume?"

Lee hesitated before, reluctantly, shaking Choyce's outstretched hand.

"You know this guy?" Lee asked, turning to me.

"Yes," Choyce answered for me. "We go *way* back."

He wiggled his eyebrows at me, and I rolled my eyes. He knew I couldn't tell Lee we'd met in the early nineteen hundreds. I bit back the slew of expletives I wanted to call him.

"I've just transferred in." Choyce added.

"Really?" Lee arched a brow. "Did you go to the same

71

school or—"

"Definitely not," I replied before Choyce could make up another lie.

Choyce smiled. "I'm transferring from Lawrenceville School. Perhaps you've heard of it?"

I frowned, hoping that wasn't another innuendo to the first time he attended this school under his birth name Lawrence Bartholomew.

It's a real school, Choyce's voice echoed in my mind, and I nearly jumped. I hated that he could do that.

Lee shrugged. "Never heard of it."

"Well, I was going to meet Kia at the cafeteria. Care to join?" I asked Lee.

"Absolutely," Lee said as we made our way down the path.

Why was Choyce trying to make it so obvious we knew each other from way back? Did he want everyone to know what we were? I wasn't fond of the prospective web of lies Choyce was likely to create. He was going to get us killed. Suddenly, I regretted agreeing to help him.

Choyce waltzed up beside us. "I was heading to the cafeteria to meet Kain. Mind if I join you?"

He didn't wait for an answer as he walked along with us. Lee seemed tense, his shoulders squared, and I knew he was not comfortable with Choyce around. I grimaced, knowing how we must've looked when Lee happened upon us. I cringed inside, wishing I could tap into that time-traveling power right then and there. What made matters worse is that Choyce didn't seem to be helping. He didn't care about Lee, or me, for that matter. Why had I agreed to help him?

7
A HISTORY LESSON

- Kain -

My eyes flew open as the constant beats and tune of some high-pitched pop artist sang in my ear. The guys from the basketball team had decided to celebrate the last night as it was the last free night before classes began, and it'd turned into an all-night video game tournament. It was a lot of fun, but now it was the first day of class, and my pounding head was making me regret the long night.

"You up, sleepyhead?" Choyce asked, pulling his hair into a man bun and smoothing his eyebrows.

Grunting, I pulled myself from the bed, fingers

fumbling to find the stop button to the most annoying song in the world.

"Did you mess with my alarm tone?" I asked, rubbing my eyes groggily.

"Not really my thing." He popped the collar on his black button-down before grabbing his book bag. "As for Duran and Laurent? I can't say their alibis will hold up."

"So dumb." I shook my head, finally shutting off the alarm and quickly changing it back to something normal.

Pulling on a vest with the school's emblem on it over my shirt and a clean pair of pants, I followed Choyce out of the room for our first class.

"US history," he read off his class schedule off his phone. "That should be an interesting class."

I smirked. "'Cause, you lived it?"

"Of course!" He grinned. "And to see what lies they're teaching you all these days."

"Sure." I grabbed the shoulder straps of my backpack as we followed the group of students piling into the classroom.

"Sleep well?" Duran asked as I sat next to him and his brother, Laurent.

They laughed as I plopped my backpack beside me. "I'm going to need to change my lock screen code."

Lee shifted uncomfortably as Choyce sat next to us. He seemed to have a chip on his shoulder.

"Hey, Lee!" Izzy greeted, kissing him before sitting at

the desk to him.

Gross, I thought, and I knew Izzy had heard me after she gave me a dirty look. They could at least keep the PDA down.

"Welcome back," Mr. Web called. "Hope y'all had a good summer and all that jazz."

The classroom quieted as Mr. Web gained most of our attention.

"Mine was good. Spent it with the family." He smiled. "My kids are a little young, and they're at that age where they think the summer is an eternity. About halfway through the break, they're already asking me, 'Dad, why are you here?'. You're probably already asking the same question about yourselves."

Laughter filled the room.

"So why are you here?" He asked, leaning against the front of his desk. "To get a history lesson. So let's dive in. Open your books to chapter six. The Social and Political Impact of Prohibition."

Opening the thick hardback textbook on my desk, I leafed through it to the correct page.

"Now, I know you've slept since then, so let's recap where the United States was at this point." Mr. Web stood up, walking to the chalkboard. "World War I ended, opening us up for industrialization which presented new issues"—I grimaced as the chalk scraped the board with each word Mr. Web wrote down—"causing a push for social reform. One of these being the prohibition movement." He turned back to us. "So. How did it begin?"

I slumped in my seat, hoping not to get called on.

"With the ratification of the 18th amendment," Lee answered.

A scoff echoed through the room, and I looked in the direction it came from. Choyce sat there; a smirk spread across his face as he doodled in his notebook.

"Good, someone's been studying." The teacher congratulated Lee. "That was the beginning of the prohibition amendment, but the idea of prohibition and temperance actually began about a hundred years prior when drinking had become a three-times-a-day habit for men."

"That's the life." Duran snickered, his brother nudging him to stop.

"Not exactly, Mr. Black." Mr. Web chuckled. "In fact, drinking became even more of an issue as beverages with higher alcohol content were being made."

"How did they function?" A girl asked. It was Leslie, Amadeus's girlfriend, and one of the drama people from Izzy's group. "How could society function with a bunch of drunks running around?"

"That's just it." Mr. Web exclaimed. "This influx of alcohol consumption caused a lot of issues, particularly for women and children. Imagine, the sole provider of a family in those days was the man. Now, if they're consuming high amounts of alcohol every day, they're no longer able to function at work. It caused poverty, starvation, and all of this tragic loss built up a moral issue against alcohol."

The room grew silent for a moment as the teacher paused. I usually wanted to drown everything out by listening to music, but not in history class. There was something fascinating about learning how humanity really hadn't changed, despite modern technologies and advances. No matter how much we thought we were different from back then, the human condition was always the same.

"At the turn of the century, temperance movements spread like wildfire"—Mr. Web paced in front of the classroom—"and soon, alcohol became the largest political issue of its time."

"Even during prohibition?" Izzy asked.

"Even then," he replied. "After the 18th amendment was ratified, it became even harder for the government to enforce it. These once genuine businesses were now in the hands of gangsters who became so rich off of bootlegging that it became impossible to stop."

Another cocky laugh echoed, and this time, all eyes turned on Choyce.

"Have something to add, Mr. Barton?" The teacher asked, raising a brow.

"Sounds like you've covered everything in the

textbook." Choyce laughed, closing the book. "If only that was the whole story."

"Care to elaborate?"

"For one, these businesses were always legitimate. They were run by businessmen regardless of what the government chose to label them." Choyce waved his hand emphatically.

"History shows a very violent past for these *businessmen*, as you call them," the teacher replied. "Which is why they were called gangsters."

"They were labeled gangsters because they continued to run their businesses. To distribute alcohol." Choyce's mouth twisted grimly, and I wondered if he was reliving a particular moment in his life. "Despite the government calling what was once legal against the law. A government that did hideous things to try and stop it."

A thick silence billowed through the room, causing me to sink further into my seat.

"The government actually had very little power to enforce prohibition." Mr. Web contradicted.

"*Little* power?" Choyce arched a brow. "They had a lot of power. Including the power of kerosene."

"Kerosene?" The question flew out of my mouth before I could stop it.

"Kerosene, chloroform, acetone, take your pick," Choyce replied, the passion in his voice apparent. "The government used it all to poison as much of the supply as they could get their hands on before letting it get distributed to hundreds—even thousands of unsuspecting citizens whose only crime was that they enjoyed a drink now and then."

"That can't be true." Lee scoffed. "This book doesn't even back that up."

I sat up in my seat, skimming the first page in the textbook to see if it mentioned anything about it.

"It wouldn't, would it?" Choyce snorted. "The government even denied doing anything wrong, basically saying that the victims brought it upon themselves."

"How do you know?" Lee pushed.

We were talking about an era that Choyce had experienced firsthand, not that he could tell Lee or the teacher that. I wondered if he'd lost any friends to this injustice.

Catching a knowing glance from Iz, we both wondered the same thing.

Choyce smirked. "Look it up."

Just then, the bell rang, putting a pause to the debate and derailment of Mr. Web's class.

"Okay, guys!" Mr. Web called as we grabbed our things. "Your assignment is to write a two-page, twelve-point font, double-spaced essay on chapter six. Due by Friday."

Everyone groaned as we headed to our next class. I stood from my seat, heading for the door.

"What a prick, right?" Lee said in a hushed voice as he

walked with me to drop off our books. "How can you stand being that guy's roommate?"

"It's alright." I shrugged, not wanting to get in the middle of whatever drama existed between the two of them. I had enough of that as it was.

Lee was my friend, but Choyce was the only other person besides my sister who was like me. He could help us develop our powers; the only way I knew for sure, we'd be strong enough to take down the nightwalkers. I wouldn't risk losing that.

"Something's not right with that guy, right?" Lee asked.

"I guess," I said, opening my locker and dumping my history book in. "I wouldn't spend too much time on it."

We didn't need another person to worry about. I didn't want to think about what would happen to Lee if he found out about us or the school's secret. I'm sure Choyce wouldn't hesitate to get rid of him if Lee kept challenging him. By the looks of things, that was likely to happen.

"See any new potential for the basketball team?" I asked, hoping to distract Lee by switching subjects as I grabbed another notebook and a spare pencil.

"A few," Lee replied, taking the bate. "But it's looking like we'll have roughly the same lineup as last year."

I nodded. "You've got English next?"

"Nah, Calculus. I'll see you later." Lee said, heading in

the opposite direction.

I hoped Lee would get the hint and continue to focus on the basketball lineup for this year and less on Choyce. We didn't need another reason to watch our backs, and who knows what would lead Lee down the path of finding out who really was responsible for his mom's death? Even though I didn't support Iz for continuing the relationship, I definitely didn't want him to find out about us. If he knew, I was sure he'd report us. That's what I would do. And then the nightwalkers would definitely kill us. But what if he didn't stop? What could I do to keep him from discovering the truth?

8

HALF LIGHT

- Izara -

"Ugh, I'm so glad first period's over." I sighed, taking the seat next to Kia at our large work area in the chemistry lab.

"Was history that bad?" Kia asked, looping her bag over the wood and metal chair.

"Mr. Web's lecture was great, as always," I replied. "But Choyce was there. He's such a know-it-all. You should've heard him today. He got on my last nerve."

"Hey, I don't even know the guy, but maybe you should consider switching classes?"

"Yeah, maybe." I agreed. "I'll try."

The room became very still as Mr. Valkyrien floated in, his long cape-looking coat fluttering as he made his way to the front of the class. It was definitely too hot outside for anyone to be wearing something like that, not to mention a little more suited for a wizarding school.

Kia rolled her eyes. "It can't be as bad as what we're going to have to deal with in this class."

Mr. Valkyrien was famous for his slow and dull teaching style. He also was creepy to look at. His pale complexion almost glowed as the sun beamed through the opened windows lining the right side of the classroom. He squinted for a good minute, his eyes unwavering from mine. I frowned. Was he staring at me? I looked for the key around his neck, but it was either hidden under his cloak or not there at all. Did he know that I'd used it last year? Did he know about Kain and me?

I glanced at Kia and the other classmates to see if anyone else noticed the teacher staring at me, but it didn't look like it.

Mr. Valkyrien's head wobbled on his long neck as he quickly pressed a button on his desk, causing blackout shades to lower over the glass windows. The mechanism controlling the blinds buzzed as they dropped, the sun disappearing with it, and soon the room was in darkness.

A large projector whirred to life as a screen lowered over the whiteboard, and class began.

"W-w-what is Ch-ch-chemistry?" Mr. Valkyrien's penetrating voice echoed, causing shivers to run down my spine. "W-w-what is m-matter? These are the q-q-questions we will b-b-be exploring."

Kia leaned over to me. "Why does the room have to be so dark? It's creepy."

I just shrugged. What was creepy was that Mr. Valkyrien continued to stare at me. Why was he singling me out? If he knew or suspected that I'd used his key to activate my time traveling power, would he turn us into the nightwalkers? Were we on death row? I balled my fists up, trying to calm my shaky nerves.

"So, what's with you and this new guy, anyway?" Kia wondered, totally ignoring the presentation. "I've never heard of him, but it sure seems like you two know each other."

Glancing over at her as she rested her elbows on the desk in front of us, I paused. How was I going to explain it to her? I imagined telling her about all the dreams I'd had about Lawrence Bartholomew. That he was now over a hundred years old and was calling himself Choyce Barton; here to teach Kain and me how to control our powers so we could time travel to 1911 and save his brother. She'd think I was a lunatic for sure. But she wouldn't be wrong. I was definitely losing my mind. The line between reality and fiction was crumbling, leaving me helpless. I was losing control over my abilities, my dreams, what was next? My existence?

How was I supposed to explain how I knew Choyce? He was the guy I was about to help save his brother from the past? But how? We already tried? Choyce had repeatedly assured me that he had a plan, but he had yet to share exactly how he planned to do this with us.

"I knew him back in New York." I chose to go with Choyce's lie. It seemed like the path of least resistance.

"Oh." She nodded. "He's your ex, right?"

"What?" I stiffened. The thought of that was horrifying. "No, definitely not."

"Huh, could've fooled me." She turned back to face the front.

"Why would you think that?"

"Seems like you two have a lot of history and sexual tension," she replied. "A little too much not to have dated in the past."

My eyes widened, swallowing hard. I was going to be sick. "Choyce and I are more like ex-acquaintances. I definitely never dated him."

Kia snuck a peek at me, smiling. "Okay, good 'cause I love you and Lee together. I wouldn't want anything to jeopardize things between you two."

I cringed inwardly. I was already doing that by lying to him, even if it was to protect him. Telling Lee the truth would kill him.

"Hey, have you noticed that the teacher's been staring at us nonstop?"

I glanced towards the front of the class, and, sure

86

enough, Mr. Valkyrien was still looking directly at us. Only I knew it wasn't us he was looking at. It was me. "Yeah. I thought it was just me who noticed that."

"No, it's kind of obvious."

"I don't know why." Wishing he would just look away or open a window and stare at one of his beloved squirrels.

"He's just a creep."

Suddenly something glistened around the teacher's neck as he absently clutched his chest. It was the key. It had to be tucked underneath his cloak.

His lips moved as a pinching sensation assaulted my temples, and suddenly, a voice echoed inside my mind. *Izara.*

I jumped, glancing around, hoping no one had seen that. Mr. Valkyrien's eyes were glazed over and locked on mine. His voice was still teaching the class, and the presentation was running as if nothing was different, but whatever magic the golden key was helping him communicate with me. It was definitely his voice, but somehow it was smoother. It was still high-pitched, but the stutter was gone. How was this possible? Was he a shifter, too?

She's close...

Another shiver rippled through my body as the ghostly sound rang in my head.

Take care... do not let them into your mind... you and Kain will save us...

"Izzy?" Kia's worried voice was far away. I tried to

87

respond, but I couldn't form the words as unconsciousness threatened. "IZZY!"

My eyes rolled back into my head as I fell, hitting the floor with a thud as everything faded away.

**

The wind lashed around me, blowing my natural black hair over my eyes. Tucking the loose strands behind my ear, I wrapped my hands around me, protecting myself from the cold breeze that filled the dimly lit room. I blinked.

What happened to the classroom? I wondered.

The row of blackout blinds was gone, replaced with dark, moss-covered stone walls that seemed to go up forever without a roof insight. Where the projector should've been, a group of seven cloaked figures sat in a circle, their robes billowing as the cold air lapped around them. I pushed myself onward, needing to ask where I was, and figure out how to get back to class.

"Excuse me," I called at the group, but no one looked up. "Can someone help me?"

Still nothing. I pushed myself through into the center of the group and realized no one could see me. A shiver ran down my spine as I noticed a single golden key hanging on a chain around each of the cloaked figures. The keys all had a crown of gemstones at the bow, but each one a different gem.

What were they for? Did it open something? Did it give them magic? Or both?

"You know the risk in letting this go on," an oddly familiar voice hissed behind me.

I spun around to see another hooded figure. "The Assembly decided long ago that unnecessary killing of human life should be prohibited. If we proceed with this plan, we will be violating our very own decree."

"It is a necessary sacrifice," a woman replied.

"Silence!" A low voice commanded, waving a long, bony hand.

The figure with the familiar voice stood up in protest, his hood falling back in the process, revealing his face.

"Mr. Valkyrien?" I gasped.

At first, he seemed unchanged, from his long, wobbly neck to his translucent skin on the top of his bald scalp revealing shadows of his skull. But his beady eyes glistened like emeralds, much more vibrant than I'd ever seen his eyes before, and his large ears came to a point like a bat.

"Osbel, sit down," the figure seated at the front replied, the same one who had silenced them before.

This must've been the Assembly I'd heard about when I first met with Principal Chomsky. She'd been holding the key, and I'd heard voices talking about the return and shifters of the light and dark. And the man sitting at the head of the group must've been the leader.

"We're all wanting the same thing," the leader continued, "The Academy's goal is to rid the world of the offspring. You know the prophecy. We can't risk him gaining power. He cannot return."

Who were they trying to prevent from returning? Whose offspring were they getting rid of? And what did it have to do with the school and the Assembly? My head was reeling with questions.

"But they're killing humans!" Osbel bellowed. His voice rang through the air, causing a flood of bats to rush down from the darkness above.

"How dare you use your power on us!" The leader hissed, his expression tightening.

Osbel's arm shot up, his hand balled in a fist, and the bats nearly ran into each other as they retreated to where they came from. All of the hooded figures leaped to their feet, wings shooting out from their backs. Some were pure white, while others were black like mine on the full moon.

I frowned. The Assembly was filled with shifters? How were they able to transform so quickly? Were they not controlled by the full moon like us? And, if not, why?

The woman who'd responded earlier let out a shrill cry. "How dare you!"

Looking over at her, there was something familiar in the way she said that. Like I knew her. I still couldn't make out who she was as her hood remained pulled over her eyes. Her wings glistened white, flapping ever so slightly as she stood tense, ready to pounce at any moment.

The leader lifted a bony hand once more, gaining everyone's attention. Somewhere in the distance, a water droplet hit the floor. It echoed in the silence around us. This was probably a good time for me to get out of there. I carefully crept past the dozen hooded figures, taking one last glance at Mr. Valkyrien before sliding past the last chair in the circle. The hooded Assembly member sitting in it sniffed the air, turning towards me, and I froze. He swept a monstrous hand the size of my head through the space I was standing, my body shimmering as it went right through me, leaving me unscathed. Was I a ghost?

"We are the Assembly." The leader's low and emphatic voice stopped me in my tracks. I wanted to know what he was going to say next. "Half from the light and the rest of the dark. And for the sake of our factions here in the Transitioned World, we must stand together now. United. We must trust one another if we are to triumph."

The tension in the room was palpable, and I tried to control my breathing, hoping the being that was still staring at me would leave me alone. My heart pounded, and I swore someone would notice.

"You and Osbel will go to the school." The leader concluded. "If there are any signs of the return, report them to the Assembly, and we'll prepare to intervene."

Murmurs flooded through the Assembly at this announcement before quieting down.

"We are not alone," the giant man next to me whispered, breaking the silence.

He braced his enormous hands on the armchair, heaving his giant frame to a standing position. Removing his hood, the veins in his neck tensed as he flexed the muscles around his neck. Each tendon was perfectly defined and enormous like he was a professional wrestler. His giant white wings towered above everyone else.

I sucked in a breath of air, stepping back as he glanced down at me. His eyes glowed when they locked on mine.

"I can feel its beating heart. It's human, but"—he sniffed the air and gasped—"it has his power flowing through its veins."

It? Was he kidding? I most certainly wasn't an 'it.' Why was he referring to me like that? I'd of preferred the gender-neutral third-person singular pronoun. It was better than referring to me as some object. But I wouldn't tell that to the beast in front of me who could probably eat me for dinner.

All heads turned towards me, and I realized I had more important things to worry about. Leaving care to the world, I spun on my heel and raced back down the dark corridor I'd come from, not knowing how I was going to get out of there. My foot hit a groove on the floor, and I pitched forward, my arms flailing to catch my fall, and suddenly everything went dark once again.

9

WEIGHT OF THE WORLD

- Izara -

"Izzy!" A voice called in the distance.

My body was being moved, but I couldn't feel my arms or legs.

I still had those, right?

I blinked, the smell of dust filling my lungs, and I doubled over coughing. Someone grabbed my shoulders, pulling me up into an upright position and propping me against something hard. My blurry vision slowly came into focus, and Kia's strained face appeared inches away from my own. I caught the students' astonished faces peering down at me from behind Kia, and, lastly, I caught sight of Mr. Valkyrien.

Our eyes met, and a look of realization flooded across his face before he turned to leave. "C-c-class is dismissed."

"Mr. Valkyrien!" I cried, but it was too late. He'd already disappeared from the class into the hallway.

I pushed myself up, ignoring Kia's protests that I should rest a bit. He knew. He knew everything. What we were, that I was human, but had some demon blood inside me, or something, and that both the school and the Assembly wanted me dead. I wasn't going to let him out of my sight until he told me everything.

"Mr. Valkyrien!" I shouted again, running down the empty hall just as he disappeared around a corner.

Sprinting as fast as I could, I followed where he'd gone, and I stopped in front of the same janitor's closet I'd seen Principal Chomsky disappear behind last year.

Heaving a sigh, I squared my shoulders and gripped the round knob firmly. Swinging the door open, I was once again met with a soppy yellow bucket and the stench of old rags. How did this keep happening? First, Principal Chomsky walked through the door, disappearing without a trace, and now Mr. Valkyrien?

Then I remembered the identical golden key with shimmering gemstones at the bow that they both wore around their necks. That must've been how they kept disappearing through random doorways. It was a key that allowed them to transport themselves into a different time or place just like I'd used it to travel back in time. Each of the seven Assembly members had one. It had to be what allowed Mr. Valkyrien and Principal Chomsky to communicate with the other members. But was this also how they could avoid the full moon? And did they know I'd used their key to time travel?

Defeat swept through me as I pushed through the glass-paned doors of the cafeteria. I had a thirty-minute break before my next class and needed some caffeine if I could make it through the rest of the day.

"Iced latte, please."

"Of course, sweetie." The woman behind the counter smiled as she bustled off to fetch my drink.

A cold chill shook me as the last words forced me to relive Chuck pouring a bucket of freezing water against my limp chest.

His rotten egg perfumed the air around me, his hot breath on my cheek as he slid a needle into my arm.

"You think he's not the one who assigned me this task?" he had said. *"He taught me how to hunt the disease you are."*

Frozen from the trauma of the memory, I didn't even notice when the woman set my drink on the counter before me.

"Hey!" I jumped as someone tapped me on my shoulder.

Glancing over, Kia's rose gold hair made me blink back

to reality. She furrowed her brows, eyeing me carefully. "Are you feeling okay?"

I shook my head. "I'm fine, just a bit lightheaded."

It took all of my strength to shake the horrific memories of being kidnapped and nearly killed by the school's president's nephew. That combined with the vision, I wasn't sure how I would keep up a normal conversation. I couldn't very well tell her I'd just witnessed our biology teacher and principal in a secret meeting with a group called the Assembly who was from someplace called the Transitioned World. She'd think I was crazy, and I was afraid that she wouldn't be wrong.

"Can I get you anything?" The woman asked Kia.

"I'll have what she's having and two scones, please."

After ordering, we took a seat near the window.

"So, for the fall productions," Kia began after taking a sip of her coffee, "I've got a prediction."

"Let's hear it," I replied. I could use some normalcy right about now before I spiraled into the void of what-ifs. For now, at least. Plus, I loved figuring out who would be cast for which character. It was a pleasant distraction to the weight I was carrying on my shoulders.

Kia grinned, leaning in excitement. "Leslie says we could be doing Alice in Wonderland."

"Nice! There's lots of energy in that one."

"Right?" She agreed. "So, I thought I'd be the Cheshire Cat."

I snorted my coffee, nearly spilling it. "What? Why? I thought you'd rather be Alice."

"No way, the mischievous spirit of Wonderland is way more up my alley. You'd make a much better Alice. Anyway, that Britney chick would be the Caterpillar or the Queen of Hearts. I can't decide."

"Which Britney?"

"You know, *the* Britney? The girl who's staying in the room next to ours, who's the president's niece?"

"Oh, yeah, the awful one." At the mention of one of the Tompkins, everything I'd been trying to distract myself came rushing back. I was sure being in such proximity to any of the Tompkin offspring would be the death of me. Which reminded me of the vision I had of the Assembly.

"The Academy's goal is to rid the world of the offspring. We can't risk him returning."

These words plagued my thoughts, repeating on a never-ending loop. Whose offspring were they talking about? It definitely wasn't the offspring of the Tompkin's that this school was after. It was after Edwin back in 1911, and now it seemed to be after us, but last I checked, I wasn't even remotely related to Edwin or his brother.

"And that kid who always falls asleep will definitely be the Dormouse. I don't even know why he tried out for drama this year. He doesn't even seem to like drama, don't you think?"

"It does seem like he's using drama as a blow-off

class." I chuckled, hoping Kia didn't notice I'd only been half-listening.

"Seriously." Kia took a sip of her coffee, glancing behind me. "Oh! There's Leslie. I wanted to see what she thought about me auditioning for the Cheshire Cat. Do you mind?"

"Go, I'll see you later." I waved as she pushed the metal and plastic chair out.

I gazed out into the forest as I thought about the vision of the Assembly and the seven keys again. Remembering Mr. Valkyrien's protest of killing humans made me wonder if he was somehow on our side. If so, why wouldn't he have warned us from the beginning? Why would Mr. Valkyrien be avoiding me now?

Light flashed before my eyes, and suddenly, my vision blurred as a million images flooded before me like a malfunctioning projector. Embracing my head in my hands, I squeezed my eyes shut as the pain brought tears to my eyes. It was as if someone was kicking the side of my skull over and over again.

A large, bulbous man in overalls. A basketball court. A foggy bar with a closed sign in the front. Shouts and whistles and screams filled my mind, and with each new image, a new wave of pain flooded through me. The episodes I was experiencing were definitely getting worse.

Finally, able to open my eyes, a large head of dark

brown curls came into view, and it was enough for me to identify the source of my agony.

"Amadeus." I glared in his direction.

He grabbed a soda from the machine, glancing over at me before heading back towards the entrance—a smug look on his face.

Huffing, I pushed myself up from my seat and marched right on over to him.

"Amadeus!" I growled, this time loud enough so that he could hear me.

He turned. Our eyes met, and another piercing jolt of pain hit me.

"Why are you doing this to me?"

He frowned. "Doing what?"

I huffed. "The thing where flashes of images appear in my head whenever we meet eye contact?"

His eyebrows rose. "I—"

"Never mind, I don't want to hear any of your lies. But you should know." I took a threatening step in his direction. "If you do it again, you'll be sorry."

I glared at him, pushing through the glass door next to him. I was sick and tired of all of the mind games. I wanted it all to end, and I knew exactly how I would finally get control. The full moon would rise soon, and I would be ready. Choyce was going to help us and, even though Kain and I both didn't really trust him, with a school bent on killing us and anyone else who threatened their way of life, we were running out of options. I needed some sense of control, and I wouldn't stop until I found it.

IO
CREEPING INTO THE DARK

- *Kain* -

"Ready for this?" Choyce asked.

The full moon would rise in just a few hours, and we'd agreed to help Choyce. In return, he would give us the journal, show us how to untie ourselves from the curse of the full moon, and gain control of our powers. We didn't know what the vision of Mr. Valkyrien meant or if he was an ally or not, so for now, we only had ourselves and Choyce. We need to get stronger to protect ourselves, and he was our only option.

Choyce had yet to reveal how we would go about untying ourselves from the full moon, and for some reason, he'd chosen the full moon to do so because he said it was necessary for the process. I tried to point out that that was when we were most likely to lose control. To become our dark alter egos, but none of that changed his mind.

"You do realize we've got that quiz tomorrow, right?"

"History's a breeze," he said, blowing it off. "This'll be fun. Our first full moon together. I wouldn't miss it for the world."

"Speak for yourself," I said as we snuck out the back exit of the dorms and darted for the woods. The air was thick, the setting sun casting shadows through the trees as the cicadas sang an ominous tune. "I'm not so into the whole head-splitting torture thing or the feeling of bones tearing through my flesh."

"You get used to it over time." He shrugged. "Eventually, it becomes something you enjoy. I can control all of my powers, and I'm not tied to the full moon."

Was he crazy? Who would want to go through that kind of pain?

He glanced over his shoulder, ensuring I was keeping up. "I can transition at whim. Whenever I want."

"So…" I trailed, trying to wrap my head around this as we continued through the brush towards the girls' dorm. "Does that mean you don't have to transition on the full moon?"

"I still transition. It's just different. Kind of hard to explain."

I had no idea what he was trying to say, but it sounded

better than the excruciating pain we experienced each full moon.

"Come on, we're here," Choyce said, pointing to a building just beyond the trees, barely visible as the sun had finally set, drenching everything in inky blackness. "Which window's hers?"

"Not sure."

"Well, then how were you planning on getting her down here?"

"There're these things called cell phones," I replied, my tone dripping with sarcasm. "I was planning on using one."

He rolled his eyes as I reached for my pocket and brandished it. "It's no Excalibur like back in your days, but it'll do." I swung my arm around in a sword-like motion.

"I know what a bloody phone is. Just call her." He sighed.

I laughed, unlocking my screen and sending Iz a text.

My phone beeped minutes later with her response. "She's coming down. We'll meet her on the other side."

I led the way across the backside of the dorm, taking care to keep in the shadows. Technically we weren't supposed to be in this area after dark.

"It's almost time. We need to get to the creek and out of sight."

"She's on her way," I whispered, bringing a finger over my lips to shush him. I was anxious to get this over with. But I also didn't want to get caught sneaking around by any of the monitors.

"Why are you whispering?" He asked in an equally hushed tone.

"So no one can hear us, obviously. If someone hears us out here, we'll really be in trouble."

A twig snapped, and we looked up, startled by the sound.

"Wow, you two are jumpy." Izzy's voice met our ears, and we relaxed, knowing it wasn't someone else.

"You're late," Choyce said as she waltzed up to us.

"I don't remember a schedule being sent out," she snapped.

"Can we focus?" I asked, pointing to the sky. "The moon's coming."

"Right." Choyce agreed, heading for the forest once again.

We followed him back into the woods, our vision disappearing little by little as the night swept over us. I looked up and knew the full moon was close. Our bodies would be on the ground, enduring the pain I dreaded. I hoped that it would go quickly so we could get to Collings Castle. After the transition, the darkness was so intoxicating that if we didn't get to the castle, it would make us do things we'd regret. I tried to explain all of this to Choyce, but he was determined not to start our transition at Collings Castle. He said that it would hinder the process of untying ourselves from the full moon, but if it was the only place the darkness couldn't get to us, couldn't that be helpful?

"Just so you know," Izzy's sudden voice jolted me from my spiraling thoughts. "I'm only doing this so that we can protect ourselves and the innocent students from this school. Oh, and hopefully saving your brother in the process."

"Well, of course, my lady," Choyce said, tipping the brim of his invisible hat.

"Do you even hear yourself? You can't call me things like that."

"Like what?" Choyce asked with a hint of laughter in his voice. "Love, I thought I was being nice."

"You know how tense things are between Lee and me right now since he saw you—you—"

"Guys, come on." I rolled my eyes, not wanting to know what drama happened between the two of them.

"After I hugged you?" he retorted.

I chuckled but immediately regretted opening my mouth when a small elbow rammed into my side. "Ow!"

That's what you get for taking his side. Izzy's voice slithered into my mind.

You're not helping yourself, either. I replied.

You know I can hear every word when you use your telepathy. Choyce's words silently echoed around us before speaking aloud. "And I don't think I can be blamed for that whole thing since you hugged me back."

"WHAT?" Izzy exclaimed, her voice jumping an octave higher.

Gurgling water and mist assaulted my senses, indicating the river was close by. *Knock it off, you two. We're here.*

The water glistened as the dark clouds overhead opened up, revealing the full moon in all its horrific glory.

Looking upward, my eyes burned red as every single bone in my body cracked and twisted as if I was in a giant meat press. The blood under my skin churned as the heat rose from my core, sending me into a fit of shivers. I tried to stay upright. But my muscles shook, causing me to double over from the pain.

Crack. Snap. Pang. All my tendons stretched and twisted like a rubber band, sending me over the edge. My fingers crashed into the rough fibers of a tree trunk, supporting my weight as the feeling of bugs crawling up my spine took over. Waves of pain jolted me, and I fell, crashing to the earth, my jaw hitting the rough, dead leaves.

I arched my back as the crawling sensation continued up my spine, through my shoulders, and down my arms, sending another wave of pain that reached all the way down to my toes.

What's wrong with you? Choyce asked us. *You must control it. Don't let the pain take over. Use it.*

How? Izzy's thoughts were strained as she fought the same transformation I was.

Embrace the pain, Choyce replied. *Breathe it in. Fill your lungs with it.*

A howl escaped me as my wings shot out from my shoulder blades, expanding to their fullest. *How the hell do we do that?* I growled just as knives punctured through my cuticles. Black claws grew, taking the place of my nails one by one.

Accept it, Choyce replied.

Easier said than done, Izzy retorted.

Each muscle in my body contracted as new fibers fused together, forming new strands and expanding. Choyce's cliché life-coach psychobabble wasn't helping at all as my reasoning faded. The decadent scent of blood wafted through the air, tantalizing my nostrils as everything flashed red before me. My heart exploded as Izzy's racing heart thumped within me, and then another, much quieter heart pumped within my chest.

Glancing up at Choyce, I asked, *Is that you?*

Yes.

My eyes finally cleared, color returning as my night vision allowed me to see everything in the pitch blackness. Izzy was still crouched by the river, blood-caked around her scapular and trickling down her back. Blinking twice, I thought I was going crazy. Choyce hadn't changed at all. His eyes were black as a bird's eye, but other than that, his porcelain skin was shown bare in the moonlight, not a wing in sight.

How are you not shifting yet? I asked.

He closed his eyes suddenly, stretching his arms out wide as he sucked in air.

I am shifting. His voice echoed in our minds.

Then why aren't you convulsing violently? Izzy growled. *I was very much looking forward to seeing that.*

Choyce chuckled. *Because I've accepted my torture. I've untied myself from the full moon, always in a state of transition, but now I call the shots.*

And how do we go about doing that? I asked. *You still haven't told us how we untie ourselves.*

You'll see, he replied. *Tonight, we will perform the ritual.*

His face suddenly sunk into his skull, and he took a step back, snapping his arms to his side as wings immediately burst out from his back and stretched to their majestic length. Iz stood from where she was, both of us mesmerized by the sight. The full moon didn't seem to have control over him, a trait Izzy and I both wanted.

One last shiver ran down my spine as the pain settled into my chest. At that moment, my thoughts and desires weakened as the darkness crashed within me. The evil cravings that I'd fought so hard to overcome last semester crawled into my mind, taking control. This time it was different, deeper, and the desire for blood was more potent. I licked my lips as the scent of iron made my mouth water. I could sense where our victim was, hear their thoughts, smell their flesh, and every nerve in my body craved to be in their presence. To take their sweet life in my hands.

Stop it! I cried to myself. I couldn't do it. Not again.

Choyce grabbed my biceps just as I was about to flee to the castle as fast as I could fly. *Don't.*

I growled. *How is giving into the darkness a way to take control? It feels more like giving up what makes us human.*

I know, Choyce replied. *But it will all soon make sense. Trust me.*

A million images assaulted my vision, and suddenly I knew where we were going.

Come, Choyce ushered us to follow him into the night. *You know what happens next. Embrace it.*

II
NIGHTFLYERS

- Kain -

We leaped into the air, rising above the treetops, and headed southwest towards Ardmore. Following the scent of the one we sensed, the one the darkness needed. We soared over the Arbuckle Mountains and down US-177 with Choyce leading the way. The wind tickled my feathers as we glided inches from the asphalt going well over a hundred miles per hour.

A smile spread across my face. I liked the freedom flying brought. I could go anywhere whenever I wanted. The thrill of the danger made my heart beat faster. Each turn or curve in the road threatened to bring us face-to-face with an unsuspecting driver. I laughed, wondering if anyone would believe it if they saw us. Probably not.

I let out a holler as I pulled my wings in, turning my body in a barrel roll. I grinned as I heard my shouts echo back.

A flicker of light popped and sizzled in the corner of my eye. My eyes shot in its direction, realizing Izzy's hands were on fire as she flew beside me. She didn't even notice.

Hey, you're on fire, I warned, not that it would hurt. She was practically invincible. *Someone might see you.*

I don't know how to stop it, she replied.

Breathe in, Choyce advised. *Calm your heartbeat and think of the full moon washing over you.*

Would you stop telling me to breathe? Izzy snapped. *What do you think I'm doing, suffocating myself?*

I sighed. Some things, not even the full moon, could change. These two still bickered like an old married couple.

Breathing helps you relax, Choyce explained. *It is the same movement you use to access your power. Drawing your abilities inward to your core to stop them from surfacing. Once you learn that, you can tap into it at any time, after untying from the full moon, of course.*

And how do we do that? I asked for the millionth time, hoping to get answers.

Just then, the metallic scent of blood grew stronger as we flew over Ardmore towards Broadway street. Our wings

112

formed shadows on the empty streets below as we swooped under the dim streetlamps. Landing on the lawn of a church, every hair on my arm stood upright, and I knew we were close.

It's not here, Choyce replied. *The scent we need is coming from down there.*

He pointed down the street.

So, this is you helping us untie ourselves from the full moon? I asked, realizing we were following the darkness's desire. It was controlling us, pulling us down 1st Avenue towards the blood it craved. It was the opposite of control.

You'll see, Choyce promised, stepping ahead of us as he burst through the front door of a theater. *You enjoy Anatomy of a Murder, right?*

My heart skipped a beat, hoping what I suspected he was leading us to do wasn't true. The scent of human blood met my senses as we followed him into the small auditorium, and I wondered who would be here so late.

"What do you say there, counselor?" A man on the stage was saying, script in hand.

This is an excellent play. Choyce chuckled, rubbing his hands together.

I swallowed hard as the darkness inside me quivered in greedy anticipation. I loved and loathed it, all at the same time.

Izzy and I shared a glance, and the pain in her eyes told me she was struggling with the same dilemma. It was like leading a hungry wolf to a meat shop. Choyce wasn't leading us to control our powers. He was tantalizing us with what the monster inside of us wanted the most. Tempting us to lose control.

"You're quite suspicious." the man on the stage continued.

"No, no, no, no!" Choyce exclaimed aloud for all to hear. "You've got this all wrong."

The group of about ten people sitting in the front row turned from the scene where the two actors on stage were practicing to see who'd interrupted them. A woman in her late twenties covered her mouth, holding back a scream. I could taste her fear, the sweet, intoxicating anxiety that made her forehead perspire.

Choyce's arm shot out, his fingers spreading wide. A man tried to shoot up from his seat, but something froze him in the air, preventing him from moving.

I need to get out of here, I thought to myself, but my legs would only move me forward. *Why did I ever listen to Choyce? This was wrong.*

Shut up, Kain, a voice that I knew wasn't my own echoed in my mind. *This is what you were meant to be.*

A rush of energy swept through me, taking with it my reality, my humanity.

"You must feel it." Choyce flew up onto the stage next to the six-foot-tall man holding a script in his hands. The air blew, from Choyce's movement, fluttering through the man's chin-length brown hair, and the scent of his blood nearly brought me to my knees.

It was him. His was the one it desired.

"Watch and learn." Choyce grabbed the script from the man's shaking hands.

I shook my head, snapping out of my reverie. This was definitely wrong. We shouldn't have come here.

"Choyce." I hissed.

Izzy glared at me, her red eyes unrecognizable. *You shouldn't use our real names.*

"Oh, my apologies." Choyce chuckled. "I must let the true actor run the show."

He bowed low before flapping his onyx wings, soaring into the air to stand behind Izara in the center aisle.

His long, thin fingers gripped her shoulders, bringing his lips to her ear. "Do you feel the power of the full moon?"

"Yes," she whispered.

"Channel its power, focus on it. Then go to the one you sense, the one we need."

She sucked in air, eyes closing briefly, and I growled.

Stop this! I sent my thoughts to both of them, but they ignored me. Were they that far gone?

"You smell his blood, don't you?" Choyce asked my sister, who nodded. "He's right there on the stage, waiting for you."

The man dropped his script, turning to run away when

Choyce's hand shot out once more, forcing the man's knees to lock and fall with a crash onto the wood stage floor.

"You know what you need to do to untie yourself from the full moon's limitations."

My eyes widened as she drew in a deep breath, the metallic decadence washing over us as he scrambled to his feet again. Her hand shot out just as Choyce had, causing the man on the stage to freeze before he could get up. I'd only ever seen her use that power once before when she accidentally froze the whole cafeteria. She'd meant to communicate telepathically to me, but instead, she'd used this power.

"What the hell?" The other actor on the stage cried, waving his hand in front of the face of his co-actor.

"Did I say you could speak?" Choyce growled, his wings expanding as he flew onto the stage.

My mouth dropped in horror as he raised his clawed hand to the man's cheek, almost caressing it. He shimmered into nothingness, disappearing as the innocent man gasped. A whimper escaped him as a thin, red line appeared on the man's neck. My heart raced rapidly, the iron scent of his blood tantalizing me. I had to fight the urge to fly up and rip into the man's flesh. I couldn't give in to this temptation. What was Choyce thinking? Bringing us here while we were like this?

I tried to run up and save the man, but suddenly my body froze against my will. The tang of blood filled the air as it spilled over the seam of the man's neck.

A woman in the front row shrieked, and against my will, my hand stretched outward towards her, feeling an instant connection. What was I doing? Why couldn't I stop myself from doing this? An all too familiar rage slithered from my body, and the darkness inside of me ushered me forward, removing the distance between the horrified lady and me.

This is what you were born to do. Embrace it. The darkness hissed inside my mind.

Her body began to convulse as I floated towards her. I jerked my head away, trying to move my legs and wings in the opposite direction, but nothing helped. Nothing could prevent the darkness from making me do his bidding. My consciousness weakened, and I knew I would disappear soon.

Everyone seated around her was paralyzed by fear. I could smell the adrenaline pumping through their veins, and a grin that wasn't my own spread across my face. Some brave souls glanced in her direction, only to shiver as crimson burns spread like wildfire across her face and arms, leaving a rash in its wake. Orange blisters popped up as a reaction to the boiling heat I caused within her. She shook uncontrollably. Her body wouldn't be able to endure much more of the scalding temperature.

I gasped. What the hell was I doing? This woman wasn't even the one the darkness wanted. I had to stop.

It's the only way. A dead voice whispered to me. *Forget yourself. Give in.*

The darkness swept through me, it's power more potent than ever before, taking me with it. The woman's heart suddenly stopped as the last gasp of air escaped her lips. It was finished.

"Yes! Bravo!" Choyce's voice filled the room as he shimmered back into his form. "That's how it's done. Round of applause, shall we?"

Choyce's eyes widened, his hands stretched out, and suddenly the front row of actors began clapping with him.

How are you doing that? I asked.

I'm Izara's counterpart. Choyce answered. *She communicates with the past as I see the future. She can freeze people. I can move them.*

But how? Izzy's thoughts interjected. *How can you do this outside of the full moon?*

You will know soon enough. He continued. *Eventually, you'll not only be able to freeze people completely but freeze certain parts of them. Or just slow them down entirely.*

The clapping stopped. As soon as it did, a man stood up when he thought we weren't looking and made a shot for the illuminated exit sign. I flew over the seats, grabbing his collar and throwing him across the room, sending him tumbling onto the stage.

Yes, but what exactly does untying ourselves from the full moon entail? I growled, picking myself up off the floor and returning to stand next to my sister.

A smile spread across his face and, with a flourish, he grabbed the human we needed and pulled him to his feet. Choyce opened his mouth wide, his canines extending like a vampire, and he plunged them deep into the man's neck. His shoulders and legs shook against Choyce's grip before they slumped against him.

"What the hell?" I cried aloud.

Choyce lifted his blood-drenched face, tossing the body over the stage. It slid to our feet.

Drink, his order filled our thoughts.

I took a step back, swallowing hard. Was he serious? No way was I doing that. I was a monster, but I wasn't a vampire. I glanced back up at Choyce just as his eyes sunk into their sockets, reminding me of the vision I'd seen at Lee's mother's funeral. It had looked like a skull. Was it him? But how could it be? At that point, he was still in the past. Or was he?

Drink, he growled once again.

The words echoed as I stared in shock at the limp body before us, his red blood blending into the cheap carpet. The scent of his blood made my mouth water, and my eyes flashed red.

I looked over at Izzy. Her lip was trembling, and I knew she was having a harder time resisting. Her heart fluttered nervously inside of mine, and I knew she was more afraid of herself than she was of anything else. She wanted the power. She needed it.

Kneeling in front of the body, she leaned into the body and opened her mouth. Fangs grew as she latched onto his neck.

I blinked, suddenly snapping out of it as my consciousness flooded back. I couldn't give in to the darkness—the monster in me.

Izzy! Izzy, stop. I tried to send my thoughts to her, but she wasn't listening.

Why do you think you hunt each full moon? Choyce asked. *Why else do you think you're so drawn to the blood?*

I shook my head, not wanting to believe what I was seeing or hearing. There had to be another explanation of why. I remembered taking the hearts, draining the blood into vials. They weren't for our consumption. They were for something else. For what, I didn't know, but I had to believe it was for something else.

With this blood, he hissed at me. *Your powers will be enhanced. It is what allows you to harness the power of the full moon. To control it rather than be controlled.*

Izzy finally rose, blood dripping from her lips as she towered over the dead body. She turned towards me, and her red eyes flashed to the normal blue ones we shared. Was the full moon over? She blinked again, and her red eyes returned.

She's in control now, Choyce whispered.

She turned to the stage as balls of fire erupted in the

palms of her hands. She threw them towards the curtains, igniting the stage with smoke and fire.

You must drink, Izzy thought, locking eyes on me.

I glanced down at the body, the blood taunting me. The blood was so intoxicating that I didn't even care to notice the survivors fleeing from the fire down the back aisle. I knew that they wouldn't get far. It was wrong, but right all at the same time. I wanted to unlock all of my powers and control my transition, but did it have to be this way?

12

DETECTIVE SHANE WALKER

"Detective," one of the officers at the scene called, trying to get Shane Walker's attention.

He'd been called to the scene shortly after the firefighters had quenched the flames that had threatened to burn the entire Ardmore Little Theatre down. He usually wouldn't have even been called here, except that the police department had gotten word that he'd worked several similar cases in between Davis and Sulphur. It seemed as though they had a serial killer on the loose. He remembered hearing about the first on TV. It'd happened in Oklahoma City to a businessman named Bradshaw. His heart was pulled right out of his chest.

One seemed to happen each month, except for during the summer and winter holidays. He didn't know if the killer went on vacation or what. Perhaps it was just some sort of mind game.

The night he got the call to his own home flashed in his mind whenever he walked onto a scene nowadays. The sinking feeling he had when he realized where the call was taking him. The pitied looks his fellow officers gave him as he pushed his way into his house. Some days he forgot his wife, Sara, was gone. He'd reach out for her in their king-sized bed, but all his hands would hold were empty sheets.

He choked back a sob as he looked away from the lifeless body on the ground before him in the charred auditorium. He shouldn't have even been called today after what he'd been through. It was inappropriate, but there wasn't anyone else familiar enough with these types of cases. The strange and supernatural issues were the only ones he got assigned to since his promotion to detective.

"Yeah?" He finally glanced over to the crime scene technician who'd called him.

"There are no signs of fingerprints. I'll have to take the blood samples back to the lab for further testing, but something's interesting about the second body on the stage."

"And what's that?" He asked, folding his arms across his stiff button-down shirt.

"Due to the condition of the bones," the technician began, motioning to the corpse. "The body had to of fallen over three stories postmortem."

"But this building's only got one floor." He glanced up, eying the beams above. "The ceiling in here must be eighteen- or twenty feet tops."

"Exactly." The technician agreed. "It doesn't make any sense."

He grunted. The only thing he hated more than trying to solve cases that could only be explained by the supernatural was the damn ties he had to wear.

Shane shook his head. "What I don't get is why there are so many bodies. Our killer is usually a one victim kind of monster. But this? We've got at least ten bodies."

Unfolding his arms, he rested his hands at his waist, curling his course thumbs into the belt loops of his slacks. He'd forgotten a belt, and he was pretty sure his pants hadn't been washed in weeks. His wife was always the one to take care of those things. Without even asking, she would meticulously hang the freshly starched shirts and pressed pants in such a way that all he had to do was walk into the closet and grab a hanger. There was so much about her he was going to miss. Not just how she took care of him, but her reassuring voice, her smile, and her intellect. She was always the voice of reason.

He couldn't help but think about how often he'd forgotten to thank her or to say that he loved her. If he'd known that would be the last time, he'd kiss her lips, if he'd only known...

But one thing was for sure. He was more determined

than ever to find the one who murdered the people in the Ardmore Little Theatre last night because it was the same one who'd taken Sara from him.

"Detective." The technician once again pulled him from the sea of his own thoughts. "There's more."

"What?" He barked.

"There are signs that there were three."

"Three what?" He didn't know what she was getting at, and his patience was thinning.

"Three perpetrators." She clarified.

"That's not possible." He knew that this guy had a pattern, and serial killers didn't usually work in groups.

"Look." She pointed to the first body, drenched in blood. "See the size of the footprint there?"

He grimaced. "Yeah. Adult male, we've already identified this."

"Yes, but look at this near the second body over here."

He followed her to the first row of seats where a lady sat, eyes hung wide, with red blisters all over her body like she'd been boiled.

"It looks like this floor has been sticky for quite some time," she said, pointing to various spots near the body. "Somebody must've spilled a soda or something, but if you look closely, you can see another footprint."

She clicked her pocket flashlight on and angled it to illuminate the floor so that he could make out the faint outline of the second pair of footprints she was referring to.

"It's a whole size larger than that one over there."

"Okay, so where's the third?"

"That's where it gets interesting." She motioned him to follow her up to the half-burnt stage.

There were two bodies on the stage. One had apparently fallen to his death, and the other burnt to a crisp from the fire.

"Careful." She warned, stopping him before he could step any closer to the body. "Look at this."

She signaled to an odd shape burned into the stage's floor.

"What's that?"

"It's another footprint." She grinned as if she'd made the most amazing discovery.

"How's that a footprint?"

"See the toes?" She pointed at little curvatures sticking out of the disfigured burn mark. "If I'm right, then this print had to belong to a woman."

Running a hand through his balding hair, he let out an exasperated sigh. This was starting to not fit anything he'd ever seen. He was usually good about finding patterns, but he couldn't wrap his head around this one.

Out of the corner of his eye, he spotted an officer coming out from backstage.

"Y'all need to come see this!" The young officer called

urgently to the detective and technician.

They carefully followed the officer across the burnt stage to the rooms behind the curtain. The officer held the door to the dressing room open for them; the stench of old blood mixed with cosmetic chemicals made him cough.

"What in the—?" The technician gasped, gazing around the room.

Shane followed her gaze, and he could've sworn he heard his jaw hit the floor. He half expected to see more bodies or even blood, but nothing could have prepared him for what was in that room.

Wisps of black feathers filled the entire space, from the walls to the fans. It stuck to the vanities, covered the couches, and even stuck to the costumes hanging on clothing racks.

"What in the hell happened here?" Shane scratched his head.

The case had officially moved beyond weird.

13

THE DAY AFTER A NIGHTMARE

- Izara -

Shuffling footsteps woke me from my deep sleep. Every bone in my body ached as if it'd been broken a dozen times over. A strange metallic taste lingered in my mouth, and I tried to swallow it away, but it just made the tang more potent.

Opening my eyes, the bright sun glared down on me. I must've slept in.

"Good morning." Kia greeted as she slipped into a romper.

"Morning." I wiped my eyes, still groggy as I swung

my legs over the side of my bed.

Something damp that must've been drool lingered on the corner of my lip, and I wiped at it with the back of my wrist. Glancing down at my hand, my heart skipped a beat when I saw something red and sticky left behind. Bringing my wrist to my nose, I sniffed. Panic set in as the stench of iron filled my nostrils.

Quickly glancing over at Kia, she was too busy picking out what shoes to wear to notice, so I decided to make a dash for the bathroom. I was grateful that I didn't have to run down the open hall anymore for a sink. Locking both doors, I turned to the mirror. Beet red lips met my reflection, and suddenly everything I'd been blocking out from last night rushed in like a tidal wave.

I had drunk blood.

My stomach lurched at the thought, and I dashed for the toilet. Convulsing over the seat, I tried to rid myself of the horrific contents, but nothing came out. Falling to the bathroom wall, I slid to the ground as tears streamed down my cheek. What had Choyce done to me? I was already a monster, so why did he have to go and make things even worse?

Numbness gripped me as I swallowed back the last tear. My heart pounded in my chest as I hardened my eyes. Choyce couldn't' get away with this. In one night, he'd redefined what a monster was, and now countless people were murdered by my hands because of *him*.

Remembering the vision I'd had last night of Lee's dad, Shane Walker, investigating the spectacle we'd left behind made me wish I could turn back time.

Pulling myself up off the ground, determination filled me as I walked over to the sink. I was careful to avoid the mirror and meet my reflection until I'd thoroughly washed my face and mouth out.

Brushing my teeth, I took particular care in flossing out the blood that had seeped into the corners. Suddenly, another heartbeat erupted inside of me, and I grabbed my chest.

You're no longer tied to the full moon, Choyce's voice filled my mind.

"Get out!" I cried panic-stricken.

You can now reach your true potential, he continued.

Out! I growled, my blue eyes dissolving into blood red.

I froze when I met my reflection in the mirror. But the full moon was over. My eyes were supposed to be normal. Shaking my head, I tried to blink them away, but that didn't seem to help. A crawling sensation crept up from my fingers, and I glanced down just as endless lines of black, spidery veins wormed their way up to the tips of my fingers. They snaked their way up to my cuticles, puncturing through the skin as I bit my lip to keep from screaming.

Tears swelled as black claws speared their way over my nails. What was happening to me? How the hell was I supposed to go to class like this?

"Izzy?" Kia called through the door.

"I'll be out in a minute."

"Do you want me to wait for you? I was going to head to the cafeteria."

Glancing at the state of my red eyes and claws, there was no way I was going to let her wait for me. "Go ahead. I'll meet up with you for history."

She paused. "I've got pre-calculus first period."

"Oh, right. Sorry, I forgot." I shook my head, trying to focus. "I'll meet you for chemistry then."

"Okay, see you then."

I waited until I was sure the door to our room closed behind her before I entered. I had to get to class somehow, but not looking like this. I scavenged through my close, looking for something that would provide the maximum amount of coverage without looking too conspicuous. Checking the temperature on my phone, I rolled my eyes. It was roasting outside. Not the best day for this to happen.

Without any other options, I grabbed a long-sleeved cardigan with giant pockets. I paired it with jeans and a top, and I shoved my hands into the pockets of the cardigan before glancing at my reflection in the mirror hanging on the closet door.

I sighed. I looked relatively normal, except for my red eyes and giant bags under my eyes.

Makeup. That was the only answer.

Running to the bathroom, I turned the metal knob, but it stopped.

"I'm in here." Britney's snotty voice called, the niece of the president of Tompkin's Academy.

I slapped the palm of my hand against the door. "I need in the bathroom."

Rattling the doorknob, I growled. I was so not in the mood for her nonsense. She was probably just staring at her own reflection.

"Come on!" I banged on the door again.

"I said, I'm in here!" She shouted.

A surge of anger shook my entire body, and out of nowhere, I gripped the handle, and smoke billowed from it as the metal burned red hot before melting away, allowing me to yank the door open. "I said, I need the bathroom."

"What the hell?" She cried, glancing at me in the reflection.

I quickly looked away, hoping she hadn't noticed my red eyes.

"That was locked." Her face flushed red in anger.

"And now it's not. Get out." Glaring at her, another heatwave rushed through my veins.

I extended my hand towards her just as she made a lunge for me. Her body immediately went still like a statue, her arms stretched out to protect her face, and a look of terror frozen in her eyes as if I was going to hit her. Taking a step closer, I looked into her wide eyes. They didn't even blink. She was utterly still. Not even an eyelash flickered. I'd frozen her completely.

Not knowing how long that would last, I dashed to my drawer by the sink and quickly pulled out my cosmetic bag. Dabbing concealer under my eyes and smearing a bit of tinted lip balm on my lips. Glancing down at my hands, they were still covered in black veins. I squeezed a bit of foundation on top of each hand and fingers, carefully blending it in. Letting it dry, I decided it looked significantly better. Just slightly purple and veiny, instead of black. It would have to do.

I met my reflection in the mirror, my eyes in a constant shift between red and blue. Was I turning into the monster I shifted into on the full moon? This was not what I signed up for. Grabbing a pair of sunglasses for my eyes, I returned to where I thought I was standing before Britney froze. How was I supposed to unfreeze her?

Taking a deep breath, I tried to remember how I'd unfrozen the cafeteria last year on accident. I closed my eyes, slowing my racing heart as I focused on my breathing. In through my nose, out through my mouth. The full moon filled my thoughts as a familiar tingling erupted in my fingertips. Squeezing the palm of my hands shut, suddenly Britney burst to life.

"How *dare* you hit me!" She roared. "I'm going to report this."

I smirked. "I didn't hit you. I was reaching for my towel."

Grabbing the towel from the hook beside her, I spun on my heel and left. I was already late, so I picked up my bag from the room and headed straight to class.

***

- *Kain* -

I didn't remember falling asleep, only dreaming. The memories of the past flooded my unconsciousness, unfolding before me as if I were reliving them. I stood on the doorstep of the school's library, only not in our present-day but back in 1911. I remembered standing on these same steps last year when he time traveled.

"Look." I pointed to the group of men across campus. "They're heading for the woods."

"They must be close to catching the brothers," Izzy muttered.

A feeling of déjà vu swept over me as we said and did the exact same things we had done before. Pushing forward, we ran after the nightwalkers as fast as we could. Damp pine and skunk weed wafted through my nostrils as we dove into the trees surrounding the Academy. Feet shuffled, squirrels chattered, and the branches moaned as they twisted in the wind. My hands burned with fire, and I glanced over, startled to see myself running next to me. I must've transferred consciousness again.

Why did this keep happening? Was it because I was dreaming? Or was it trying to tell me something?

"I'm not strong enough!" Lawrence called from somewhere up ahead.

A shiver ran through my body as I forced my mind back into my own.

"We've got to help him!" Izzy cried.

"They'll kill us," I shouted back, and suddenly we stopped running.

I glanced over at my sister, and I froze in my tracks. Her eyes were no longer her own but black as coal. Exactly like Choyce's were when he shifted.

I frowned. "Why are your eyes like that?"

He will return. *A dead voice hissed inside my mind and, though it was coming from Izzy, it was definitely not hers.*

A promise made will be kept, *the voice continued.*

What was the voice talking about? Was it talking about the promise we'd made with Lawrence and Edwin? And whose voice was talking right now? It didn't sound like any of the brothers. Certainly not my sister.

You know his face. *The low hiss surrounded me.* Beware the wrath of the night.

Izzy's eyes suddenly flashed and went back to their usual blue.

"What happened?" She asked.

"I don't know." I shrugged. "It's like someone was possessing you."

"Are we dreaming?" She asked.

"Yeah. Apparently, we're dreaming about the night we time traveled and saw Edwin get murdered. Again."

"Then why can we communicate like this?" She asked. "We've shared reams before, but this feels... different. It feels real."

"I think it is real."

"What's he doing?" A man called.

We looked to our left and spotted the group of nightwalkers, pitchforks, and rifles in hand.

"He's using his magic. Stop him!" Another bellowed

"It's happening again, isn't it?" Izzy asked, just as the trees melted into liquid, enveloping us into a familiar darkness. My stomach flipped as a falling sensation took over, spiraling everything into nothingness.

Suddenly I landed on something cold and wet. Opening my eyes, a familiar building appeared before me. Pushing myself up off the rugged concrete, I spotted a road sign reading 1st Street. I was back in Sulphur in front of a four-story hotel. It was The Artesian Hotel from my visions of Choyce attending a party under the pseudonym Bart Bessler. Only the hotel was different, much older than how I remembered it from the dream, and the cars parked at its side had to be from the fifties or sixties. A light flickered on in one of the windows. A drape was pulled back, and a woman stood at the windowsill, her yellow eyes beating down at me.

Tucking her red hair behind her ears, her voice filled my head; He's coming. The return is near.

***

- Kain -

Waking up with a start, it took me a minute to remember where I was. How had I made it back to the dorms last night? I gripped either side of my head, trying to remember what happened. Images flashed in my mind so quickly I couldn't distinguish what they were. The fair-skinned redhead from my dream was the only thing that came out crystal clear. She was trying to warn me about something, but whatever it was, I totally didn't get it.

"Time for class, mate." Choyce was standing at the mirror hanging from a closet door, wadding his ridiculously long hair into a man bun.

Realizing how late it was, I grabbed a pair of workout shorts lying nearby. Pulling them on, I hopped out of bed.

"Catch." Choyce tossed a paper bag in my direction. "It's a bagel. You'll need your energy after last night."

"Thanks," I replied, groggily rubbing my eyes.

Realizing how hungry I was, I tore into the bagel as if

it were my first meal in weeks.

"So, what happened last night?" I wondered out loud, taking a bit into the toasted bread.

"Well." He let out an exaggerated sigh. "If you'd followed in your sister's footsteps, you would have clearly remembered this morning. Instead, sadly, you're the only one still tied to the full moon."

"I've transitioned and retained my memory before." I pointed out.

"But you've never truly let go of your power before."

I shrugged, not knowing what the difference was. It didn't seem much different from what I could remember all the other times I transitioned. Choyce still turned into the monster. If, after doing whatever had to be done to be untied from the full moon, you still had to transition, then what was the point?

"The *point* is you're more powerful when the full moon can't control you."

"How did you—?"

"Look—!" Choyce said as his arms shot out, ignoring my question.

He closed his eyes for a moment and pulled his fingers up into fists. He snapped his arms down to his sides as a ripping cloth echoed around us. Black, silky wings tore through the back of his shirt, causing shreds of fabric to fall to the ground.

"See? *I* control the transitions."

My jaw fell open. I never imagined it would be possible to grow wings on impulse outside of the full moon. How did he do that?

"Your sister will be experiencing a flood of power. It will be overwhelming at first, but once she gets used to it, she'll be able to use all of her powers whenever she wants."

"That's pretty cool. So how do you untie yourself from the full moon?" I asked.

"You drink the blood of the one you sense. The one whose blood is different from the others," he said, heading for the door. "Now, get dressed so we can get to our history quiz."

My stomach lurched, and I swallowed hard. "Wait, what?" I asked just as he left the room.

But Izzy had untied herself from the full moon. Did that mean she…? I couldn't even finish that thought. Dropping the half-eaten bagel on my desk, I pulled open my dresser drawer. Putting on the first school-issued polo I could find, I paired it with my trusted hoodie before grabbing my rucksack and rushing out of the room.

Spotting Choyce heading down the path to the main campus, I picked up the pace to catch up.

"What do you mean you have to"—I stopped mid-sentence, realizing I was surrounded by other guys heading to class and lowered my voice—"that you have to drink blood?"

"I mean exactly what I said," he replied like it was

nothing.

"So, you're saying you drink blood?"

"Each full moon."

I grimaced. "Do you know how that sounds? Completely wrong, not to mention insanely gross."

Shaking my head, I couldn't figure out how I could've forgotten about my sister drinking blood. I was sure something like that would be ingrained in my memory. Maybe I was blocking it out somehow?

Choyce shrugged. "Look, you can either join in next month or stay your old feeble self. There's nothing that can be done now."

I opened my mouth to argue with him but quickly shut it when I heard my name being called.

"How's it going?" Duran called.

I glanced over my shoulder, spotting Duran's older brother Laurent and Lee walking down the path towards us.

"Hey," I replied, hoping my face didn't reveal the weird conversation Choyce and I were having.

"Gonna join us on the court after class?" Laurent asked.

"Yeah, for sure. What else is there to do?" I joked.

"What about you, Choyce?" Duran asked.

"Definitely not," he replied. "I'm much more interested in the drama club myself."

At the mention of Choyce, Lee's face contorted for

about a millisecond before melting into a look of disinterest as we continued the trek to class. I didn't even want to know. Whatever drama seemed to be developing between Lee and Choyce, I didn't want to be involved. I had enough of my own right now. Like, what was Izzy thinking when she drank blood last night? I shouldn't have eaten that bagel so quickly. I was going to be sick. How could she do something like that?

Once we got inside the building, Choyce and I headed straight for Mr. Web's class while the others split. We filed into Mr. Web's classroom, the scent of freshly sharpened number two pencils welcoming me as we took our seats. While the other students were concerned about the upcoming quiz, all I could think about was what had happened to my sister last night to bring her to the point of drinking someone else's blood. I like the idea of being in control of my own power, especially knowing it was the only way we'd really be able to fight off the school's own monsters. But was it worth doing something like that?

Izzy entered the room with Lee, who was apparently having a one-way conversation with her. Something wasn't right, and it wasn't just because she was wearing sunglasses inside. Her skin was grayish, and she kept her hands shoved inside her cardigan even when Lee tried to hold her hand. I tried to communicate with her, but it was as if we were disconnected for some reason. Even though most of our powers were on lockdown until the full moon, our telepathy usually worked. But now, when I tried to send her a message, it didn't go anywhere, leaving a tingling sensation at my temples.

Perhaps it was the whole being tied versus untied to the full moon thing? Whatever it was, I didn't like it. Did she remember what she did? If she was like Choyce now, then she probably did. How was she not violently ill? My insides churned just thinking about what she did, and I hoped that I didn't vomit.

"Good morning, love," Choyce greeted as Izzy and Lee passed by his desk.

Lee glared as he placed a protective hand on her waist. Izzy didn't even look in his direction, and I could tell she was pissed. They weaved through the aisle to sit on my other side, pointedly not sitting anywhere near Choyce.

He turned in his chair to face me. "Was it something I said?"

I shrugged. "Probably more to do with last night. Why does she look so sick? Is that normal?"

"That's to be expected," he replied. "She's experiencing a flood of power, the kind of power you only get during the full moon only now it's all the time. It takes a bit for the body to get used to that kind of strength."

Was it worth it? If she was that strong now, we'd probably have a fighting chance. Then I remembered how that was done, and I shivered. My sister was like a real-life vampire now.

142

Why are you talking to him? Izzy's voice hissed in my mind.

Ouch! I complained, hoping she could hear me. *That was loud.*

Whatever, she replied, obviously able to hear my thoughts. *Don't avoid the question.*

I can talk to whoever I want. I replied. *Why do you care?*

Okay, books off your desk!" Mr. Web announced, beginning the class. "It's quiz time."

Because, she replied, ignoring the teacher. *He's a murderer. And dangerous.*

Placing my book back into my bag, I pulled out a clean sheet of paper and pencil.

Aren't we those things? I retorted. *I mean, we're not exactly innocent. He seems to know how to handle this whole curse.*

Do you even remember what we did last night? She shouted, making me wince once again.

Could you take it down a notch?

You boiled someone! She cried. *I drank someone's blood, and we murdered like fifteen innocent people between the three of us. All for what?*

My heart sank. I hated the darkness that took us over on the full moon. The powers were nice, but what they made us do scared me more than anything. I couldn't take any of it

143

back, but I knew that we needed Choyce. He was the only other shapeshifter like us that we'd met, and with him, we were one step closer to bringing all of this mess to its knees. For better or for worse, we were better off sticking together.

Listen, I thought. *Whether we like it or not, we need Choyce. Besides, we already promised that we'd save his brother.*

I'm not so sure that's a good idea anymore, Izzy replied.

Why? What's going on with you this morning? I asked, but my question was met with silence as she broke off the connection.

14
NO GOING BACK

- Izara -

I will return… I will return… I will return…

A voice kept ringing in my head, repeating those words on loop. It didn't belong to Choyce or Kain, so who could it be? It was a man's voice, a deep voice so dead it sent chills running down my whole body. It was a voice I'd heard before, but never so urgent as now.

You know my face… I will return…

My head pounded, and I knew I'd get a headache soon if that voice didn't stop. I tried to focus on my locker, entering the correct combination to get my things for class.

Beware...

I slammed my fist on the locker door.

"Whoa, there," a soft chuckle started me, and I glanced up to see Lee coming to stand next to me. "Everything okay?"

"Oh, hey." I flushed pink, embarrassed that anyone else saw my mini-meltdown. "Yeah, the lock was just stuck. It's all good now."

He tilted his head, leaning in to give me a quick kiss. "Can I walk you to class?"

"Sure." I smiled, needing a distraction.

After grabbing my books, we headed for the stairs to the second floor.

I tried to listen as Lee went on about the OU vs. Tulsa college football game, but my head hurt so much I just wished we could walk in silence. He gave me a play by play of what happened, but my brain was being bombarded with strange images. The first was the vision I'd seen after the funeral for Lee's mom. A close friend of the family had met for a reception at their house, and I couldn't take it anymore. Every inch of that space reminded me of the horrific event that had taken place there.

I recalled storming out the back and heading for the fields where they kept their horses. A flash of light and a gust of wind sent me flying. When the light subsided, a team of what looked like angels stood before me. They marched towards me; their faces contorted in anger before they

146

evaporated as quickly as they'd appeared.

The second image was of the face that looked like a skull. It reminded me of how Choyce's face looked when he first transitioned.

"Anyway." Lee continued, pulling me from my thoughts. "It was an epic game."

"Sounds like it," I replied, trying to sound natural.

"Anyway, I was planning on going to see my dad this weekend," he said as we entered history class. "Want to join me?"

My heart thumped at the sight of his mother falling limp as I ripped her heart from her chest. I blinked, shaking off the vision. I'd been reliving that nightmare all year long.

"Uh, I think Kia and I already made plans." I bit my lip, unable to keep from feeling guilty as the lie slipped so easily. It'd become almost a habit to lie, and I hated myself for it.

"No worries." He shrugged as we took our seats, and Mr. Web started the projector with the list of questions.

***

I quickly grabbed my things as history class came to an end. I was definitely not waiting around to give Choyce a chance to talk to me. I was going to try and stay as far away from him as possible. I was almost as mad at him as I was at

Kain. How could he be chatting with a monster like him? Remembering the events that took place the night before, it was apparent Choyce was only looking out for himself and his brother.

He didn't care what happened to me or what he put my brother and me through. All he cared about was number one. Was I going to wind up just like *him*?

I shivered at the prospect and prayed that it would never happen. Leaping from my seat when the bell rang, I rushed into the hall.

"Whoa, what's the rush?" Lee asked, not far behind.

"I just don't want to be in that room anymore."

Something tugged at my heart, and I knew Choyce was trying to communicate with me, but I forced myself to push it away. It seemed I was actually able to block attempts at communicating with me telepathically. Was this a reaction to being untied from the full moon? I didn't know, but whatever it was, I was thankful for it.

"I know what you mean." Lee rolled his eyes. "That Choyce guy gets on my last nerve. Plus, that way he looks at you really gets under my skin."

I was glad when Kia joined us at the lockers. I didn't want to talk about Choyce anymore.

"So, it looks like Mr. Valkyrien is out today," Kia said. "We're supposed to go to homeroom."

"Lucky you." Lee laughed. "I'll see you at lunch."

He gave me a quick peck on the cheek before heading off to his next class.

"You two are so cute." Kia linked arms with me as we headed for the staircase.

As we walked, I wondered where Osbel was. I had to find him, but it seemed like he was avoiding me. What had he meant when he told me not to let 'them' into my mind? Had he caused me to see that vision intentionally?

"Oh, there's Leslie!" Kia exclaimed, interrupting my thoughts. "I need to get her notes from Friday. Catch you up in a second?"

"Sure." I shrugged as she disappeared down the hall.

I followed the other students piling into the room, and as I did so, a thick head of blond, wavy hair caught my eye. I couldn't believe my eyes. Choyce was marching his way into my classroom.

Taking a deep breath, my blood ran hot as I pushed past the students between us. I grabbed him by the shirt and pulled him outside of the classroom. I didn't care about the strange looks the others were giving us.

"What are you doing?" I growled, shoving Choyce up against the wall.

"Ooh, hello, love." His eyes lit up, making me want to smack the smile from his thin lips. "I was just going to class, but if you're interested in other things..."

"Ew, shut up." I instantly let go of him. "I meant, why

149

are you entering this room? You're not in this class."

"I wasn't," he said as if to correct me.

"What?" I shook my head.

"I *wasn't* in this class. Now I am."

"Why the *hell* would you be in this class?" I asked.

"I tried the calculus thing, really, I did. But it just didn't work out for me. So now I'll be taking chemistry second period and Algebra II fourth period."

The corner of his lip curled ever so slightly upward as if he were fighting laughter. He was trying to infuriate me, and it was working.

"That's a lie." I shook my head. "You're like a century old. You've got to know more than basic math by now."

He placed his long, bony fingers on either of my shoulders, spinning me around and pinning me to the wall.

"You're right," he whispered in my ear, his honeyed breath sending shivers down my spine. "I didn't need to change my schedule, but I do need you. And, like it or not, you need me. This is why wherever you are, I will be. You feel the powers inside of you growing, and it scares you to death. That's why you hide behind this cardigan and makeup."

His fingers attempted to lift my sleeve, and I pushed him away.

"I don't need you," I growled. "So you can change your class schedule back to whatever it was before. Preferably so we don't have any classes together."

150

I knew I was probably wasting my breath since Choyce didn't seem to ever listen to me, but I had to try. This was getting ridiculous. We couldn't have multiple classes together if I was going to keep my sanity.

He winked, backing up as he headed for the classroom. My mouth fell. What game was he playing? Frustrated and annoyed, I followed him into the room, making sure to find a seat on the opposite side of the room.

When the homeroom teacher started talking, I found I couldn't focus on anything he was saying. I kept getting the feeling like I was being watched and that someone was trying to invade my mind.

It was probably Choyce, and I was actually thankful that I wasn't tied to the full moon for once today. If I had been, then my mind wouldn't be able to protect itself from intruders like him. I kept resisting the urge to look in Choyce's direction, even though I really wanted to give him the death glare.

"Ms. Torvik?"

The sudden mention of my name jolting me from my thoughts. "Uh, yeah?"

"You're going to have to remove your sunglasses," The teacher said, motioning to my eyewear. "Class policy."

What? I had never heard of that policy before.

"Sir, I have a horrible migraine. I won't be able to focus on my studies if I do."

"I'm sorry." He shrugged. "Either that or I'm going to

have to ask you to leave and make your way to the principal's office."

The classroom echoed with a few students muffling their snickering and mocked me. I fumed. They had no idea what they were up against. I whipped my head around, and without even realizing what I was doing, I threw my pencil at one of the giggling students.

The room fell silent, followed by a piercing cry as the student's eyes froze on the pencil stuck in his hand—blood formed around the wood as gasps spread like wildfire throughout the classroom.

What had I done? How in the world was I supposed to explain this? I didn't know how that even happened. Glancing around the room, all eyes were on me, and my chest tightened. I couldn't breathe. Without another word, I hurriedly grabbed my things and rushed for the door.

"Ms. Torvik!" The teacher shouted after me, but I'd already left the room.

I would probably get reported, but I didn't care. I couldn't believe how close I was to exposing us if I hadn't already. What had come over me?

I threw my things into my locker and stormed out of the school. I couldn't go back in there. I didn't really know where I was going, but before I knew it, the old familiar scent of pine welcomed me as I dove into the woods as fast as I could.

I will return...

The voice was back, filling my entire consciousness. I grabbed my head as I fell to my knees. Tears spilled over the corners of my eyelids; I had no more fight in me to stop them. I couldn't take it anymore. My vision blurred, and soon I was staring at a group of cloaked figures surrounded by a brilliant light.

"This is your end." The leader of the cloaked figures said, her patronizing voice almost familiar.

I stood, noticing my feet had large, muddy toes that didn't belong to me but to a man. What was happening? Whose feet were these?

Looking up at the group of shifters before me, some had black wings, and others had white. I sensed their disgust as it rose inside the pit of my stomach. A chuckle escaped me, a low guttural sound that took me by surprise. This wasn't my voice.

"Why do you laugh?" The leader asked. "You do know that this is your demise."

I continued to laugh against my will. "You think this will kill me?" The words slipped through my lips, but I knew they were not my own.

"We don't plan on killing you." The leader said from underneath her hooded robe. "We've learned from our mistakes. This time, you will be neutralized."

One of the figures gripped a glowing white stake, and a

smirk spread across my face. I knew that whoever's body I was in was amused for some reason.

"You laugh, even though you know that this is the end of your heinous existence?" The leader asked, her white wings bristling.

"How foolish!" The deep voice bellowed from within me.

"The only thing that is foolish is you," the leader replied. "You're an abomination."

The cackle returned, and my face contorted against my will. "You," I hissed. "You are the abomination."

My hand rose, my index finger pointing towards the group. "The end is near. I will return."

At that moment, one of the winged angels grabbed the stake from the leader and flew at me, plunging it straight into my heart. As the blade crashed into me, pieces of glass exploded from my body, sending millions of silvery splinters out in every direction. Black spidery veins crawled across my vision, enveloping everything in darkness. The cloaked figures faded into nothingness and the voice within me that belonged to someone else dissipated...

Sharp twigs pushed against my cheek as the scent of dry leaves and dirt assaulted my senses. Tree trunks groaned as birds playfully chirped. It was somehow comforting knowing I wasn't in the presence of those angels anymore. But where was I?

You know my face... the dead voice echoed in my mind. *I will return... this is not the end...*

My heart sank as I realized this was anything but the end and that this voice would continue to haunt me. Who was he, though? Was he the one the Assembly wanted to prevent the return of? And how did I fit into all of this?

"Izara."

My eyes flew open when I heard someone say my name, hoping it wasn't the Assembly come to finish the job. Scanning the woods before me, the light cascaded through the treetops casting ominous shadows. My fingers curled into the uneven ground, pushing myself up off the ground. Someone grabbed my arm, and I looked up.

"How are you feeling?" Choyce asked, his brow furrowed as he helped me up.

It took my brain a second to register who this was, and I instantly shoved him away.

"Stay away from me." I took a step back, sending him a warning look.

"Iz." His eyes softened.

There was pity in them, but I wasn't falling for it. "Did you know this would happen to me?"

He opened his mouth to speak but hesitated, giving me all the answers I needed.

I shivered with rage. "All this to bring your brother back?"

"You have to trust me," he whispered with a hint of guilt in his words.

"How dare you." I shook my head, the heat bubbling within me and settling in the palm of my hands. "You accuse me of using you, and then you trick me into drinking someone else's blood?

"I didn't trick you." Choyce took a step closer to me. "And I *am* sorry about accusing you of using me."

He was crazy. How could he say something like that and then apologize so quickly? It couldn't be honest. No matter how sincere he was acting.

"I was upset," he explained. "A part of me blamed you for losing my brother because if you hadn't asked us to search for the journal all those years ago, I might still have Edwin."

My face hurt from the heat of fury that was rising up from my core, threatening to surface.

"It was what put the nightwalkers on our tail," he continued, "it is what resulted in Edwin's death. I also blamed you for not using your powers to stop them that night."

"You blamed *me*?" I scoffed. "Kain and I both were powerless!"

"Yes, I know that now. I resented many things in my naiveté, but I now know that blaming you was wrong."

More like ignorance, but I shut my mouth. I didn't want to talk to Choyce longer than I had to.

"So you thought you'd get back at me? Turn me into a

vampire to torture me? Make me even more guilty than I already am?"

"No, you've got it all wrong." He sighed, rubbing the back of his neck.

I couldn't see how anyone with half a brain could misunderstand what he was saying.

"None of this is coming outright." He took a deep breath, his head bowed low as he rubbed his temples. Bits of his wavy blond hair fell across his fallen face from the knot it was in.

I could sense the agony he was in, but I wasn't going to fall for this act again. I would stand my ground.

"Look." He finally faced me straight on, his eyes glassy. "That was my first reaction. It was wrong. Losing my brother was the worst day of my life, but I shouldn't have blamed you. I shouldn't have said any of that."

Choyce stood before me, vulnerable and open, and I knew he was sincere. But stubbornness reared its ugly head, and I didn't want to give in. This still didn't change the fact that he'd been the one to push me over the edge. To do such a horrible thing like drink someone's blood. There was no going back from that.

"I know you didn't want anything bad to happen that night. You wanted to stop them but couldn't." Choyce's voice turned desperate, filling in my silence. "I know that now."

He finally removed the space between us, and I

instinctively took a step back.

"I didn't trick you into untying yourself from the full moon." He lifted his hands up when I flinched. "You drank willingly. I would never force you to do anything you didn't want to do."

I shook my head. I didn't want to believe my memory. That I would do anything that horrible by choice.

"I know what you're going through." He finally took my hands in his. "This is just your body adjusting to the surge of power. It's a lot to take in, but you'll get used to it."

"How do you know?"

"Because." He tilted his head, massaging comforting circles on the tops of my hands. "I've been through this. I know what you're going through, and I'll be with you every step of the way. With each full moon of partaking, you'll gain more control."

"Wait." I pulled my hands from his. "You mean I have to continue drinking blood?"

That was definitely not a part of the deal.

"Only until you've mastered time travel so we can save my brother. Then you can do whatever you want."

My heart raced, threatening to burst through my chest, and I backed away from him.

Heaving a sigh, I knew what I needed to do. "No. I can't help you."

With that, I turned and fled from the woods.

15

BART BESSLER, 1919

- a.k.a. Lawrence Choyce Bartholomew -

Lawrence found himself frozen, staring at the unusual couple that caused his heart to beat rapidly. The whole world seemed to disappear as the yellow-eyed woman, and her friend became his sole focus.

The two moved together as one, leaving the party behind, and he followed, drawn into their orbit. They increased their step as they neared the staircase. One row led up to the second floor, while the other went down to an underground level. They darted for the stairs heading upwards, seemingly unaware that they were being followed.

He wondered what these two were up to. Slowly

making his way up the stairs, he reached the second-floor landing when he came face-to-face with the redhead, her black claws drawn and fangs extended.

"Why do you follow us?" The woman hissed, a hint of a British accent touching her lips.

Lawrence was so startled by the intensity of her glare that he forgot how to respond. His eyes darted between the two in a feverish panic.

"Answer her," her companion growled, flashing wolf-like teeth that were white as pearls against his grizzly black beard.

"I—I don't know." Lawrence was dumb. He'd never imagined that one would be able to use their powers outside of the full moon unless these shapeshifters were an entirely different type of monster than he was.

"You must leave." The woman warned.

"Why?" Lawrence finally managed to ask, curiosity getting the better of him. "Why can I feel your hearts beating?"

The man rolled his eyes. "He's going to ruin the plan."

The woman tilted her head, her red locks draping over her bare shoulder. "He's one of us. Shouldn't we at least warn him?"

"We have to leave that up for *him* to decide," the wolfman said, gruffly.

Who were they talking about? Lawrence wondered.

And what did she want to warn him about? What plan?

He had so many questions, but they were soon lost as a feeling that he shouldn't have followed them washed over him. They were the ones he sensed, but there was something very dark and ancient about them that struck fear in him. They probably wouldn't help him get his brother back, anyway.

Out of nowhere, the yellow-eyed woman reached for him. Her cold fingers wrapped around his face, and suddenly she snapped his neck, causing his world to disappear.

***

He didn't know if he was alive or not. Everything was dark, and the last thing he remembered was the redhead breaking his neck. He had to be dead, right?

"You said it yourself," a gruff voice echoed around him. "He can't be trusted."

Lawrence wiggled his fingers and decided that he was still alive. But how? That woman had definitely snapped his neck. He didn't know how long he'd been out, but as he gained consciousness, he concluded that he needed to get away from that couple as soon as possible.

"Please, Abram," a quiet and calming voice whispered. "We needn't act with such haste."

They spoke as if they belonged to another world entirely. Lawrence snuck a peek, his cheek lying against a damp, hard surface with small cracks in it. Was he still in the hotel?

A bare bulb light with a string pull hung from a low ceiling, illuminating the couple standing beside a row of shelves filled with dusty cases of wine and preserves. He assumed they must've been in the cellar of the hotel.

The wolfman huffed, his dark, muscular arms flexing as he folded them. "The full moon is upon us. We don't have time for this."

"My love," the woman said in an attempt to calm him down. "We must have patience."

"We are so close," the man named Abram growled. "If we don't do this now, we shall have to delay yet another month. He won't be happy about that."

She placed a hand on his cheek, stroking his curly beard. "It will all be okay. Stay with me. Stay with the light."

Lawrence took this moment to stand up, careful not to make a noise as he crept towards the wooden staircase nearby.

"The lad is waking." The woman whispered without even looking at him.

His heart leaped into his throat as he dove for the staircase but met the pair standing in his way before he could make it.

He stopped. "Let me go. I won't cause you any trouble. Just let me pass."

Their heartbeats erupted inside of his chest like a million pitter-pattering raindrops in a thunderstorm. Suddenly, the door at the top of the stairwell creaked open, casting light down the dusty steps. A man in a perfectly tailored suit and neatly trimmed black hair stepped through the doorway. The steps groaned as he made his way to the basement floor. The door slammed shut, and the distant echoes of the party disappeared.

Lawrence couldn't feel this man's heartbeat, so he must've been human, but he didn't even have a pulse either. It was as if he was dead, but he knew that couldn't be true. The man was clearly alive, and the way he looked at the couple made Lawrence think that this man knew them well. Was this who they were talking about?

"Who are you?" Lawrence finally asked.

"Silence," Abram growled at him before turning his attention to the strange man. "Should we just get rid of him?"

The unbreathing man finally took the last step, the couple carefully backing away from him. He made no response as he walked past them, taking in his surroundings as he tucked his hands inside his suit pants. He took his time until he turned on Lawrence, getting a closer look.

"Chain him." The human ordered the wolfman.

Lawrence panicked, throwing care to the wind as he grabbed the handrail, determined to get to the top of the staircase.

He only made it halfway up when the wolfman's arms wrapped around him, pulling him back down. Before he even had a moment to fight back, he was shoved against a wall as his ankles and wrists were shackled.

"You have questions." His voice was as smooth as silk, soothing the tension in the darkness. "But you must have patience. For, you see, the destiny of shapeshifters, such as yourself, is about to come to fruition."

"The only thing that will come to fruition," Lawrence spat, not appreciating being chained up, "is me escaping these chains and killing you all."

"Of course, you would kill your own kind." The human sighed as he turned to the woman. "Do it, Emma."

The woman he'd called Emma glanced to Abram as if for reassurance. Lawrence cried out, hoping someone could hear him. He shook the chains that bound him, but it was no use. He could make himself invisible, but this didn't change the fact that he was a tangible form. He would just have to wait for the full moon, which luckily would begin any hour now.

Emma squeezed Abram's hand before turning to Lawrence. Her hands stretched out wide on either side, and the whole room shook as little strands of light rushed from the ceiling and through the walls. They flew in a string towards her fingertips, lighting up her arms as she sucked in all the light. Even the light from the little bulb dimmed as she pulled in its energy. She closed her eyes as she looked up, her entire body absorbing the light. Lawrence had never seen anything like it.

As Emma fed off the light, Abram moved around her,

drawing strange curly symbols on the floor. It looked almost like cursive, but not in any language Lawrence knew of. What were they for?

Something crashed above them, startling them. Lawrence prayed it was someone that could save them.

"What was that?" Emma asked, ceasing to draw in the light at the interruption.

The door croaked, opening as unsteady footsteps made their way down.

"Are you sure about this?" A lady's voice giggled, obviously intoxicated.

"Of course." A man's voice confirmed. "This is where they keep their finest."

"Oh, I like the sound of that." Another woman's voice replied.

The three found their way, unsteadily, to the bottom of the staircase and stopped when they saw that they weren't alone.

"Oh, pardon the intrusion," the man slurred, tipping an invisible hat. "We didn't realize this vessel had company."

The two women laughed as if they'd heard the funniest joke in the world.

"But you, my dear, why aren't you the most delectable..." He reached for Emma, her skin glowing bright with light.

Abram stepped in front of her, growling as he exposed

his sharp fangs. His eyes flashed gray, and the man jumped back.

"I meant no offense." He quivered. "We shall just choose a bottle and be on our way."

The human companion stepped towards them, his calm countenance sure and calculating. "Abram, would you show our guests what happens when we're interrupted?"

A smile curled across Abram's face as he leaped forward like a lion, biting into the neck of one of the drunk women. Lawrence flinched as their screams filled the cellar walls. He couldn't believe what he was seeing, but soon it didn't matter as his entire body shuddered.

The full moon. It was here. His muscles contracted, and he shuddered as a crawling sensation snaked up his spine. Black veins crawled down his arms towards his fingertips. He cried out in pain as they stabbed through his cuticles, growing sharp, black claws in the place of his fingernails.

"Emma, you must continue." The man in the suit urged. "It is our last chance."

Knives pierced through either of Lawrence's shoulder blades as he twisted in agony until he shuddered. The full moon took control of him, and he knew that, even though he was captive to its power, he was free of these feeble chains. He heaved a sigh, focusing his energy on the chains around his ankle, and moved his clawed hand through the air. Suddenly, the metal snapped away.

That was a new power, Lawrence thought gleefully.

Maybe his powers were finally advancing? The realization of what he'd just done sent a thrilling shiver down his spine. He'd just moved the metal without even touching it. He hadn't gained a new power since his brother was murdered eight years prior.

The three humans that had interrupted them hung at odd angles, blood drenching the last step. Abram wiped his mouth but froze when he saw Lawrence standing before them, wings extended.

"Go!" Their human companion shouted to Emma and Abram just as Lawrence grabbed his collar.

"Who are you?" Lawrence hissed, trying to fight the tug that pulled him in the opposite direction.

The familiar darkness crept into his mind, threatening to take over. Another heart thumped within his chest as the metallic scent of the one the darkness longed for took over his senses. His knees nearly went weak from it, but Lawrence had to get some answers first. He couldn't leave without getting something back. They'd owed him that.

"*GO!*" The human shouted again.

"I will be right behind them." Lawrence threatened.

"You can't hurt us." The companion chuckled. "Look at you. You're still tied to the full moon. It's calling for you to do its bidding."

"Try me," Lawrence growled, making a point to

168

investigate if there was a way to untie oneself from the full moon. Lawrence wasn't about to let this man think he didn't know what he was talking about.

Emma continued to give Lawrence the death stare, the light exploding from her pupils blinding him.

"What are you doing?" Lawrence cried, squeezing his eyes shut.

When the light subsided, his fingers rubbed together as the man he was holding disappeared. Glancing around the dark cellar, he found himself alone. The couple, their human companion, and the three intruders were all gone. Everyone had vanished, and the only thing that remained was a strange feeling in the pit of his stomach that something had gone terribly wrong.

16
CONSEQUENCES

- Izara -

I was afraid. Afraid of myself, of what would happen next, of everything. Would I get expelled for losing control in class? Most likely.

I shook my head, not knowing why I'd been so stupid. I wanted everything to stop. How could I be a good student, girlfriend, or even a person when my body seemed to be losing control?

I tapped my foot nervously as I sat in the lobby of Principal Chomsky's office. After the incident, I had been put on probation until the school's 'powers that be' could decide what to do with me, which meant weeks of detention and a lot of extra homework. They'd finally decided on my fate, and I prayed it didn't involve getting expelled. How would I be able to bring down this school from the inside if I was kicked out?

"She'll see you now." The secretary called from behind her desk, startling me from my thoughts.

I nodded, standing up and making my way down the hall. My hands shook uncontrollably, and I crossed my arms. I was sweating and yet ice cold all at the same time. How was that even possible?

Taking a deep breath, I stopped in front of the last door. This was it. Whatever happened, I had to be strong. I had to get through this. I'd faced worse things in my life, hadn't I?

"Come in." Principal Chomsky's shrill yet stern voice came from behind the door.

No turning back now, I thought to myself.

Turning the doorknob, I slowly opened the only barrier between me and the unknown.

Principal Chomsky barely glanced up from her computer as I took a seat across from her. She held a document in her hand while the other clacked against the keyboard. I sat there in painful silence. The constant ticking of a clock reminded me that every turn of the hand was a second closer to my fate.

Out of nowhere, the document flew from her hand into the air, placing itself in the filing cabinet before the drawer shut itself closed. My eyes widened in disbelief. Did that really just happen? I turned my gaze back to Principal Chomsky, who was now staring at me intently, arms firmly folded on the desk.

She pursed her lips. "It's been challenging for us to figure you out." Her calm voice contradicted the intensity of her stare.

"I'm sorry?" I asked, wondering what she was getting at.

"You and your brother, of course."

"And what have you figured out?"

She sighed, obviously irritated by my question. "That you and your brother are exactly what this school has been searching for."

Goosebumps covered my arms, understanding what she couldn't say. This school was made to rid the world of those with powers, like Kain and I had. But then why was I still sitting here? If she knew what Kain and I were, why hadn't she sent the nightwalkers after me?

"You can't hurt us."

"Oh, we can." She chuckled darkly. "But I've been advised, against my better judgment, not to *expel* you both."

The way she emphasized expel made me shiver. The gunshot that killed Edwin echoed in my head, knowing this was Principal Chomsky's preferred way of removing students. A knot twisted in my stomach at the thought.

"What do you want?" I asked.

"We want to prevent the return."

"The return of who?" My nerves on edge as I realized I

might finally be getting the answers I'd been searching for.

"The darkest being of them all, an abomination." Her words rang around me as she gripped the key around her neck, causing my vision to blur.

Suddenly, I was once again standing in front of a group of angels—some with black wings and others with white. We stood in a field of roses. There was a man on the ground. His black wings bent at odd angles as he picked himself up from the thorny brush. The angels removed their hoods, and their glowing eyes flashed at him as a warning.

I took a closer look at the man and gasped. He looked a lot like I did when in transition. Only instead of black irises like Choyce or red like mine, his were pure white. His face was sunken in, exposing the bones of his skull through translucent skin. His fingers and toes were crooked as if they'd been broken many times. Blood dripped from the corner of his lips, and his winks twitched in pain.

"You are an abomination." The angel at the lead hissed. She looked identical to Principal Chomsky, except that she had giant white wings.

Without hesitation, she swiftly grabbed a glowing white stake, flying towards the beaten figure.

NO! I screamed, but the words were never heard.

The stake met his skin, tearing through his heart. I watched in horror as his body turned limp.

I blinked as my sight returned to the principal's office.

I sucked in a breath of air. My heart beat nervously as her eyes bore into me. I was more terrified of her than I'd ever been before. She was an executioner. My whole body shook as the realization sunk in.

"We have reason to believe this evil has returned." Principal Chomsky interrupted the silence. "And I believe he is calling himself Choyce these days."

I frowned as the night Choyce appeared in Lee's backyard while playing flashlight tag popped into my head. I remembered his round scar on his chest as he removed his shirt I'd lit on fire. It was in the exact spot where Principal Chomsky had stabbed the man from my vision. But how was this possible? They didn't look anything alike.

"His true name is Lawrence Bartholomew." She continued. "He arrived at the school when it first opened but got away before we could capture him."

I shook my head, unsure I was hearing her correctly.

"Unfortunately, I'm under strict orders that we must be certain he's the one before we can take measures into our own hands."

"What do you mean take measures into your own hands?"

"That's none of your concern," she said sternly. "I've been asked to take a milder approach. That's where you come in. Your assignment is to get close to Choyce, get him to trust you, and to confirm his true identity."

174

"How am I supposed to do that?" I asked. "I don't even know who you think Choyce is."

She paused for a moment, considering what to say next. "He is the most powerful being ever to exist. His abilities go far beyond any of ours."

"Ours?"

She fell silent, and I could tell she was deliberating on what to say to me. "Hidden from this world, another exists. One where shifters, like myself, exist. Some belong to the night while others belong to the day."

The room grew cold as each word she spoke sunk in.

"An assembly was made to maintain order and keep the two factions separated. Unfortunately, someone disobeyed the order of things. A shifter of the light fell for one of the night, mixing their powers creating something more powerful than anything we've ever witnessed. It tore through the veil that keeps us from the human world, allowing hundreds to escape the Transitioned World into yours. Thankfully we've been able to build up a wall, locking our world up, but the prophecy says he will return soon. Which is why we're here."

That must've been what the keys were for. It was the key to their world, but then why had it sent me back in time when I used it? Perhaps I was using it wrong? I was so confused.

"I still don't see how this has anything to do with me," I replied, my head spinning from all this information.

She cocked an eyebrow. "Isn't it obvious, child? Somehow, from where he lives underground, he's been moving his powers into humans. Perhaps to preserve them, and you have one of them. The ability to manipulate matter as you did in class a few weeks ago."

I realized then that she knew very little about what I could do. She had no idea that Kain and I had many other powers besides moving things about with a wave of our hand. It seemed as though she didn't know about the full moon, either. Was the full moon somehow connected with the glass that shattered when Principal Chomsky stabbed that man in the chest? Was it a curse?

"Powers like his were never supposed to exist," she continued. "He threatened to spread, to make others like him, and as of yet, that hasn't happened. The Assembly's main mission is to make sure that doesn't happen."

I wasn't so sure about that. If she only knew about our other powers, she'd kill us for sure. Whoever this shifter was, he was the reason we had these powers.

"Anyway, we believe he's transferred his consciousness to Choyce. As I've said before, we want to be sure this is the case before we proceed."

Transferred his consciousness? Was that even a thing?

"I will make sure you are unharmed by the nightwalkers." Apparently, that was their official name. "And in return, you'll give a full report to Chuck each week."

My heart fell at the mention of that name. "Chuck?" I gasped. "The one who tortured my brother and me for weeks?"

"Yes, I heard about that." She smirked. "He will be keeping an eye on you. Consider this an extra incentive."

I gulped, her threat resonating loud and clear.

"How do you expect me to get Choyce to trust me?" I asked.

"I heard he signed up for drama club. That should give you two some good bonding experience." She chuckled as my jaw dropped. "Ms. Morgan has been kind enough to step down—"

"WHAT?" I cried.

"—so that Chuck can take on the position." She concluded, ignoring my interruption.

Bile rose in my mouth at the idea. The only class I enjoyed, the one time I could genuinely distract myself from it all, and now it was going to be ruined by spending it with the tagalong I was trying to get rid of and the psychopath who nearly murdered me. How had he escaped wherever Kain plopped him last year? What would prevent him from trying to kill us again?

"I don't think Chuck is the best person for the job, not to mention I don't trust him."

"I've taken care of that. For now."

"And what about Kain?"

"Your brother will be safe as well," she confirmed,

177

although I wasn't so sure how much I trusted her word. "As long as you are doing what you are told, you need not worry."

I wanted to lash out, to say what I wanted to. She was manipulating me. Just the thought of doing as she asked made my blood boil. But I bit my tongue. She had me cornered, and I could see there was no other way out that kept the people I loved safe. I would just have to be careful and keep my mind closed off so Choyce couldn't read my mind.

"Fine," I hissed through clenched teeth.

17
WATCH ME WATCH YOU

- Izara -

Lee and I walked to lunch in awkward silence. After hearing through the grapevine that Choyce was in all of my classes, he freaked out, and I couldn't blame him. I didn't like it either. He didn't understand why I couldn't just switch my classes, and I couldn't tell him the truth. That Principal Chomsky was forcing me to get close to Choyce to see if he really was the devil incarnate she thought he was. I'd had to lie again, something that was becoming all too common in our relationship.

"Are you okay?" I asked, just as he opened the door to the cafeteria for me.

"Yeah." He sighed. "Just be careful, okay?" I don't know what it is, but something's off with this guy, and I hope you at least try to keep your distance whenever possible."

"I'll definitely try," I agreed. My inner desire to keep far away from Choyce was even greater than it had been before. Lee might've suspected something dark about him, but if he knew what I did, then he'd be sure of it.

After grabbing our food, we scanned the room for a place to sit. I didn't see Kia or any of the others. Had they eaten earlier?

"There's a spot at that table." Lee nodded towards a table with a few seats left. "Come on."

We marched over to the table as several students I hadn't seen before glanced up. They glared in my direction as I neared, and I wondered what their problem was.

As I pulled a chair out, the person next to it dropped a backpack in the seat.

"Excuse me," I said.

The girl looked up at me and smirked.

"I was going to sit there."

"No, you weren't." She barked.

"Was someone else sitting here?" Lee asked.

"You can." She nodded towards him. "But she can't."

I frowned. "I don't see why you can't just put your bag on the back of your chair or on the ground where it was." I retorted.

I shrunk back as the girl stood up, her tall frame easily six feet tall. If we weren't in a crowded cafeteria, I'd easily take her. My fingers tingled as flames threatened to ignite, but I held back. I couldn't risk anyone seeing me use my powers.

She shoved me back. "I said you can't sit here."

I stumbled back into Lee, who grabbed me before I fell. "What's your problem?" Lee glared at the girl after making sure I was okay.

"Come on." I tugged on his shoulder, pulling him away. "I see some of the guys from the basketball team over there. Let's see if we can sit there."

It took Lee a second to back away. I gripped his hand tight, hoping he'd just let it go.

"Fine. Let's go." He turned to leave, but before I could follow, the large girl stepped closer to me.

"We'll be watching you."

My eyes widened as I realized what she was implying. She was a nightwalker. My mind raced as we left her table behind. The girl I'd met in 1911 flashed before my eyes.

"They surround the school in the dark, looking for students." Her voice was haunting as it echoed around me.

"The school killed Edwin's love… they killed her dead. Nightwalkers!"

We'd learned a lot that night we'd witnessed Choyce's younger brother murdered by the school's nightwalkers, but no one told us that we had to worry about students being

181

nightwalkers, too. But how could they motivate students to hunt each other and keep it a secret? They couldn't pay them overtime like they could the instructors. Maybe they got less homework? Or extra credit? The idea of students being undercover nightwalkers was terrifyingly brilliant. What better way to spy on the students and figure out which ones the nightwalkers should bury in the quarry? I shivered at the thought.

"Hey!" I barely heard Kia above my own blood pumping in my eardrums. "Izzy, come on."

She tapped on my shoulder, and I glanced up.

"Ready for drama practice?"

"Oh, yeah," I said, hopping up from my seat. "I'll see you after practice?"

Lee nodded. He hadn't said a word to me since the incident at the other table. I wondered if he'd heard what that girl said. If he had, he didn't show it.

"I'm so glad Leslie and Ms. Morgan agreed to cast me as the Cheshire Cat." Kia squealed. "It's going to be so much fun!"

"Me too. I think you'll be great at it," I replied.

I couldn't bring myself to tell her about the change in leadership. She loved Ms. Morgan and knew she'd be just as devastated as I was that she was gone. Although, she didn't realize Chuck was the one who'd kidnapped my brother and me last year.

182

The thought of Kain reminded me I still needed to tell him that Chuck was back, but I hadn't had a chance to yet. He was going to be furious, but that would be a problem for another day.

"Hurry up, we don't want to be late," Kia said, practically skipping all the way to the auditorium as I reluctantly followed behind.

For once, I wasn't excited about drama class, wishing I could just crawl into my bed and wake tomorrow with all of this being a stupid dream. But it wasn't a dream. It was real. So I decided I'd be the best actress I could possibly be. I didn't want to give the nightwalkers any reason to hurt us. Again.

***

- Kain -

I left the cafeteria and headed for basketball practice with the guys.

"Ya know we're playing Davis next week?" Duran was saying.

"Are you worried?" Lee winked.

"Nah, we'll crush them." Duran laughed.

"They're more of a football town, anyway." Laurent agreed.

"Hey, isn't that the president's nephew?" Duran asked, nodding towards a scrawny guy up ahead, walking towards us.

My heart thumped nervously, hoping he wasn't talking about who I thought he was.

"I thought he was missing," Lee added.

The stench of rotten eggs met my nostrils, and the hairs on the back of my neck stood up on end, confirming my suspicion.

"Pardon me," Chuck said as he strolled by us. Our eyes met, and he chuckled, shoving his glasses back up his nose.

I froze, unable to move as I watched him walk on by. My body shook with rage, and all of my instinct urged me to follow, to finish the job I should've before.

How was this possible? I'd dumped him in the middle of nowhere without a cell phone. It wasn't possible. Unless the president had made another deal with the Assembly.

Seeing him again brought up everything that I tried to forget about last year. Being chained and tortured by that man who walked free before me.

"What's your power?" he'd asked me.

The bat he'd held scraped against the floor; I could hear it now like it was happening all over again, sending shivers down my spine.

"No words?" his snarl was embedded in my memory. *"Well, maybe this will jog your memory."*

He wound up like a batter, slamming the metal against my chest, knocking the air out of me. I stood there, breathless as the memory repeated on loop until Lee's hand on my shoulder set me free.

"You okay, man?" Lee asked.

I gasped for air, blinking as I realized where I was.

My jaw clenched as I swallowed hard. "Yeah. Fine."

Finally, able to move my feet, I followed the guys to the court. I needed to blow off some steam, and practice seemed like an excellent way to do that. I was powerless now, but, come the next full moon, I would correct this mistake. Chuck had to die.

18
HERE IT COMES

- Izara -

We entered the auditorium, and Choyce's heartbeat tugged on mine. Balling my hands into fists, I used all my strength to block him from my thoughts. I didn't know what Principal Chomsky was expecting me to be able to find out. I couldn't just suddenly be okay hanging out with him. That would be incredibly suspicious. If he was as dangerous as she said he was, then I had to be careful.

Following the other students, as they took their seats in the front row, I stopped Kia before we got to the row Choyce was sitting.

"Let's sit over there." I motioned to the opposite side.

She didn't seem to notice; her focus was on the script she had in her hand. "I have *so* many words to memorize." She sighed. "I should've been the White Rabbit. Want to switch?"

"No." I laughed. "You'll just have to practice a lot."

"Welcome, ladies and gents," Chuck called for our attention, his oversized suit pants fluttering as he marched to the front of the room.

Kia frowned. "What's he doing here?"

I just shrugged, not knowing what to say.

"As some of you may know, Ms. Morgan has stepped down from heading the drama department." A wave of gasps echoed throughout the room at his announcement. "I will be taking over—"

"What? That can't be right!" Leslie stood up, placing a hand on her hip. "I'm the president. If this were true, I would've heard something about it."

"Oh, dearie." He leaned his skinny head to one side. "This decision was a bit above your pay grade."

Leslie balked at his condescending comment, slowly sitting back down.

"Anyway, before I begin roll call," he continued, grabbing a clipboard, "there's another order of business I must bring to your attention, and that is the matter of fall productions. We will no longer be doing Alice in Wonderland. Instead, we will be covering Romeo and Juliet."

More protests erupted at that.

"But we don't have time to learn a whole other play!" A student cried.

"Now, now, there's no use in protesting!" Chuck called, trying to silence the riot.

"Well, I guess I don't have to worry about my lines." Kia frowned, tossing her script on the empty seat next to her.

"The decision is final!" he called out. "This is the play that the school has requested us to do. I don't know what kind of drama club Ms. Morgan was running, but our job is to implement them if the school requests changes. If anyone has a problem with this, you're free to leave. The show will go on."

The room fell silent.

"Good. So we're all on the same page now." He chuckled smugly. "I've already taken the liberty to assign parts to those I think would be the best fit for the role."

"Seriously?" It was my turn to complain.

It was one thing to insert a spy into the club to 'keep an eye' on me, but it was another to remove any chance to audition for parts we wanted.

"Wait, so now we don't have a choice?" Kia asked.

"Here are your scripts." Chuck ignored her question. "Your assigned part is highlighted."

No one seemed happy about the recent turn of events, and I wondered how many complaints Principal Chomsky would receive after class.

Chuck's stink nearly made me puke as he handed me my script. "Don't mess it up."

I rolled my eyes. If only the other students could smell him. He was as rotten on the inside as he was on the outside. Unfortunately for me, that little ability of his only worked on those with shapeshifting powers.

"I got Lady Capulet," Kia replied, scanning over the new script. "Far less interesting than the Cheshire Cat, but with fewer lines. Who'd you get?"

I opened the folder on my lap and glanced down at the first page. "I guess I'm Juliet."

"I'm going to be your mom." Kia burst out laughing.

"Careful, mom, or you'll pull a muscle." I teased.

Chuck cleared his throat, gaining our attention again. "I'll also be assigning you a co-actor. You'll consider this your partner, and you will be required to practice outside of our daily sessions on your own time. At least two hours a week until the time of our production."

How could he expect that? With homework, learning an entirely different script last minute, and everything else, we'd hardly have any free time. He was turning the drama club into a nightmare.

"The back of your packet will list who your partner is," Chuck concluded.

Flipping the pages, I glanced at the name listed. Of course, it was Choyce Barton. Rolling my eyes, I wasn't even surprised. I mean, the school did want me to get close to him, so why not require me to spend every waking hour with the one person who irritated me the most?

"Miss me, my lady?"

My insides lurched when I heard the words drip from Choyce's lips.

"Not in the least," I said as I stood in our designated section of the stage to practice our lines.

"Still hate me, I see," he mused, tucking his long curly blond hair behind an ear. "Don't worry, that'll soon change."

"What do you mean?"

"Love, what part of being psychic don't you get?" He wiggled his well-trimmed eyebrows.

"I thought that your power didn't work so well for you nowadays."

"Cruel to remind me." He sighed dramatically.

"Let's just practice our parts, okay?"

"Oh, good idea. Let's start with…" He paused, flipping through the pages. "How about scene five? The kiss?"

"In your dreams," I replied. "That won't be happening."

"But it's in the script." He gave me his famous crooked smile, his brown leather eyes glistening with delight.

He was enjoying this too much. "You think I'm going to kiss you? Especially after what you've done to me?"

"Listen," he whispered, stepping closer. "I know

190

you're blocking out the crucial bits of what happened that night because you're in what they call *denial*, but the facts speak for themselves."

"Which are?" I raised an eyebrow.

"That you chose to drink." Cinnamon and teakwood surrounded me as he whispered in my ear. "You chose to be the monster. You gave in to our true nature, and you know what?"

I couldn't respond. I just stood there, unable to move, not wanting to hear any of it.

"Even though you're hiding your thoughts from me right now, the beat of your heart tells me that you enjoyed it."

Why was he telling me lies? They had to be just that.

"You don't just like the power. You need it. Crave it," he finished.

I sucked in air quickly, realizing I'd forgotten to breathe since he started talking.

"No," I finally replied, shaking my head. "I don't want this. I never asked for this."

"We never asked for any of this." He gripped my shoulders, anticipating my fall as my knees weakened. "But this is the hand we've been dealt. You need to accept this."

"Why is this so important to you, anyway?" I asked. "About me accepting whatever this is inside of me?"

"I told you." He let go of my shoulders, glancing away from me for a second as he tucked his hands in his jeans. "To save my brother."

191

"But that's impossible."

"You traveled back in time before." He shrugged.

"Yeah, but that was with a key that didn't even belong to me."

"Yeah, that's why I'm trying to get you to accept who you are. You have all the power you need inside of you to travel back in time just before he was shot."

His eyes begged me to believe him, but I didn't want this power. I hated how it made me feel. It was curious, though. As much as Principal Chomsky was determined that Choyce was this great evil, right now, he was very much the Lawrence Bartholomew I remembered. A protective older brother who desperately wanted to save his brother. I frowned. She had to be wrong. If he was as powerful as she thought he was, why would he need me?

"I don't want to kill anymore." I swallowed back the tears that were bubbling up. It was all too much for me right now. "Couldn't we take the blood without killing anyone?"

"I guess that could work. Have any suggestions?" He asked.

"Maybe we use syringes?"

"But what about the darkness that takes over us? The desire to kill grows even stronger after being untied."

"Well, it's worth a shot." I lifted my chin, determined to try.

"I thought you weren't willing to help me." He

narrowed his eyes, obviously suspicious of my change in heart. "That you couldn't partake again?"

My heart skipped a beat as he eyed me carefully. I hoped he still couldn't read my mind at the moment. I figured if he believed that I would help him, he would reveal something to me eventually. If Principal Chomsky was right about Choyce, I needed to find out for myself and knew that this would be the best way.

"Yeah, but your brother. He didn't deserve to die. If saving your brother means you'll leave us alone, then I'm willing to help."

That seemed believable enough. Choyce hesitated but seemed to let it go, and we focused on practicing our lines for the rest of the last class period.

19

LEE WALKER

"Dad, I'm home!" Lee called, inserting the metal key into the lock of the front door. He turned the handle and gave it a push, it always stuck, but this time it came to a complete halt.

Was it jammed?

"Dad!" He shouted, but there was still no response.

His dad was definitely home. His car was in the driveway. Hopping off the front porch, he walked around the side of the farmhouse. The grass brushed his ankles as he made his way around back.

The yard really could use a good mow.

Taking a mental note to do that before he went back to campus, he bent to peer through the window next to the back door, but the drapes were pulled. Reaching for the knob, the back door swung open, and he was yanked inside by the shirt.

"What the—?" Lee started, but his dad quickly brought

a finger to his lips.

He reeked of sweat, his graying hair matted as if he hadn't washed it in weeks, and he had giant bags under his eyes like he'd been up all night. The end of his dad's police-issued Glock pointed squarely at his chest. Lee widened his eyes.

"You shouldn't be here," his dad hissed.

"What's going on?" Lee whispered, matching the low volume. "And why the heck did you pull that on me?"

"I wasn't expecting to see you." His dad lowered the weapon.

"Jeez, you nearly gave me a heart attack." Lee sighed.

"Sorry. Are you okay?"

"Yeah, but why do you have that out?"

"It's not safe. They could be anywhere."

"Who could be anywhere?" Lee asked.

His dad didn't respond.

"Dad, you sound like a crazy person."

He sighed, letting go of Lee's collar as he motioned for him to follow. "It's this case. I don't want to get you involved. Anyway, I was fixin' to make a cup of coffee. Want some?"

"Sure." Lee let the last syllable draw out as he followed his dad into the kitchen.

A fly buzzed around the piles of dishes in the sink and the dozens of empty chip bags and ramen packages covering the counter space. "Love what you've done with the place." Lee teased.

"Yeah, I know it's a mess." Shane chuckled halfheartedly. "Your mom sure did take care of a lot. I don't know how she did it."

Lee softened his expression. He knew his dad was still hurting. "Sorry, I shouldn't have said anything. I was just joking."

"Oh, I know. Don't worry about it." He ran a calloused hand on the back of his neck as he placed the gun strategically in the only free spot on the counter. "So that coffee, let me find the thingamabob."

Shane reached for the carafe with old coffee burnt to the bottom of it from the warming plate.

"Here." Lee placed a hand on his dad's shoulder. "Let me get that. You should go relax. I'll fix us a fresh pot."

"Are you sure?"

Lee nodded.

Shane's shoulders slumped as if a huge weight had been lifted from him. He really did need some sleep.

"But you should put that away first."

"Hmm?" Shane asked.

"The gun." Lee motioned towards the firearm still on the counter.

"Oh, sure," he replied as if he hadn't heard Lee.

Lee shook his head. His dad was going mad.

"He's still out there, the bastard." His dad muttered to himself as he turned to leave the room.

Lee worried about his dad. This didn't make any sense. He'd seemed to be getting better towards the end of summer, but ever since he got this latest case, all his progress seemed to fly out the door.

"Dad, seriously put that thing away," Lee called after him. "You don't want to accidentally shoot me, right?"

"Oh." Shane's eyes widened as the words finally resonated with him. "Yeah, let me get that back into the safe."

"Good. You do that and then have a seat on the couch." Lee let out a sigh of relief, glad he'd finally gotten through.

Lee grew concerned about his dad living here all by himself. It wasn't healthy.

"I'll get us some coffee," Lee finally said, shuffling back to the kitchen.

After scrubbing the carafe clean and wiping out the filter basket, he got a new pot started. Drying his hands on a reasonably clean dish rag, he decided he would get to the dishes after checking out the rest of the place. He wanted to see if he could find any clues about this case that was making his dad go insane. His nostrils were met with a foul stench of dirty clothes as he opened the guest room. He coughed, quickly shutting the door. Shane must've been sleeping there instead of the master upstairs.

Lee turned towards the door on the opposite side of the small hallway, adjacent to the kitchen. His dad's office. That would definitely have something, Lee concluded. He ducked inside, shutting the door before flipping on the lights.

When he turned towards the room, his jaw fell open. The desk was covered with empty coffee cups, candy wrappers, and endless files piled next to his dad's computer. But what caught Lee's attention was the giant tack board on the wall beside the desk. Every inch of it was covered with photos of dead bodies, all lying in mangled directions.

Taking a step closer to get a better view, he suddenly realized there was an order to the madness. The far left was a photo of the killing in Oklahoma City. Lee grimaced at the image of the man lying with a giant hole in his chest. His heart had been completely removed. Who would do something like that? There was a colored sticky note underneath it, and he smoothed the edges out with his index finger.

"September twenty-third," he read aloud.

There was a piece of yarn tacked up connecting it to another photo below it, and this time Lee closed his eyes, wishing he hadn't seen the image. A woman lay, frozen. Her eyes wide open, cold, and lifeless. Tears spilled over the corners of his eyes. He recognized the woman in that photo.

"Mom." His lip quivered as his voice cracked.

He shook his head, trying to push through the pain that threatened to paralyze him. There was no time for that. Dragging his fingers over the rough fibers of the tackboard, he gently pushed the corners of the corresponding sticky note down.

"February eighteen." He knew the date well, moving on to the next image.

It was a news article about a guy who had his heart yanked out at a New York City subway station. It was just like all the other victims. This one had happened only a few weeks before school started. Before Choyce had arrived. He was from New York, wasn't he? Could it be he was part of all of this? He shook his head. That was crazy. Most of the murders had happened in Oklahoma. But was it possible he'd been in Oklahoma around the same time as the businessman? Or when his mom was murdered? Deciding it was not impossible, he continued his snooping.

Another photo caught his eye, this was of a half-burned auditorium very much like the one at the Academy, but instead of kids acting out parts, a group of bodies lay charred and bent at odd angles.

Glancing down at the note below it, this one had two. "Ardmore Little Theatre. September twelfth."

This happened just a few weeks ago. This must've been what had his dad all up in arms. It was curious; only one of the theater bodies actually had a removed heart like the other murders. Why kill the rest differently? And why so many? What had caused the killer to change his pattern?

"What have you gotten yourself into, Dad?" He thought out loud.

"I'm much more interested in the drama club myself."

Choyce's words echoed in his mind as he continued to stare at the photos taken in the theater.

Taking a step back, he pulled his cell phone out of his pocket and snapped a quick photo. He had a feeling he was going to need it for future reference. He grabbed the ergo mesh desk chair, rolling it back, and plopped down. He was determined to get some answers, waking up the sleeping machine. It buzzed to life, the overworked hard drive spinning as he pulled up a browser to PublicPages search engine. The keyboard clacked as he entered the name Choyce Barton and selected New York City, NY from the city and state drop-down menu.

He held his breath, clicking enter, and waited for the page to load.

No results found.

He frowned. That couldn't be right. Maybe he didn't live in the city? He broadened the search to the entire state.

Still, no results were found.

He was in New York, right? What was the name of that school Choyce said he was transferring from? Torrance—or Florence—ville? Lawrenceville? That was it.

He glanced over his shoulder and, after making sure his dad hadn't caught him yet, he quickly opened a directory of that school. He was surprised when a school in New Jersey popped up as the top result. He'd half expected it to be a school Choyce had made up. Clicking over to the student registry, a login page appeared and he realized it wouldn't be publicly accessible. Clicking the contact page, he decided to give them a call.

His palms began to sweat as the adrenaline kicked in, punching in the number into the old landline. He couldn't believe his dad was still holding on to that thing, but grateful he still remembered how to hide caller id on it.

"Thank you for calling Lawrenceville High," an automated voice greeted him. *"For the dean's office, press one. For admissions, press two—"*

He pressed two before the voice finished spouting off the options and prepared his best southern drawl. He would use his dad as inspiration, not that he would impersonate him per se. Lee didn't want any of this coming back to bite him in the end.

"Lawrenceville admissions office, this is Claire. How may I help you?"

He cleared his throat. "Howdy, ma'am, this is Officer John Schumer. There's been an accident involving a former student of yours. He transferred over to a boarding school here in Oklahoma, and we need to get in touch with the family. Unfortunately, the school doesn't seem to have an up to date phone number for him. If I provide a name, would you be able to get me that information?"

"Oh." The woman seemed ill-prepared for the request. *"I'm so sorry, but I can't share any personal information like*

that over the phone."

"I understand," Lee said, thickening his accent. "I know this is an odd request, but please, ma'am, if there's anything you could do to help, it would be greatly appreciated."

"Well." Claire hesitated, then lowered her voice. *"I guess if you gave me the name, I could see if I could call them for you."*

"Oh, thank you, ma'am. That's mighty fine of you." Lee bit his lip to keep from laughing. If he was an actor, he was sure that'd win him an Oscar. "The name's Choyce Barton. C-h-o-y as in Yankee-c-e." He couldn't help but add that last little flourish.

There was a brief pause on the other lines as the woman typed in the information.

"Sir, I can't seem to find that name, are you sure—"

"CLAIRE!" A woman shouted in the background and proceeded to shout incoherently at the poor secretary. Whoever it was didn't seem very happy.

"I was just—" Claire protested. *"Yes, I'm aware of the rules, but isn't this a special circumstance?"*

A muffled noise hummed as the upset woman came on the line. *"I'm sorry, sir, but we can't give out personal information over the phone. If you need anything, please come in to file an official request."*

Before Lee could respond, the line went dead. Wow,

that lady was definitely in a mood. He was glad that Claire had answered the phone first. She'd confirmed his suspicions. He sat there in calm silence, given what he'd just discovered. There were many things he couldn't be sure of, a ton that was still unclear to him that he didn't know how to begin to find the answers for. But there was one thing he knew for sure without a doubt, and that was Choyce definitely wasn't who he said he was.

20
SOMETHING IN THE WATER

- Izara -

"You're not focusing!" Choyce cried, taking the script from my hands. "What's going on with you?"

We'd been practicing for what seemed like hours that weekend and had made very little progress. The school was expecting me to get evidence that he was this great power they were looking for, but so far, I'd only learned that his favorite color was blue and his full birth name was Lawrence Choyce Bartholomew. Not really anything I thought was important enough to report. If he was truly this villain, he had yet to prove anything but a major pain in the butt.

"Iz! Seriously!" He clapped his hands, gaining my attention.

"I think I need a break." I sighed. "These lines are all starting to jumble up together."

"All right." He put his script on the desk.

We'd stolen an empty classroom to rehearse in as there were too many people in the auditorium.

"Want to grab a snack from the cafeteria?"

"Sounds good." I was happy to get out of that stuffy classroom and into some fresh air.

I took a deep breath of the crisp Autumn breeze. It was a surprisingly chilly day for Oklahoma this time of year, but I wasn't complaining. It reminded me a little bit of back home in New York. I frowned. Even just thinking about New York as home felt weird now. It's been so long since I'd been back there. So where was home for me now, I wondered? Was it here? I cringed at that. Perhaps I didn't have a home right now. That was oddly more comforting than either of my other ideas.

While Choyce got a sandwich, I grabbed a sparkling water and found a seat near the window. I gazed out into the endless row of trees, their orange and red leaves clinging to the branches for dear life. It would be sad to see them go, but just like the full moon, there was no stopping it.

I glance up just as Choyce placed his food on the table, sitting across from me.

"They've really done an upgrade on this place." He

205

commented.

"You never actually told me what the school was like back then," I replied. "You know when you went here the first time?"

He paused, chewing his food as he gazed out through the glass. Swallowing, he turned back to me. "It was grand."

Sadness flickered in his eyes, but he quickly blinked the emotion away. It vanished as soon as it materialized.

"It was much like it is now, I guess." He shrugged. "Homework, teacher conferences—you know, the usual."

"What was that?" I asked.

"What was what?"

"That look. Before you gave me that crap about 'the *usual*.' It looked like you were about to share something real."

He smirked, looking away. "You don't care about all that."

I frowned. "Why would you say that?"

"You only care about saving my brother because you saw him get killed out of some strange sense of morality, or something like that. You don't really care about him or me. And how could you? You don't really know either of us nor do you want to. You've made that very clear."

My jaw dropped. How could he think that? Did he really think I was that shallow? And how had I made it clear that I didn't want to know his brother? I understood how he might've gotten that impression about him, but not someone innocent like Edwin.

He leaned in, the intensity in his eyes catching me off guard. "I'm only accepting your help because I *need* you."

I didn't really like him, so I was surprised by how much that stung.

"I think we're done for today," he said, suddenly hopping up from the table and left.

Frozen in place, I just sat there. I swallowed hard, realizing that he was right. I did feel obligated to save his brother, but who wouldn't after witnessing an innocent person murdered? No. He was wrong about me, not caring. I may not have known them personally or care for Choyce, but after the visions I had of them last year, I knew I would always care for Lawrence.

I blinked back the tears and stood up, dashing for the front door in time to see Choyce disappear into the woods. Careful not to give me away, I followed him. My heart raced as we neared the river where he had told his brother for the first time what he would become. It had seemed so real. If Choyce was like he'd been back then, I wouldn't have doubted for a second that he wasn't evil, but after that full moon in that theater in Ardmore? It made me wonder. What had changed in him since then? What had the last century done to him?

"Want a glass?" Choyce asked, interrupting my thoughts, and I jumped.

I didn't realize he'd noticed me follow him. "No,

thanks."

"Suit yourself." He poured himself a cup of whiskey as I sat next to him near the riverbank.

His eyes closed as he drank. "A hundred-year-old bottle, you know."

"Fancy," I replied as he took another sip.

A comfortable silence fell between us as the bubbling water sloshed over the rocks.

"You're wrong, you know," I said.

"About what?"

"Me. About all of it."

"Oh, really?" His eyebrow rose. "Do tell me, love."

"I *do* care. About Lawrence and Edwin, that is." I paused, considering my next words before continuing. "And not just because I saw what happened, but because I knew them. My visions showed me you, or the you back then when you were Lawrence. It showed me the good."

Choyce chuckled darkly, taking another swig of whiskey.

"I know you've been with your brother for a long time. I can't imagine having this darkness for as long as you have, especially without my brother, but if there's any way you could remember who you used to be—if you could just be that person again—"

"That person died." Choyce hissed, looking me straight on, his voice even and sure. "He died when this school killed his brother."

"I know, and I want to help you," I said quietly. "I mean, I want to help Lawrence, at least. He annoyed me less."

I winked and saw a crooked half-smile spread across his face. "I like that."

"What?"

"That smile," I replied. "It's a good one."

We sat there in silence for a while, leaving me thinking about what a mess I was getting myself in. I was torn between feeling sorry for who this man used to be and hating the one he'd become. I knew if he really was the one this school was after then everything I'd seen and all he'd told me was a lie. But what if they were wrong? What if he really was just Lawrence? As I thought about how betrayed he would feel if he found out, a knot formed in my side. If he was innocent, then it wouldn't make me any better than this school.

"This place,"—Choye motioned to the surrounding areas—"this academy, it was the only place that made any sense. Despite all the crap that went on, it was always better than being home. As soon as Edwin and I arrived, we knew there was something different about it."

I watched him closely as he spoke, watching for any signs of a lie. So far, there was none.

"It may have looked like any other, but it felt different, you know? There was an energy about it that made all of our senses heightened."

I nodded. Now that I thought about it, I knew what he meant.

"Some sort of pulse runs through this whole place, and I know it holds all the answers to why we're like this. I just don't know exactly where they are."

Listening to him here and now, I didn't hear the obnoxious Choyce, but the protective older brother he once was. I looked away, not being able to think straight. It was easier to hate him when he was acting full of himself.

"What've you been doing for the last century? I asked, finally pouring myself a tiny glass of whiskey.

"Well, if you really must know"—he winked—"I've been traveling every crevice of this world."

I laughed at the dramatic response.

"But I've mostly just been looking for a way to go back in time, to change all of this."

I nodded. "Why do you think we're like this?"

Choyce took a deep breath. With glassy eyes, he stared at his feet. "All I know is that I was born this way."

An empty hole opened up in my chest, and it felt as if my lungs would cave. I didn't want this, any of it, but each time I got to the point of no return, I inevitably fell, each time falling harder than I'd ever fallen before.

"But I think we were born to find each other. So we wouldn't have to suffer like this alone." He concluded.

A tear escaped me, and I batted it with my fingertips.

"I'm dreaming of a place where we could just be, you know?" I didn't know if it was the strong drink, but I was vulnerable, and there was no one else in the world who understood what I was going through more than the guy sitting next to me. "A time and a place where all of this darkness would just disappear. Where we could tell all of the bad stuff to suck it."

We laughed, both knowing how unrealistic that was.

I brightened, trying to change the subject before I turned this into more of a sob fest. "What were the fifties like?"

"I don't really know." He shrugged.

I frowned. "What do you mean?"

"There's a whole section of my life that I don't remember," he replied. "Maybe I was drunk. Who knows?"

"Really?" I smirked.

"Maybe." He grinned. "It was bound to happen."

"Of course." I giggled.

"You know," he began, eyeing me. "You're the first person I've been able to talk to about all of this since... well, you know."

"Yeah, I know how you feel."

"You do?" he asked, looking doubtful. "What about your brother?"

"Yeah, but I can't talk to him like this. Not really."

"Like how?"

"Like..." I trailed off, trying to put it into words. "Like

211

this. Completely honest. I mean, he's my brother. I want to protect him, not dump my fears on him."

"Isn't he the guy? Isn't he supposed to protect you?"

I rolled my eyes. "That doesn't matter. We're both human, we're siblings, we're mutually supposed to keep each other safe. Or at least sane."

"Sounds like you're taking on a lot of responsibility."

"Maybe." I shrugged. "He's my brother. I've got to watch out for him, right?"

I met his expectant eyes as he leaned closer to me.

"And where do I fit into this picture?"

I gulped, taking another sip of my drink, which was probably a mistake. "How about the ketchup?"

"The what?" His eyes widened, a wholehearted laugh escaping his lips.

"Don't overthink it." I rolled my eyes. "Just be the ketchup to our weird little sandwich."

Now I didn't understand what I was talking about.

"Okay, I think you've had one too many cups of the sauce." He took my rusted tin cup.

"Oh, well, you asked," I said, my words slightly slurred.

"So, I'm something to you? I thought you hated me."

"I don't hate you," I retorted, a bit offended by the words.

"Yeah, you kinda do."

"I don't hate you, Choyce," I repeated. "But you have become kind of a dick."

"Hey!" He scolded, looking half offended for less than a second before bursting into laughter once again. "Okay, maybe you're right."

My lungs hurt from laughter. "A bit."

"But only a little bit." He agreed, licking his lips before biting the bottom one. He tucked a loose strand of his long, wavy blond hair behind his ear, and I found myself unable to look away from him.

"Why do you have to be so annoying most of the time?" I asked, my head spinning as the alcohol took its toll on me.

"Why do you have to be so beautiful?" He whispered, the sunlight glistening in his deep, leather brown eyes.

I gasped, not expecting that response. "What?"

"You know you are." The words slipped effortlessly from his thin lips.

"No." I shook my head. "You can't say things like that."

"Why not?"

"Because you're not supposed to be someone I could actually like," I replied. "You're supposed to be—ugh, you know, always saying stuff that irks me. You're supposed to be a jerk now. You're not supposed to be Lawrence."

"But I am." My breath caught as his hand brushed

213

against mine.

"I'm so confused," I gasped, moving my hands as I rubbed my eyelids. "Why'd you have to go and get under my skin?"

"I did? How'd I do that?" He asked, his eyebrows rising, feigning innocence. "Please tell me, I'll need to put this in the books for future reference. I never thought I'd be able to get under your tough skin."

"Don't be smart."

"Izara," he replied, gazing deeply into my eyes. "We're the perfect pair—two peas in a pod. If I'm getting under your skin, it's only because we're the same. We were meant for each other."

He stretched his hand out for mine, and I looked at it for a moment, unmoving. There were a million things wrong with this, but against my better judgment, I took it, giving in against all of my inner protests. I had no more fight in me to resist.

21
WHAT POSSESSES YOU

- Kain -

After discovering Chuck's return, I was determined to learn more about this school and headed straight for the library. I mean real, hard facts. There had to be something somewhere about the keys or Thomas Tompkin, the founder of this school, and the deal he made. Something that could be used to get rid of Chuck once and for all. Not just that, but this school. I knew to keep away from online resources and resorted to reading through stacks and stacks of local history books that all turned out to be a dead end.

I wasn't sure when I'd fallen asleep, but I knew I had to be because I was standing in Principal Chomsky's office. A blue fog hung in the air, curling across her desk, only it wasn't

Principal Chomsky sitting behind it, but Mr. Valkyrien. He was glaring across a stack of papers at Principal Chomsky. A plaque rested on the desk reading Principal Valkyrien. Was it a dream? Or was I having one of those memories? If it was a memory, it was before Ms. Chomsky took over the school. What happened to make this change?

"You c-can't possibly be c-considering this!" Mr. Valkyrien stuttered.

"I've considered it," Ms. Chomsky replied. "And I've determined that there's no other way. They must be eliminated."

"But they're human!" he gasped, leaning forward in his seat to rest his hands on his desk.

"I should remind you that I have the full support of the Assembly."

"And you should remember that I am the p-principal," he squawked.

"You've been out of the dark too long. Your voice reveals it." She ignored his threat, calmly standing up. "Perhaps it's time I advise the Assembly on some much-needed changes in leadership."

"Whatever happens"—Mr. Valkyrien shook as he stood from his seat—"it will be on your c-conscience. M-mark my words, Evelyn. Both the light and the dark factions c-can not hide from him. Even while the Transition World lies behind lock and key."

216

"Yes, well, that's why we must put an end to them." She turned to leave but paused before she opened the door to go. "Do say hello to the bats for me."

With a sarcastic chuckle, she disappeared and with her the dream.

***

My eyelids flew open, a bit turned around as my eyes adjusted to the dim room. Waking up from that memory—vision, or whatever it was—was utterly disorienting. The whirring of the old heater pushing out air with hints of old carpet reminded me where I was. The basement of the library.

A piece of old paper from the book that doubled as a pillow stuck to my cheek as I sat up. How long had I been asleep? I glanced at my phone lying on the table next to the stacks of books, but the screen was black. I tapped the screen, but nothing happened. I sighed. It was dead. Great. I probably didn't even bring a charger for it. It would've been nice if Izzy had been there to help, but she'd been spending her weekends practicing for the play. While she did that, I spent my time in the library trying to find some clues on this Assembly and how to get Chuck off our case for good.

Wet drool clung to the side of my lip, and I reached for a tissue, my elbow knocking the book I'd been sleeping on, clattering to the floor.

"Crap!" Rolling my eyes, I bent to grab it when something moved out of the corner of my eye. I jumped up, ramming my elbow on the corner of the table as I stood from my seat.

"What the hell?" I cried, meeting the intense stare of Mr. Valkyrien, who was sitting in a chair opposite me. How had I not noticed him before?

"S-sleep well?" His high-pitched voice made me wince.

His glazed eyes scanned my reading material, and suddenly, I felt self-conscious about my choices. Did he know? Would he suspect what I was doing? I wasn't sure if he was on our side. From the dream I'd just had, it seemed like he might be, but for now, I wouldn't trust anyone aligned with Chuck or this school.

"You," I gasped. Seeing him then and there, I lost it. "You're one of them. You and Principal Chomsky are part of the Assembly. You're *murdering* your students!"

His lifeless gaze never left mine as he gave a single nod, his head wobbling on his long neck.

"Why do we keep having visions of you?" I asked. "Why did you run away from Izzy when she tried to get answers from you?"

"It's not s-safe." He hissed. "The s-school and the Assembly have their s-spies everywhere, but this is the only s-safe p-place on c-campus."

218

"The *library*?"

He gave another single nod. I rubbed my brow, a headache coming on as he continued to be vague. That was my worst pet peeve.

"What is the Assembly?" I asked, hoping he would give me a straight answer for once. "And what do they have to do with this school?"

He uncrossed and recrossed his long, spindly legs. He must've sensed my annoyance, clearing his throat before responding. "They b-both want the s-same thing." His voice was barely above a whisper as if he was afraid someone else would hear us in the basement of the library, a place no one would come unless they had to.

"And what is that?"

Mr. Valkyrien leaned his gangly head to the side, rocking his folded leg as he considered his next words. "To r-r-rid the world of a g-great evil."

I frowned. "Me?"

"Your p-power comes from the g-greatest b-b-being there's ever b-b-been."

I blinked as my vision suddenly blurred. I stood in a rose field surrounded by a group of people with wings, some with pure black wings and others with white. Principal Chomsky stood at the front, her white hair glistening against the sun. They stood, united against a man, crumpled on the ground. His black wings bent at angles, his brow dripping with blood.

"This is not the end." The man growled, wiping the blood on the back of his hand. "I will return..."

Shaking my head, I nearly fell as I returned to the library. Grabbing the side of the desk for support, it took a moment for my ears to stop ringing. Obviously, having a vision like that while awake had side effects.

Before I could get my bearings, Mr. Valkyrien's voice erupted inside of my head. *The school was built to rid the world of shifters like you. The Assembly allowed the school to continue because the power that runs through your veins is the same as Credan.*

Something about interacting with magic must've fixed human deficiencies because his lisp was entirely gone when speaking telepathically.

"Credan?" I asked, speaking out loud out of habit.

"It's the name of the powerful man you've heard speak to you since your first transformation."

I tossed the name around like a cough drop in my mouth, considering what I thought about that. It oddly fitted for some reason. "But why?"

Chills ran down my arm as Mr. Valkyrien spoke to me telepathically once more. *The Assembly believes he stored his power in individual humans so that these humans could be powerful enough to bring him back. And now they think he has returned. It's only a matter of time before they come to neutralize him again. They believe he's among you.*

"Who?"

Choyce.

"That can't be." I shook my head. "He's Lawrence Bartholomew. The school murdered his brother. You're telling me that he's also Credan?"

Mr. Valkyrien gave a nod, confirming.

"How can Choyce be two different people?"

That's a good question. Mr. Valkyrien replied, the corners of his lips turning upwards. *Of course, one can't be, and they're running around blind with fear. I tried to stop them from making this terrible mistake. You are human, and we swore to protect you from all of this.*

I slumped back into my chair, my head spinning from this new bit of information. "And what about that key? What's the story with that?"

Mr. Valkyrien glanced down at the golden key peeking out from his robes. His glassy eyes met my expectant stare. *Long before Credan was neutralized by the Assembly, he waged war against the Transitioned World—*

"I keep hearing about this *Transitioned World*"—I put in air quotes—"but what is this place?"

It's a place adjacent to the human world, separated by a veil. Mr. Valkyrien continued. *The Assembly was formed to create an order, a balance, and we could not enter the void beyond. What we now know as the world of man.*

But there were rumors of a way out, a way to escape.
Many began to disappear. Credan was never supposed to exist.
A being of the light and the dark, with powers far beyond the
Assembly's control.

I tried to keep up, my head spinning from all the information Mr. Valkyrien was filling my head with. "What do you mean a being of the light and dark?"

Within my world, there are two factions. One that remains in the night while the other roams the day. Species that belong to the night cannot unite with the day and vice versa.

I frowned. This sounded like segregation. What sort of sick people were they?

I know what you're thinking, and it's nothing of the sort. Mr. Valkyrien's expression softened. *It is for the protection of all species.*

I still didn't like the sound of that, but he had yet to answer my question. "What does all of this have to do with that key?"

Because, Credan is the reason they exist, Mr. Valkyrien replied. *In 1739, he waged war on us by organizing one of the greatest breakouts we've ever seen. The beings you know as vampires, werewolves, faeries, and wizards, he led thousands and thousands of them out of our world into yours, endangering human life.*

"But I thought you said you all called it a void."

We did. Mr. Valkyrien nodded. *But this was to protect*

222

humankind from the likes of us. After the breakout, we had to be smarter. And so, the keys were forged, locking our world down once and for all. Only Assembly members can wield them.

I shook my head. "But my sister did. Last year, she used it to time travel."

Mr. Valkyrien nodded again. *The key showed me this.*

"You said that only Assembly members could use it, though."

The one that created the keys was of the species with time-traveling capabilities. When he died, the species went extinct until your sister. A talisman is always loyal to the power that made it. This is why the Assembly has worked hard to make them extinct.

His head cocked to one side as if his pointed ears heard something.

Your sister is in danger. The words curled inside of my mind, causing my heart to race in panic.

"What do you mean?"

They're going to use your sister to kill Choyce. Mr. Valkyrien replied. *Then they'll come for you both.*

"I've got to find her." I stood up to leave, and, with a speed I'd never seen before, he appeared before me, blocking my path.

"S-stop." Mr. Valkyrien gripped my shoulder, his palms cold and damp like a lizard. "P-proceed with caution.

They're watching."

I took note of his warning, ducking around his towering frame, and raced for the library exit. I had to find Izzy. If the school was using her, then this was news to me. She should've told me what was going on. Why would she keep working with the school a secret from me? If she was in danger, then we had to work together. We were siblings, after all. I thought that would mean something to her, but I guess lying came easy for her these days.

Feigning to walk casually across the quad, I hoped the nightwalkers weren't watching. If they suspected anything, then I was sure they'd have no problem kidnapping me again. I was convinced that'd make Chuck happy. I tried calling her, but her phone went straight to voicemail. She always had a bad habit of letting her phone drain. I made it across the bridge leading to the dorms when Iz stumbled out from the woods, followed by Choyce.

"Oh!" She stopped when she saw me, covering her mouth as she suppressed a laugh. "Kain, what're you doing here?"

"Trying to find you." My eyes darted between the two of them, and I frowned.

Choyce smirked, tucking his hands in his jeans while Izzy bit her lip. Did they realize how guilty they looked?

"What's going on?"

"Nothing," Izzy replied, a little too quickly.

224

"Anywhosers, you said you were trying to find me? What's going on?"

Her eyes were a bit unsteady, and she over-enunciating every word.

"Were you two *drinking*?" I asked.

Choyce made no response, but when Izzy's eyes widened, I sighed. She was so transparent. Her lips folding over her teeth as it seemed to sink in that she'd been caught.

"Come on, Iz, we need to talk."

"Well, this sounds like a sibling thing. I'll leave you two here." Choyce brushed past us, winking at my sister.

Giving Iz a disapproving look, I motioned for her to follow me back across the bridge.

"We were just rehearsing."

"Sure, you were." I rolled my eyes.

"Seriously, Kain. That's it."

I just shook my head. "What did Choyce give you?"

She giggled, wrapping an arm across my shoulders. "Just some whiskey. Are we going to the cafeteria?"

"NO!"

Izzy made a face at my thunderous response.

I lowered my volume. "No, we're going to the library to talk. The basement would be safest."

Izzy dropped her arm to her side and pouted. "Weirdo."

"But it might be a good idea to grab some waters, first," I said, realizing she wasn't in any state to listen to what I had to say.

We made a quick stop at the cafeteria for water and a quick bite to eat before heading back to the library. It seemed Izzy was feeling much better by the time we got there, or at least a bit more alert.

"So, what's this all about?" she asked, sipping on her water as she sat crisscrossed on one of the chairs. "And why couldn't we talk in the cafeteria?"

"The library is the only safe place. The only place the nightwalkers can't hear us."

She frowned. "What do you mean? How do you know this?"

"Listen, I know what this school is trying to get you to do about Choyce because of who they think he is, but you need to know that they're wrong."

Her eyes widened as the shock set in. She didn't deny it, which confirmed what Mr. Valkyrien told me was true. "How could you not tell me? I thought we were in this together?"

She sputtered, looking away. "I—I just didn't think—I didn't want to get you involved."

"But I *am* involved," I hissed. "And as soon as you turn him in, they'll be coming for us both. Again."

"They gave me their word."

"Do you think they're going to keep their word?" I raised an eyebrow. "You're talking about people who order

226

innocent kids to be murdered. A group who exterminated an entire species just to give themselves more power. Do you think someone like that is really *trustworthy*?"

She opened and closed her mouth, obviously unsure of how to respond. After taking a deep breath, she finally replied. "How do you know this?"

"Mr. Valkyrien told me."

"Wait, he actually *talked* to you?" Her mouth fell.

"Yes."

"Did you ask him *why* he suddenly started revealing all of this to you?"

"Does it matter?" I scoffed, a bit thrown off by the question. "He's trying to protect us from this school. That makes him okay in my book. He told me the Assembly thinks we have this evil guy's power and that he is Choyce, but Mr. Valkyrien also said they're wrong. That they're using you to get rid of Choyce, but that he's actually human like us."

"Then why would Principal Chomsky give me her word that the school wouldn't harm us if I helped them?"

"Because they're using you. Can't you see that?" I cried. "Once they get what they want, they'll get rid of us too because we're like Credan."

"But I have to do this. If I don't, they'll kill us for sure."

"Well, then we'll have to figure out a different way. For now, you'd better be a good actress." I rubbed the bridge of my nose as my head pounded. "We need to get Choyce's brother back, we need to right this wrong, and then we need to bring down this school and the Assembly."

"That's probably going to mean you'll need to drink blood, too."

"I know," I said, reluctantly. Remembering how one actually untied themselves from the full moon made my stomach flip, but if we were going to live to fight another day, I knew it was the only way I was going to tap into my powers. I would just have to suck it up, pun intended.

"I suggested to Choyce that we use syringes." Izzy shrugged. "That could work, don't you think?"

"What about when we lose control? What if something goes wrong."

Izzy shrugged. "There's always a risk, right?"

I couldn't argue with that. "Next full moon, then?"

"Next full moon." She nodded.

***

- Kain -

"That's disgusting!" Lee coughed, nearly choking on his sports drink.

After leaving the library, I'd joined up with the guys from the basketball team to shoot a few hoops, and now we'd just made it back to the dorms.

"I don't believe it." Lee shook his head.

"I'm dead serious!" Duran assured them after sharing a perverted rumor I wouldn't dare repeat.

"Good job, brother." Laurent slapped his brother sarcastically, albeit a little too hard as he pushed by us. "Now, I won't be eating dinner."

"What? It's a true story." Duran protested as we entered our floor's kitchenette and game room.

"You shouldn't believe everything on social media." I laughed, opening the fridge and grabbing a water bottle.

As I took a large gulp, letting the liquid cool me from the inside out, a strange voice crept into my mind.

Has he drunk?

"No," someone whispered in the distance.

He must. All of you must be at your full potential to break the bonds.

"How can it be done?"

Keep your distance for now. See how this plays out. Then, before the next quarter, you'll know what to do.

I frowned, walking past the guys and towards the door leading into the pantry.

Quick! The dead voice hissed. *Someone's coming.*

Gripping the handle, I swung the door open, meeting the wide, green eyes of Amadeus. A pain erupted at my temples as if a drill was being pushed through my skull and I fell against the door, gasping.

"You!" I barely made the words out, gritting my teeth. "Who were you talking to?"

"I don't know what you mean." Amadeus feigned innocence, grabbing a bag of chips. "I was only looking for a snack."

I grabbed his neck, the shelf quivering as I knocked him into a stack of ramen. "Lies!"

His emerald eyes glared back at me as another wave of rippling nails attacked my brain. My vision blurred as tears welled up from the pain, causing me to let go of my grip as I stumbled back, my shoulder squashing a bag of Doritos.

"Why are you—?" I began, but once my vision cleared, he was gone. Vanishing out of thin air.

I ran from the pantry, sprinting towards the exit, but there was no sign of him. Defeated, I headed back to where the guys were starting up a video game.

"Yo, Kain, wanna play?" Laurent asked.

I shook my head, a splitting headache in the works.

"Nah, I'm good. Need to shower," I said, grabbing the water I'd left before getting distracted by Amadeus as I made my way back to my room.

Who had he been talking to? Was it Credan? Was Amadeus the one the school, had been searching for all along? And who had the voice been talking about drinking? Did he mean drinking blood? Was he talking about me?

There were so many questions running around in my

head that I just wanted it all to stop. I wanted to be ordinary. To go to school, graduate, get a college degree, and to one day, maybe work in the music industry full time. But would any of that be possible if this school and all the powers that be wanted me dead? It was a question I couldn't answer. I would just have to wait and see.

22
MIDDLE FINGER

- Lee Walker -

When Lee returned to campus, only one thing occupied his mind, and that was worrying about Izzy's safety. Spending all of her free time with this guy who could be a serial killer? Out of the question. He was determined to keep her away from Choyce, no matter what it took. He didn't care if they had to rehearse. She needed to know that Choyce wasn't who she thought he was. She didn't seem to care for him, anyway, but if she knew there was a chance he could be a killer, Lee was sure she'd think twice before being in the same room with that liar again.

"Hey, Kain," Lee said, dropping his duffle bag on the

common room floor. "Have you seen Izzy?"

"I thought I last saw her at the library."

"Cool, thanks." He didn't bother putting his things away. He needed to get to Izzy as fast as possible. What if she was rehearsing with him right now? What if this time he revealed who he really was? What if he actually was a killer?

These thoughts spun around in his mind as he entered the musty library. As usual, whoever was working the front desk was absent, so he decided to go look around a bit. The clatter of keyboards echoed in the still air; an old vent whirred as it worked to heat the enormous room. Crisp paper and dusty books perfumed the air as he headed up to the second floor, where most students went to study or read. Old couches scattered the second-floor landing, some next to the oak banister that overlooked the first floor, while others were squished in the corner.

"There you are," Lee said, spotting her on a couch near the windows as he turned the corner. Her shoes were off as she lounged against the armrest, script in hand.

She looked up from her reading. "Lee? You're back!"

Jumping up, she embraced him in a big hug.

"Yep." He smiled, leaning into her. "I've been looking everywhere for you."

"I missed you." She tucked her black hair behind a porcelain ear. "How's everything with your dad?"

Lee made a face. "Eh, it's okay. It could be better. I just

helped him clean up a bit. Hopefully, he can keep it up. I worry about him living alone, though."

She nodded, glancing away.

"But, Iz, I need to talk to you about something."

"What is it?" Her eyes widened with worry.

He couldn't believe how blue her eyes were. He'd looked into them a million times before, and each time he was captivated, but this time something seemed different. He couldn't put his finger on it, but there was something off, and it showed in her eyes.

Taking a deep breath, he was unsure of how to bring it up. The direct approach would have to do. "Look, I know you've got this play coming up, but I really think you need to stay away from Choyce."

She blinked, evidently a little confused by where this was coming from. "Why would you say that?"

"There's something seriously wrong with him."

"What do you mean?"

"I mean—everything points to him being—No, I *know* he's a"—he glanced up, wishing he'd planned this out a little more. How could he tell her what he wanted to say? He didn't have any proof, but something in his gut told him he was a murderer. He took her hand in his—"he's a killer."

Izzy shook her head, her jaw-dropping.

"I mean, I *think* he is, anyway." Lee corrected himself. "It all makes sense, though, right? He comes out of nowhere,

234

knows all this weird stuff, and has no record of ever attending school. Anywhere."

"And that makes him a killer?" she snapped.

Lee didn't like the direction the conversation was going. She was supposed to side with him. He'd hoped she'd understand, but she didn't seem to.

"No, but he's clearly not who he says he is," he replied. "There's no birth certificate in the entire state of New Jersey or New York for a Choyce Barton. Who else would need an alias, right?"

A moment of silence passed, and Lee could tell Izzy was having difficulty processing all of this information.

"You need to switch your classes. And if Choyce is in your drama club, then you'll need to get out of that, too."

"Hold up." She lifted her hands up. "Why do I need to quit drama?"

"Because he's not who he says he is," Lee emphasized each word, hoping she'd finally understand the gravity of the situation. "According to records, Choyce Barton has never lived in New York and the most certainly never went to that Lawrenceville High School."

"Wait a minute, how do *you* know that?"

It was Lee's turn to be astonished. He couldn't believe what he was hearing. Had she known Choyce hadn't gone to that school this whole time? Was it all a lie?

"You checked up on him, didn't you?" Realization

spreading across her face.

"I might've done some digging." He shrugged. "But why doesn't this news surprise you? Did you know?"

"Wow, you really have zero trust."

"Well, what else am I supposed to think when you don't tell me anything?"

It was Izzy's turn to be silent.

Lee pounded his fist against the nearby wall, and Izzy jumped.

"What's going on with you?" He shouted.

"What do you mean? You're the one punching walls."

Lee rolled his eyes. "You've been incredibly distant ever since school started. You attack a student, and now you're protecting this guy who may very well be the one who killed my mom?"

"Whoa, that's a big accusation. One I don't think you've got enough evidence for."

"Oh, no?" He raised an eyebrow. "He's lied about his identity. Who's to say he's not a serial killer? Unless you've got information, I don't?"

He waited for an answer he knew he would never get.

"I don't know what you're talking about," she finally replied, crossing her arms.

"You know *exactly* what I'm talking about."

"No, I really don't." She shook her head.

"Remember when I caught you hugging him? Going

236

along with that lie about him going to that school in New Jersey?"

"I didn't go along with anything. That was all him."

"So you admit it!" He cried, "You knew he was lying, and you've been in on it from the beginning."

"I didn't admit to anything!" She gave a nervous laugh. "Seriously, if you had a problem with me, why is this the first time I'm hearing about it?"

"Don't try and change the subject."

She threw her hands up in the air. "I can't deal with this right now." With that, she picked up her things and stormed out.

***

- Izara -

I couldn't believe how much of a mess I'd made. I not only had the school to worry about but now I had my own boyfriend digging into things he shouldn't be. If he found out the truth about what Choyce was, about what I was—I couldn't finish that thought. What if he realized that Choyce really wasn't the one who killed his mom? What if he found out it was actually me?

I shook this question from my mind. I couldn't let myself go down that rabbit hole.

Rotten eggs wafted through my nostrils as I exited the

library, and I spun around, spotting Chuck leaning against the brick wall.

"Have a nice chat with Choyce?" His words were dripping in sarcasm. How did he know who I was talking to?

"What do you want?"

"Just checking in on your progress, dearie." He smirked. "Principal Chomsky's growing impatient."

"What do you know about all of this?" I asked deflecting.

His pointy jaw clenched in irritation. "Oh no, you don't get to ask the questions."

I fumed, wanting to dig my claws into his throat, but I tried to contain my anger, taking a deep breath. "So far, he seems to be who he says he is."

He swiftly removed the space between us, his voice dropping to a whisper. "You'd better find something quick. Or you and your pathetic brother will go down with him."

My hands burned as they threatened to ignite. Smoke rose from the palms of my hands, and Chuck instinctively took a step back. Everything turned red as my eyes shifted, and black claws punctured through my cuticles.

"If you dare harm him, I will end you," I hissed, flashing him a fanged smile. "That's a promise."

For the first time ever, I truly saw the look of fear in his eyes, and I smirked. He was a coward. He might've been able to intimidate me when I was weak, but now? Being untied from the full moon gave me unlimited access to all of my powers. I wasn't afraid of him anymore.

"You have no idea who you're dealing with." He glared down at me. "Just think about what they'll do to you if anything happens to me!"

"And you have no idea who *you're* dealing with," I growled.

The library door rattled as students left, and I quickly took a deep breath, retracting my fangs and claws.

"Are we done here?" I asked, briskly turning on my heel to leave.

"We'll be watching!" He called after me, but I just flipped him off as I walked away. I was done being afraid.

23
AIN'T GOT NOTHING ON ME

- Izara -

Standing near the river, the full moon rose around us, and my heart raced. I didn't know what to expect this full moon. Everything was different since I drank blood last. Would I still shift the same? Would it hurt like it usually did? The power inside of me vibrated to life as my body prepared to transform, but nothing seemed to happen. It was like waiting for a sneeze, only it was stuck. Annoying and delightful at the same time.

A light flickered through the darkness, and suddenly Kain trembled as the full moon overpowered him. Glancing over my shoulder, I half expected myself to feel the pain of shapeshifting, but instead, there was nothing. Kain's heart thumped inside of my own, and I could sense his pain.

I looked over at Choyce, but he hadn't shifted either. Our eyes locked, and a connection between us grew, one that was much stronger than just feeling his heartbeat. It was like we were one unit. I could see his thoughts without him even having to push them to me, and I could sense his anger as he saw into my own. It was like my memories were being pulled from my mind, and soon my entire meeting with Principal Chomsky was rolling around in the open.

Choyce lunged for me, grabbing my shoulders as he pinned me against a nearby tree trunk, his livid eyes inches from my face.

Get out of my head! I glared.

You're helping them? His eyebrows drew in, the sting of my betrayal apparent as he flashed his fangs. *How could you be a part of the very school that killed my brother?"*

My claws extended, and for once, the shift was painless. With a speed I'd never experienced before, my hand shot out, wrapping my clawed hands around his neck as I pushed him away from me.

They said you were the monster who did this to us. I tried to explain, but I knew he'd already gathered this information when he read my mind.

Did you know about this? Choyce asked, turning on

Kain, who, at this point, was trembling on the ground as his wing bones pushed through the skin at either shoulder blade. His eyes flickered between ice water blue and blood red, the intensity of the pain, causing a vein in his forehead to protrude. His biceps had nearly tripled in size, giving him a bodybuilder appearance.

I can't do this right now, he replied as he cried out in agony. *Just read my mind.*

I focused on Kain's thoughts as he relived the meeting with Mr. Valkyrien in his mind, about the library, and about how he and I had decided to just pretend to help the school.

By the time the vision ended, Kain was in full form, and I could sense his power. Maybe this was what Choyce was trying to tell us before, of how he could tell that our power was great. Perhaps it was another 'being untied from the full moon' thing.

Are we good now, Choyce? I asked once he had the full picture.

No. His eyes darkened to coals, and I felt his anger rise as if it were my own. *Not even close.*

His claws peeled through his fingertips as he lunged for me once again. On instinct, I clenched my fists, and suddenly my black wings exploded through my shoulder blades. I spun on my heel and ran through the trees in the opposite direction.

You can't hide from me, Choyce cried.

Gaining momentum, my feet lifted up off the ground as I took flight.

Not so fast. Choyce wrapped his ice-cold hands around my ankles, throwing me to the ground.

My body landed with a crunch on the dead leaf-strewn forest floor, rolling down the side of a hill before hitting my stomach into the base of a tree trunk. I coughed as the blow knocked the wind out of me.

"What the hell?" I cried aloud, picking myself up.

I could say the same thing, he snapped, flashing his white fangs.

Before I could get my balance back, he waved his, forcing my arms behind my back.

Don't you dare use your power on me! I fumed.

How could you help them? Choyce asked.

I tried to push against his power, smoke erupting from the palms of my hands. My arms shook as I fought against the invisible restraints he had cast on me.

They said you were the reason we're like this. That you're Credan.

Whatever you may think. Choyce replied. *This is the first time I'm hearing of this so-called evil.*

Didn't you see Kain's memories? I asked. *Mr. Valkyrien explained that they must be wrong about you. We're on your side.*

And you believe him? Choyce cocked his blond brow.

I trust my brother's instincts, I confirmed. *But it wasn't hard to be convinced by this school. You know all these things about our powers.*

Choyce couldn't contain himself as he shouted aloud, "That's because I've been alive for over a hundred years!"

The vision of the Assembly attacking the man with broken, black wings flashed before my eyes. I'd had this vision just before Choyce visited me in the backyard of Lee's house. In the vision, I was standing in Credan's perspective, and his voice rumbled from within me. It seemed like too much of a coincidence that I'd had this vision right before Choyce appeared to me.

That wasn't me, Choyce whispered, witnessing my memory. *I was born on September twenty-fifth, eighteen-ninety-three, to Henry and Clara Bartholomew. I'm not the one who they're accusing me of being.*

"I got it," I snapped, tapping my foot. "I just wanted it to be you. I wanted us to finally have an answer so that this could all be over."

I want the same thing, Choyce replied, his expression softening.

Doubt it, I thought. *You seem to be all for the darkness.*

Why would I want to live like this? His words echoed in my mind. *Why would I want to have the same power that caused my brother to be targeted and murdered?*

He had a point, but this left us with so many problems

244

that I desperately wanted solutions to.

If you're not the one controlling us, forcing us to be slaves to the full moon, then why do you seem okay with transitioning? I wondered.

Ask me that question again after you've transitioned a thousand times. Choyce replied. *Eventually, you'll be numb, too.*

Choyce turned to leave but stopped, turning back to me. "As for your other question, I have a feeling whoever is controlling us has something to do with what happened to me at The Artesian Hotel in 1919."

"What happened?"

"The entire hotel exploded, but for what reason, they never could figure out." Choyce shrugged. "That was the first time I'd met anyone like me before, but there was this other guy. Someone who was human, but his heart didn't beat like he wasn't alive."

Chills ran through me. "Do you think that was Credan?"

"Maybe, but if the Assembly buried him, then how did he get out? Where is he now?"

It was my turn to shrug.

"I don't know where this evil being is, but if we follow the past, I'm sure we'll find something. We just need to get you and your brother both untied from the full moon. Then we'll be able to fix this. Hopefully."

24

HAUNTING OF FULLERTON PARK

- Lee Walker -

It took Lee forever to find parking in the packed streets of Davis. People from all over the area had arrived for the night's festivities, some dressed in Halloween costumes while others remained in everyday attire. The main street was closed off and, in addition to the crowd, littered with hay bales, pumpkins, scarecrows, and dozens of intricately decorated trailers prepared for the parade.

Lee met up with some of the guys to see the parade and check out the haunted trail. What else was there to do on a Friday night, right? He hadn't bothered asking Izara if she wanted to come along. They hadn't spoken in what felt like weeks, but quite frankly, he didn't care. Something had happened to them. He couldn't put his finger on what it was or when it had all started, but there was definitely an issue. He had humored the idea that maybe it was just him, but there were too many signs that clearly pointed to it being something more.

Like last December at the president's house when Izzy and her brother had disappeared for basically the entire night. And did she tell him why? No. Or when she blew him off repeatedly to practice with Choyce. Was she that dedicated? Or was she just into someone else now? He'd tried to chalk it all up to her still being traumatized by being kidnapped last year, but that was starting to make less and less sense. She was lying to him about something big, something more than just a change of heart.

The thought of his mom popped into his mind then, and he clenched his jaw to keep the tears from forming. If only she were still alive to help him now. She would know what to do.

He shook the thought out of his mind when he spotted Laurent and his younger brother, Duran, out by the Sooner Food's grocery parking lot.

"Ready to get spooked?" Duran joked, letting out a laugh that resembled a scary clown's cackle.

"If it's anything like last year's, I think I'll be fine."

Lee laughed, joining them as they walked to the back of the store towards Fullerton Park.

Ghostly sounds echoed through the park as mist floated in between the dark trees and crawled across the ground. It lapped at their ankles as they crossed East Benton Avenue towards the entrance of the trail. Beady-eyed pumpkins framed a giant *Keep Out* sign written in red paint, mimicking blood.

"BOO!" A guy's raspy voice cried behind them, and they all jumped, spinning around.

Amadeus and Leslie, along with a few of her friends, burst out laughing. "Oh, wow, that was priceless!" Leslie grinned. "You should've seen y'all's faces. I told you it'd work, didn't I?"

She nudged Tiffany and Kia, who stood at her side. They were all dressed in hospital gowns with black paint under their eyes, and blood splattered everywhere.

"Are you supposed to be zombies or something?" Duran asked.

"What else would we be?" Kia asked.

"Weak." Duran deflected, obviously a little too embarrassed that they'd been able to scare him.

"You got us, good job, guys," Lee called, being a good sport.

They got a good laugh before purchasing their tickets and joining the line for the haunted trail.

"Have you seen Izzy or Kain?" Kia asked Lee.

"Nah," Lee replied, only a little curious as to where they could be.

"Whatever you do"—a girl's muffled voice echoed from a loudspeaker from somewhere behind the entrance's archway—"don't fall asleep."

"Ha! That's gotta be A Nightmare on Elm Street." Laurent laughed. "Classic."

A giant skeleton with a top hat lurched, it's limp arm eerily ushering them inside. A fog billowed around them as they walked through the dark park. An orange light flickered in a tree filled with mechanical bats, casting shadows around the tombstones that blanketed the ground.

"Lame." Amadeus scoffed.

"I think it's pretty good," Leslie commented while her friend Tiffany rubbed her arms nervously.

"Yeah, not everyone can handle your level of scary." Tiffany mused.

Whoosh!

The sudden movement of wind above them made them jump.

"What was that?" Tiffany whimpered.

"Now *that* was pretty good." Amadeus laughed.

A cry startled them as a life-size clown with a giant red nose rose from the shadows, the clown's spikey teeth highlighted by a fast blinking strobe light.

"Well, that's a new one," Lee commented. "What do

you think about that, Duran?"

He just shrugged in response, feigning bravery.

"What about you, Amadeus?" Lee raised an eyebrow.

"It's a pity they had such a low budget," Amadeus replied, and they all laughed.

"He's got such high standards." Laurent snickered.

Whoosh! Whoosh!

The wind rustled through the trees above them once again, this time much closer.

"What is that?" Kia asked, stopping in her tracks.

"Are those—?" Leslie began as a blood-curdling scream filled the air.

They all turned towards Tiffany, who was a few steps behind. Her face had turned a sickly gray, and her eyes were fixed upwards towards the starry night's sky.

"Where'd Duran go?" Laurent asked, and Lee glanced around, noticing that he was gone.

"What happened?" Lee asked Tiffany, but she only lifted a trembling hand to the sky.

"What's wrong?" Laurent asked Leslie and Kia, who both just stood there looking stunned like they'd seen a ghost.

"He just—" Kia gulped. "He just got snatched up."

"'*Snatched up*'?" Lee frowned.

Kia nodded. "Yeah, he just kind of flew up and disappeared."

"Did you see what took him?" Laurent asked.

251

She shrugged. "Must be part of the trail."

Lee hesitated but realized he was probably just being silly. It was a haunted trail, after all. "Yeah, must be."

"Looks like they've improved things this year." Laurent chuckled, motioning for them to continue on. "We'll meet him up at the end, I guess."

Tiffany hesitated but then finally followed as they ventured through the haunted trail.

***

- Izara -

A tug at my heart alerted me that something was dreadfully wrong. I peered through the trees, using my night vision to where we'd left Kain as the full moon began, but he was nowhere to be seen.

Where's Kain? I asked Choyce.

He met my worried expression and, without hesitation, we both leaped into the air. Above the ground, we focused our energy on Kain's weak heartbeat. Finally, finding a connection, we let it lead us to where he was.

How'd he get all the way to Davis without us noticing? I wondered.

We were kind of distracted working out our issues. Choyce pointed out.

I know, I replied. *But we still should've been keeping*

an eye on him.

Choyce shrugged, picking up the pace, and I flapped my wings harder to catch up. We landed in the parking lot of the Sooner Food's grocery store. The sounds of chainsaws and ghosts echoed around us as frightened teenagers screamed in innocent delight. They had no idea the real danger that lurked in the dark. Fluorescent lights flickered as we turned the corner to the back of the old painted cinder block building. Approaching the park, a gust of wind rush past us, bringing with it the alluring scents of the one we most desired.

Your brother's close. Choyce warned.

The desperate flutter of Kain's heart reverberated inside of our chest, and I feared the worst.

Let's spread out. I suggested. *We'll cover more ground that way.*

Without waiting for a response, I leaped into the air and rose above the trees. I had to find my brother. I had to stop him from making a horrible mistake. He didn't even have the syringes I brought and, if he killed someone again, I knew he wouldn't be able to live with himself. I didn't want him to have to go through the guilt I had endured.

Sure, love, came Choyce's snarky response. *Great Idea.*

I didn't care. I closed off all my senses, ignoring the intoxicating blood and the compelling voice of Credan as I focused on my brother's heartbeat. It was amazing how being untied from the full moon weakened the temptation and force of Credan's influence. The price was high, but freedom rarely came free.

Lowering myself to a tree branch, I zeroed in on the beats of each passerby of the haunted trail. One by one, I filtered through the crowd, pushing out the rhythms that didn't belong to Kain. Keeping to the shadows, I soared through the air and landed on another branch. My claws dug into the bark, every fiber scraped against my palm, crackling under the pressure. Each pulse of life formed an image in my mind, and I could match each heartbeat with either a student at the school or a member of the community. It was as if I knew everyone and could locate anyone on the planet except for Kain.

Why are you hiding? I wondered, hoping Kain would hear me and reveal himself.

He'd never been able to hide like this before. What had changed?

A scream in the distance caused my eyes to dart to the haunted trail below me. Tiffany stood yards away from me, her eyes frozen upwards. My eyes followed her glance, but I couldn't see anything out of the ordinary, except for plastic bats hanging from the tree branches.

Izara, Choyce said. *You need to come see this.*

Did you find him? I asked.

Sort of. That was all he responded with.

I instantly took flight, letting the wind glide through

my feathers as I darted towards the purr of Choyce's heartbeat. Landing beside him, I gasped.

Black feathers were strewn across the ground around Choyce. Feathers large enough that they could've only belonged to someone with our powers. But that's not what caught my attention. Lying in a heap, a pair of giant wings dripping with blood lay at odd angles at his side. They were my brothers. They had to be.

I didn't do this. Choyce shook his head, immediately pulling into a defensive position.

Where is he? I growled, my thoughts racing with all the endless possibilities. His wings had been ripped from his back. Was he dead? It couldn't be.

Another scream bellowed through the night, causing our claws to snap through our skin out of instinct. Diving into the air, we flew towards the sound. Spooky laughter from the haunted trail reverberated through the air as we flew over, landing in the park just out of sight.

A figure turned away from us, cowering near a tree trunk with two holes in his back.

"Kain!" I gasped aloud, running towards him.

His head snapped towards my direction, and I stopped in my tracts. His eyes glowed deep red, and in his hands lay a limp corpse. Blood dripped from the corners of his lips, and soon, black liquid spewed from the holes in his back.

Choyce! I cried. *What's happening to him?*

I glanced over at Choyce, who stood next to me. His jaw fell open at the sight.

I've no idea, honestly. Choyce replied.

Black veins crawled through his ripped shoulders as the skin around the holes in his back instantly rebuilt.

How are you still alive? Choyce asked Kain, but he was currently preoccupied with consuming the human in his arms.

Recognizing the form as Duran, I darted to his side. "Kain!" I cried aloud, my desire for blood overcome by my human instinct of seeing my boyfriend's friend lying there, dead.

Gripping either side of my brother's face, I forced him to look at me, and his eyes suddenly snapped out of the trance he was in. Kain dropped the limp body of Duran as he brushed me away, not realizing who was in his arms.

"What have you done?" I cried aloud.

Glancing down at the cold face of Duran Black, my brother's heart skipped a beat within my chest.

What the hell happened? he asked.

I shook my head, unable to answer that question.

He blinked several times until realization dawned on him. *It happened so quickly. Something—someone attacked me. They took my wings and then—the blood. It was the only way.*

Suddenly, the black goo spewing from his back turned solid as bones formed, growing a fresh pair of black wings.

They bristled behind Kain, shimmering in the moonlight.

"They grew back." Choyce gasped, unable to contain himself.

How is that possible? I wondered.

It could be his own unique power developing, Choyce hypothesized. *Regeneration, maybe?*

He's not the freakin' Wolverine! I replied.

Choyce just shrugged.

"NO!" Kain bellowed, slumping near Duran's limp form, cradling his head. "You can't be dead."

He sobbed.

You do realize where we are, right? Choyce replied, always the voice of reason.

Glancing around, we were smack dab in the middle of the haunted trail's grand finale.

We've got to move. Choyce and I thought at the exact same time.

I grabbed Kain's arm, but he shoved me away.

Go. He cried. *Leave me if you must, but I can't leave him. I can't live with this. I'm not like you!*

His words stung as if he'd stabbed me in the heart. What could I do to make this right?

Come on. Choyce grabbed my hand. *We need to get out of here.*

I can't leave my brother, I replied.

The crowd's giggling screams grew closer as they

approached the end, and I knew it was only a matter of time before they saw us.

"Kain!" I tugged on his arm once more. "We can't let them see us."

A teardrop glistened as it spilled down my brother's cheek, falling onto Duran's stone-cold cheek. The pain of the loss tugged at my heart, the unfathomable torture of taking a life filled his entire being, and I wished that I could erase it all.

When I get a handle on this time travel ability, I pushed my thoughts to Kain, *I will fix this. I promise.*

Kain continued to sob over Duran's dead body but finally nodded. His shoulders slumped in defeat as I helped him up from the ground, and we disappeared into the night.

25
WHEN THE FLOOD BURNS

- Kain -

After English, I headed for my locker to drop off my stuff before searching for Laurent. I hadn't seen or heard anything from him all weekend, and I was beginning to panic. I needed to tell him everything, despite Izzy and Choyce's protests. Something had come after me. It attacked me, causing me to lose control, tearing my wings from me, and forced me to drink the blood.

It was what allowed my wings to regenerate. But it was at the cost of my friend's life. Nothing was worth that. I should've just died. It should've been me instead of him.

Pushing through the entrance to the cafeteria, I scanned the crowd.

"Hey, man!" Lee called, walking up to me. "Didn't see you in history class this morning. Is everything okay?"

"Yeah, just overslept." I shrugged. "Have you seen Laurent?"

"Yeah, he went to that study group for pre-cal," Lee smirked. "Probably just because Tiffany's there. You know he's got it bad for her."

"Where's it being held this time?"

"The library, I think," Lee replied.

"Thanks," I said, spinning on my heel to leave.

"Wait up!" Lee called, but I was in too much of a hurry to stop my jog to the library.

Pushing my way through the entrance, I headed to the front desk. Luckily there was someone there this time. It was like spotting a unicorn in real life. "Hey, would you know where the study group for pre-cal is?"

The guy behind the desk glanced up from his book. "Second floor, cube seven."

"Thanks," I called over my shoulder.

When I got to the second-floor landing, I ran into Laurent just as he was on his way out.

"Yo, man, you missed a sick haunted trail the other night. I mean, it was *crazy*!" He chuckled.

I frowned, his nonchalant reaction confusing me. He

260

should've been distraught from the loss of his brother. Why was he so happy?

"Dude, I need to tell you something," I said.

"Kain!" Duran called as he turned the corner.

What the heck was happening? Wasn't Duran dead? I had seen him take his last breath, tasted his blood, but somehow, he was standing right before me. It was all surreal. The sight of him made the black veins protrude from my arms, and I was glad that I had chosen today to wear an actual sweatshirt to beat the cold.

"You've got to see this." Duran handed the phone to Laurent and me. "People have been talking about this crazy photo someone shared from the Halloween festival."

Glancing down at the screen, my jaw dropped. The quality wasn't so great, but the photo on his phone was obviously taken towards the end of the haunted trail.

"See that?" Duran pointed to two figures hovering just above the ground and one in the distance. It was mostly blurry, but it was definitely the outline of the three of us in full shifter form.

"Who took this?" I asked.

"No idea." Duran shrugged. "A guy I know from English class shared it."

If Choyce saw this, he would freak. Luckily, it was blurry enough that no one would be able to tell it was us, but that still wouldn't keep him from flipping out. I needed to get out of there. The blood inside of me began to boil, and I was suddenly feeling nauseous. It was just too much for me to handle right now.

"That's crazy!" I hoped that was a good enough response not to make Duran and his brother suspicious. "I forgot I had to get to…someplace else."

They frowned. Great. I wasn't being very smooth.

"Catch you guys later," I mumbled before fleeing the library before I puked.

Choyce and Izzy could deal with that mess. After all, they were the ones encouraging me to drink blood. I was more preoccupied with the fact that Duran wasn't dead anymore. How was this possible? I'd drained him of blood. His body had fallen limp in my arms. The more I thought about it, the more confused I became. With all the energy that was bent up inside me, I knew I needed to go workout, so I changed my course towards the gym.

Sweat, bleach and dusty mops that couldn't entirely cover up the stench met my senses as I entered the spacious gym. I knew a few guys from the team grouped together by the bench press machine, but I didn't feel like being social. My blood was visibly boiling inside my veins, and the next person who bothered me would be sorry.

Darting for the dressing room, I grabbed my junk from my reserved locker, pulling the spare t-shirt and sweats on and sticking my earbuds in. Placing my phone in my pocket, I let the intoxicating beats of The Kills take over me as I headed for the pull-up bar.

The lyrics of U.R.A Fever replaced the fears tumbling around in my mind as I pulled my chin up above the bar. I lost track of how many reps I'd done, but I didn't care. My arms weren't even sore, and the pull-ups seemed too easy. After a moment, the clock on the far wall caught my eye, and I realized I'd been doing pull-ups for the last thirty minutes. I should've been exhausted, but my whole body was weightless. Was this the side effect of being untied from the full moon?

"Wow!" someone behind me said as I dropped to the ground.

Turning, Kia walked up with a broad smile on her face, her gym bag in hand. "Impressive. You've got a free period now, too?"

"Yeah. Nice, huh?" I grabbed my towel, barely dabbing at my forehead.

"Definitely," she agreed, eyeing my pumped biceps appreciatively. "So, you must be working out a lot this semester."

"A bit."

She winked. "Keep it up."

Her eyes lingered on my newly built body as she headed for the ellipticals. I exhaled, relieved that she was gone and glad that she didn't have any more questions. I grabbed my empty water bottle, and as my hand wrapped around the clear, reusable bottle, it slipped through my fingertips. I froze, letting it fall. Strange looking beads of water bubbled up from my palms. It was probably just sweat.

But didn't I just wipe them off on my towel? I thought.

Rubbing them again on my shorts, I tried to dry them off, but they continued to feel damp for some reason. I gave up and proceeded to pick up the bottle again. Uncapping it, I brought it to my lips, but only a drop fell.

It was empty. Great. This day kept getting better and better.

Picking up my things, I headed for the drinking fountain. I was incredibly thirsty and lightheaded all of a sudden, like I hadn't had water in a week. I grasped the dispenser's sides, pressing lightly against the metal button that triggered the water to rush through the spout. I practically inhaled the water as I drank with a thirst I'd never experienced before. Closing my eyes, the fluid rushing through my body was so satisfying.

"Ahem, save some for the rest of us." A girl behind me tapped her foot impatiently.

Glancing over my shoulder, the name on her sports jacket read *Britney Tompkin.*

Great. Another one. Rolling my eyes, I turned back to the fountain, expecting the water to rush from the spout and down through the drain. Instead, it was filling up, causing the rushing water to flow over the sides of the fountain and into my hands. I checked the floor, but the water seemed to be draining into me through my fingertips. What the hell? Was the drain clogged? Was I going crazy? I figured it must've been a little bit of both. Removing my hands from the fountain, I studied them. Tiny beads of water droplets cascaded over them as my hands absorbed the fluid. That definitely wasn't normal.

"You done?" The Tompkin girl asked again.

"Uh, yeah," I said, absently staring at my hands as I turned to leave.

The clang of her pushing the metal button echoed. "Hey!" Britney cried, and I glanced back just in time as she angrily slammed her fists against the button for the fountain. The machine made a noise as if it were pulling water, but no matter how many times she pushed against the dispenser, water still didn't flow through the spout. Each time she pressed the button, a shiver ran through me as more beads of water crawled up my hands and arms.

"He broke it!" She exclaimed, cursing as I disappeared through the doors for the guys' locker room.

Grabbing a towel, I checked to be sure no one else was in the showers. I didn't need anyone noticing the beads of water twirling up my arms and chest. It looked like sweat at first glance, but at a closer look, it was apparent the water was going against gravity. Turning the nozzle to ice-cold, I stepped under the showerhead expecting the cool water to rush over my skin, but instead, the liquid pooled over my skin for a moment before my skin absorbed the moisture completely. The water didn't even have a chance to hit the floor into the drain, and it was like the water wasn't even running. I stepped out of the rushing water noticing that the spraying water evaporated into mist before it ever hit the floor.

What was happening?

A shiver ran through me once again, and suddenly, my stomach lurched. I doubled over, my hand reaching for the cold tile for support as my whole world spun around me. My shoulders slammed against the humid floor, steam emanating from my body. My lungs heaved, trying to pull in more oxygen, but I choked on a strange, thick liquid as if I were drowning.

But how was that possible? I wasn't even underwater. I cried out as my body convulsed against the cold floor. Clambering for a railing, anything to grip and gain control over my body, I choked as I tried to expel the excess water. It was a futile attempt as each time I vomited, the water replaced itself tenfold with more liquid. Finally finding the wall again, I braced my palm on the tile, pushing myself up onto shaky feet. Stumbling to the faucet, my body landed with a thud on the shower wall as I used all of the strength I could muster to turn the lever. The water pressure slowed to a drip before I collapsed backward, black and yellow spots taking over my vision as I lost consciousness.

26

A STORM BREWING

- Kain -

I was drowning in a sea of fire. My whole body burned to the core. I couldn't remember where I was, but once the steam that surrounded me subsided, I realized I was surrounded by green and brown. My vision still blurry, I wiped my eyes. Blinking a loose eyelash away, tree trunks groaned around me as squirrels scuttled through the branches.

The sun was setting in the distance like it was a time-lapse video, and soon I was in darkness. The night sky blew around me as I finally picked myself up off the musty dirt and fallen branches. Footsteps crunched from somewhere nearby as angry voices echoed through the trees. I spun around to see a bunch of men dragging a body away. He couldn't have been more than sixteen, although he was relatively small for his age. I recognized the well-trimmed brown hair of Edwin Bartholomew as nightwalkers dragged his limp body from the fire that was spreading through the forest behind them.

"Sarge! We won't make it to the quarry!" a young lad helping lug Edwin's body away from the fire cried to the enormous man running as fast as he could, his suspenders straining to hold his britches up.

How was I seeing this? I remembered at this point, we had already returned to our time. This must've been a dream. Or was it?

"We'll drop it up yonder!" The man called Sarge bellowed. "Then"—he coughed, out of breath—"we'll come back to put the fire out."

Why wasn't this huge guy helping to carry the body? He looked strong enough to help, but perhaps he was just worried about himself. Out of nowhere, the group leader stopped running, pointing to a ditch near the creek. "Dump it here!"

As the nightwalkers dropped Edwin in the ditch, the Sarge locked eyes on mine, coming to grip my shoulder.

"What are you doing just standing there?" he barked. "Start coverin' it with dirt. We don't need anything getting a whiff of this."

My heart pumped nervously, taking a step back. How could this man see me if I was dreaming? He seemed to even recognize me, but how?

"Sorry?" Ewww, my voice was all nasally. It sounded nothing like me. Was I dreaming from someone else's point of view? If so, why?

"DID YOU HEAR ME, BOY?" Sarge shouted at me.

He shoved me towards the body on the ground, causing me to faceplant in a pile of dead leaves. I coughed, course wood scraping against my tender cheek. The man grabbed me again by the suspenders, pulling me up on my feet. "If you want to be on the team, you do what you're told. No questions."

Shivering, I looked down at the dead body at my feet, my stomach nearly expelling all of its contents. Before I had a chance to move, my chest heaved as if it were being pumped. A sour taste hung in my mouth, and I choked. Voices in the distance cried out to me, but none of them were the men around me, and within seconds, everything went black once again.

***

I opened my eyes, coughing uncontrollably. My throat burned as water rushed up from inside of me. My cheek rested against the cold, damp tile as bright, blurry lights blinded me. Panicked voices murmured above the rushing water, and then another voice spoke as if to me.

"There you go," a woman said, slapping my back when I sat up.

Water molecules continued to seep into my skin, but for now, it seemed I had emptied enough of the liquid to not drown for now. If I kept absorbing all of this water, I knew it was only a matter of time before I drowned from the inside again.

"Stop." I managed to cough out, irritated by her continuously burping me.

"Don't try to rush it," the lady replied. "You need to get yourself to the dorm room and rest."

"The water," I croaked, my throat dry as I pointed towards the running water. I couldn't take any more of it.

"I'll help you to the dorm entrance." The woman in scrubs continued to ignore me. "Then the RA will take you from there."

I finally gained focus. I was covered in a towel and, gripping it in one hand, I hopped to my feet and wrapped it around my waist. "I can manage."

"You need to take it easy," she said, standing on her feet as she reached out for me.

I ignored her attempts to help me, a little insulted. I wasn't some weakling, and in my head, I heard the guys nearby snickering among each other. I knew it was only my imagination, but I didn't want to give them the satisfaction of

271

seeing me like this. Shakily, I braced myself as I limped my way out of the showers and to my locker. Fidgeting with the lock, my focus faded in and out. I had to get to Choyce. If anyone would know what was going on with me, it'd be him.

Finally, my lock popped open, and I was able to grab my clothes. Throwing everything on, I threw my gym bag over my shoulder and stumbled towards the illuminated exit sign. A cool breeze hit me as I left the gym, which was strange because the trees gave no indication of any wind. I shivered as the wind blew against my clammy skin. The sunlight flickered on the ground as dark clouds rolled through the sky.

The hairs on my arms and the back of my neck stood upright, telling me it would rain soon. Goosebumps covered me as my body anticipated the moisture. Even thousands of feet below, I could sense how much rain was in the clouds. I swallowed hard. I would die if it started raining while I was outside. Maybe, just maybe, I would be safe if I got to the dorms in time.

Sprinting towards the bridge, thunder shook the ground as the sky cast gray shadows throughout the school grounds. I sighed with relief when I made it to the dorm's front lawn, the entrance in sight. Hopping up the two steps of the porch, I reached for the door when a drop of liquid hit my knee. I froze.

How was that possible? It wasn't raining yet, and I was under a covered porch. Several more pellets hit me, and I lifted my hands to get a closer look.

What the heck? I thought.

Droplets fell from my hand. I turned my palm face-up, and my heart skipped a beat. Tiny raindrops were falling upwards from my hand as if my hand itself was the cloud storing the water. They dropped upwards about a foot before turning into steam and evaporating. It was a strange sensation, like that tingling feeling after sitting on your leg for too long. Only it wasn't my leg, it was my whole hand, and it wasn't asleep at all.

Black and blue splotches covered the palms of my hands where I was apparently absorbing the rainwater from the clouds. At least I wasn't drowning, but what would happen if I drank water? Did I even need to remember my daily eight cups of water anymore now?

Deciding these were pointless questions as I couldn't answer them, I grabbed the brass doorknob and turned my wrist, but my clammy hand just slipped across it like a water slide.

"Come on!" I groaned.

Taking a step back, I clenched my fists and tried to calm my racing heart. I needed to focus. Taking deep breaths, I searched for the strength to overcome my own ability that was currently in my way. Wasn't I a supernatural being? Didn't I have other powers? Remembering when I first shifted and squashed a doorknob with my bare hands. If I could do that and a million pull-ups without getting tired, I had to be strong enough to get through this measly little door.

Just as my breathing slowed, the full moon flashed before my eyes, and my heartbeat soared. The fibers in my muscles fused together, thickening my arms as they visibly doubled in size. Large veins poked out from my shoulders to the ends of my fingertips.

"Sweet." I breathed, reaching for the door when it suddenly swung open.

A startled RA stopped right as he was about to plow right through me.

"Oh sorry, Kain," Joe said. "Didn't know you were there. Been working out much, huh?"

"Ah, yeah. Can't get enough." I waved as Joe continued on his way.

The door nearly closed, and I quickly shoved a foot in, slipping through before it latched.

I tried to get back to my room as soon as possible. Just because Joe hadn't been too suspicious of my newly found bodybuilder physique didn't mean others wouldn't question it. I worked out and wasn't exactly wimpy, but right now, I looked like I was on steroids in comparison.

Finally making it up the stairs and to my door, I was relieved when my hands firmly gripped the handle this time. Maybe being inside dried me out enough to be a normal person. The door rattled on its hinges when I opened it, and I sighed. Perhaps being normal was just wishful thinking. I

274

hadn't even used that much strength, and the screws holding the door to the frame looked like they were going to snap. Once inside, I carefully used my index finger to gently close the door. I sighed with relief when it closed without falling over.

I turned to find Choyce lying on his bed, tossing three hacky sacks up into the air. "I didn't know you could juggle."

"You've been avoiding me." Choyce ignored my comment, tossing them into a jar on his desk without even looking.

He snapped his fingers as he sat up. "You're untied from the full moon. How's your power treating you?"

"Awesome." I rolled my eyes, walking over to my side of the room and plopping in my desk chair as I searched for my toiletry bag.

I still had this gross, dry feeling in my mouth that tasted like moss. It had to go.

"No news? Well, your sister's in the same situation." Choyce continued even though I was trying to tune him out. I didn't have time for this. "We tried multiple times over the weekend to control her time traveling power, but it's no use. She still hasn't found a way to access it, even with the two of you untied from the full moon. Which is strange."

"Cool," I grunted, grabbing my things and heading for the bathroom.

"But you." Choyce followed me into the bathroom.

"Your power is incredible. Duran was dead, but then lo and behold he's alive again. I'm thinking you've got a little power called resurgence."

I narrowed my eyebrows. "You mean like I can bring people back to life? What, are we in some episode of *Supernatural*?"

"No, we're very much in real life. A life where you killed Duran but somehow brought him back. You resurrected him."

"You're crazy." I scoffed, uncapping the toothpaste. "Anyway, how are you still untied from the full moon? We had to get out of there quickly. I didn't see either of you have time to—well, you know."

"I may have stolen a few vials from him before we shifted back." He said as I turned the knob of the faucet.

My blood boiled as the anger rose up from the pit of my stomach as I slowly turned around. *You did WHAT?* I growled.

The water barely hit the porcelain before a swarm of shivers rushed through me as my body absorbed the water, filling my entire body. Catching myself in the reflection, my eyes shimmered as bright as the sun reflecting against the ocean. My stomach churned like waves, and I nearly vomited.

Choyce didn't seem to notice. "We had no other choice, Kain. Surely you understand. He was already dead and—Kain?"

I braced myself on the vanity as I bent my head over the empty sink. Gagging involuntarily, my stomach couldn't take any more water.

"What's going on?" Choyce asked, but I couldn't answer. "Are you sick?"

Pounding my fist on the counter as I tried desperately to control my absorption. A loud crack echoed through the room, and the granite gave way. Another rush of water entered my body as I stumbled away from the sink.

Choyce gasped, grabbing me before I stumbled back into the tub. If I didn't dehydrate, I knew I would drown again. Focusing on my hands, I tried to get the water to leave me like it had before. How did I do it last time? Being a mystery to me still, I just decided to try some things. Squeezing my hands into fists, I opened them up, extending my palms upwards.

Nothing happened except black dots began to cover my vision, and I knew it was only a matter of time before I lost consciousness.

Gripping the acrylic tub, I pushed through the pain, the fog, and the horrible flood that was within me. Stretching my hand out once again, the full moon flickered around me, and this time, water droplets exploded from my hand in every direction. "Turn off the faucet!" I was barely able to get the words out as the water flowed endlessly through me.

Choyce darted for the sink, turning the knob off, and the water slowly subsided. He stood there, frozen in place, staring at me with his mouth gaping wide.

"What?" I snapped.

"Resurgence and assimilation," he said in awe.

"Assimilation?"

"It's where one can absorb the elements around them."

I smirked. "Yeah right, like I'm an Arthur Petrelli."

"You watch too much TV." Choyce shook his head. "How else do you explain what you've just done here?"

I pushed past him and back into the room. "I'm cursed. That's how I explain it."

"This isn't a curse," Choyce said, following me. "This is an opportunity."

"Oh yeah? For what?"

He chuckled. "We'll finally be getting to use the school's pool. To see what you're truly capable of."

***

- Izara -

The bell rang as I answered the very last question on electron configurations. I would be quite okay if I didn't have to look at another dot formula for the rest of my life. I was definitely not going into a career in chemistry.

Closing my book, I dumped my things in my bag before rushing out of the classroom. I knew Kain had a free period next, and I had to go find him. He'd been avoiding me ever since Halloween, and I was beginning to worry. Each time I tried to communicate with him telepathically, he pushed me out. I knew what being untied from the full moon could do, how overwhelming it was, and I wanted to be sure he knew I was there for him.

Rushing for the exit, I welcomed the sun as it cast its warmth over me. Even though it was a bit chilly outside, being cooped up inside a freezing lab made me gladly embrace the sunrays beating down on me. Out of the corner of my eye, I spotted Lee exiting the gym, and a pang of guilt tugged at my heartstrings. I should've been brave and told him the truth when I had a chance. But how could I? I couldn't exactly tell him that I was a monster who flew around killing people on the full moon and that there was nothing I could do about it. Oh, and that it wasn't Choyce who killed his mom but actually me. That conversation was bound to be an epic fail.

Remembering the moment I finally had the guts to break up with him before the summer, trying to let him down easy. I was a nightmare, and he deserved to be with someone who could be completely honest with him. He'd been okay with it then and refused to let me go, but I knew that it couldn't last. Eventually, the secrets would get to him and put him in even more danger, but I couldn't bring myself to part with him now. When I was with him, I was almost normal. There was nothing else in the world I wanted more than that.

"Lee!" I called, and he glanced over in my direction.

Hesitating, he waited for me to catch up.

"Hi." I smiled, trying to fill the awkward silence between us.

He tucked his hands in the pockets of his gym shorts, his drawstring bag slung over one shoulder. "Hey."

"How are you?"

"Okay." He shrugged, his deep-set eyes cold and distant. "You?"

"Honestly? Not okay." I shrugged. "I've missed you."

He made a face. "I thought your new boyfriend would keep you company."

"Don't say that." I sighed. "He's not my boyfriend. He's not even my friend. He's just someone who's in my drama team that I, unfortunately, have to practice lines with."

He didn't respond, and I scoured my mind for words to make all of this right. Anything, but nothing was right.

"I'm sorry, okay?" I began. "I shouldn't have gotten so defensive. I don't know if Choyce was lying or not. I just don't want to quit the drama club. But that doesn't excuse how I responded to you, so I'm sorry."

His shoulders relaxed a bit at that.

"Can you forgive me?"

It took him a minute to respond, but finally, he removed the space between us, pulling me into a hug. "Of course. I shouldn't have even suggested it. I just don't trust this guy, okay? Promise me you'll be careful?"

"I promise."

27
THE DELOREAN

- Kain -

The fire burned, yet somehow, I had learned to live with it in my dreams. It was as if Izzy and I could share resources in our subconscious. Standing in front of The Artesian Hotel, as I'd been many times before, this time Izara wasn't there. I stood alone, gazing out at my surroundings. A brand-new Oldsmobile drove by as people walked the streets with clothing and hairstyles like the Beatles. Everything from the cars to the clothes screamed I'd hopped into a DeLorean with Marty McFly as I stood in a 1960's Sulphur, Oklahoma.

BAM!

The ground shook as an explosion burst, setting the

hotel on fire, followed by shouts and screams. Fire engulfed the building as people rushed out in droves. Not knowing what to do or how to help, I glanced around to see if anyone might know how to get in touch with the fire department, but no one listened to me.

Oh, right. This was a dream. Or was it? I couldn't tell anymore.

Out of the corner of my eye, two figures emerged from the smoke. They ran diagonally across the street. A streak of red hair was all it took for me to know that it was the yellow-eyed woman named Emma and the wolf-like man, Abram, from my dreams of Choyce. How were they here? I thought that they were here in 1919, not the sixties.

They hadn't noticed me, so I followed them. If I stayed just out of sight, perhaps I would be able to finally see what they were up to. It couldn't hurt. Well, maybe it could, but it wouldn't kill me.

Straining to keep up as they darted across Broadway and 1st, ducking into the nearby park. I grimaced as the wind blew the odorous hints of sulfur from the nearby spring. It overpowered my senses, and for a moment, I wasn't watching where I was going.

A twig snapped behind me, and I spun around, coming face-to-face with a wolf—an actual wolf with yellow eyes and teeth the size of a butcher's knife. My eyes widened as four more approached me, growling. Slime dripped from their fangs, *and I knew they were thirsty for blood.*

Backing up slowly, I backed right up into a tree trunk. They couldn't hurt me in my dream, could they?

A black clawed hand wrapped around my neck, and I sucked in air, panicking as I gasped for oxygen.

"How did we get here?" Abram hissed in my ear, his grizzly black beard scratching my cheek.

Movement from behind him distracted me as the blindingly yellow eyes of the red-haired woman met mine. Her body began to shimmer as bright as her eyes.

"Speak!" Abram's voice rang out, pulling my eyes away from her glistening skin.

"I—I don't know," I stammered, but my voice was all wrong. It didn't belong to me, but somehow it was still familiar.

"This isn't the time we were just in." Abram hissed. "We were in the middle of—"

"Careful," Emma warned him. "He's always listening. We mustn't change his plan."

"Whose plan?" I blurted out before I could think twice.

The wolves were now circling us, eyeing me as if waiting for Abram to give his okay to eat me.

Abram let out an exasperated sigh. "Whatever you did, you must reverse it."

"I honestly don't know what you're talking about." The eerily familiar voice responded through me, the sound of it feeling odd to my lips.

"You followed us down to the cellar," he barked, smacking my head against the tree. "You did this! You brought us here. You're the only one who could."

He must've hit my head harder than anticipated because soon, everything turned dark, leaving me unable to respond.

***

I couldn't focus on class at all that morning. My thoughts kept going back to my dreams of The Artesian Hotel. The one last night seemed so real it had to be another vision from Izzy's mind, but it was different. This time I wasn't looking at it from the outside. I was *in* it as if I was a part of it. It reminded me of the vision I'd had while drowning. The hot breath of the wolf barking in my ear still tingled, but it wasn't me he saw.

"You did this!" The wolf-like man's words kept ringing on loop. *"You're the only one who could."*

That had been a keyword. Who else could travel into the future? I just wanted to know how he did it. Without Choyce's brother, he couldn't time travel, but obviously, that wasn't necessarily the case unless—no. That was crazy. I remembered the vision of Choyce being shackled in the cellar, Abram killing the drunken man who'd stumbled down, and how everyone except Choyce had seemingly disappeared.

285

What had happened to them? How did they wind up in the 1960s? And what had caused the fire? These two questions must've had something to do with that night of the party in 1919, but what that was, I couldn't say.

The bell rang, signaling class was over, and I headed for the exit. The other students were making their way to lunch, but I wasn't about to make that mistake again. Not until I gained control over my newfound power. I couldn't drink water or even be around anything with fluid in it without absorbing it and nearly dying. The steaming vegetables' moisture would leave tingling droplets on my fingertips and don't get me started on what effect the soups had.

The struggle was that I still needed water, and my body seemed to crave it even more so now. It was like an addiction, a thirst I couldn't quench. Every second that passed by, I wanted it, making the least exciting thing in the world a constant temptation.

The school's drinking fountains.

But if I made contact with them, they could kill me. I couldn't control my intake yet. I thought being untied from the full moon would help me get control over my power, but apparently, that wasn't always true. It seemed to unleash several new abilities, like bringing Duran back to life. I was grateful for that power. That was the bright side of being free. The downside was I still heard this distant whisper in my head, the voice of Credan. I thought I would be free from his reach if

I was untied, but apparently, Choyce actually didn't know everything about how all of this worked.

Kain, speaking of the devil, Choyce called for me. *Meet you at the pool in five.*

Great. Another practice session to try and get me to overcome my assimilation power. I wasn't looking forward to yet another session of drowning in chlorine water. In the cold, no less. Choyce's theory was that I needed to get to my total breaking point, face a life-or-death situation to trigger my instincts. Force me to control my power, and then maybe I could reproduce whatever I did to keep myself alive. It didn't seem to be helping.

FOCUS! Choyce's demanding voice bellowed in my mind as my body landed with a thud on the cement for the hundredth time. He used his power to push me against the bottom of the pool with such a force that every single bone in my body cracked.

My fingers dislocated but healed within seconds of breaking. Another shove sent the pool waters plunging against my back, shattering my bones again, making me wish it'd kill me. But to my dismay, my body regenerated for it all to be repeated.

Finally, the weight subsided, and I surfaced, sputtering as I made it to the pool's ledge. "It's too much."

I shivered as my insides spilled out.

"You're healing yourself faster. That's a good sign."

287

I peeled my eyes open, squinting against the sunlight.

"You think you've had enough?"

I coughed. "Yeah."

"You'll have enough when you stop drowning yourself!" His harsh words didn't hurt as much as the water did as he pushed me back into the pool.

My skin suddenly became a sponge as the treated water rushed into my body, making its way into my bloodstream. It attempted to penetrate every crevice of my being, but as soon as it hit my stomach, I convulsed uncontrollably. Gasping for air, I choked as my attempts were met by swallowing more water.

The vein at my temple bulged as I flailed my arms and legs, desperately trying to latch onto anything. The surface was just out of reach as Choyce's power continued to shove me to the bottom. Why couldn't I push through this? Why couldn't I stop from drowning? Those were the last thoughts that ran through my mind as my body stopped moving, and I peacefully went into the dark.

The lights of The Artesian Hotel flickered as the party drew on into the night. Bart Bessler danced with Mary, and the bright, dazzling yellow eyes of Emma entranced me as she captured the light with her eyes. Large teeth lashed out as Abram attacked the intruders in the cellar while Choyce lay in a heap, chained to the floor.

"The destiny of shifters is about to come to fruition."

Their human companion's smooth silk voice cooed.

The world around me turned to liquid, and Izzy suddenly stood in front of me.

"You know his face." A voice that didn't belong to my sister bellowed from within her. Her irises went white like Credan's, and suddenly everything shook around me.

I will return to my children. *The dead voice repeated over and over again, and I writhed in pain.*

***

You did it. Choyce's shocked voice in my head was the first thing I was able to process.

The darkness slowly subsided as my chest moved normally again, pulling in air with tiny hints of bleach. It wasn't the best of smells, but it was better than drowning for sure. Carefully opening my eyes, I prayed it wasn't all just some delusion my brain was putting on.

Blinking several times, I couldn't believe it. I was standing on the cement floor of the pool, water surrounding me as I stood at the center of a giant bubble my hands appeared to be holding up. I didn't dare move them for fear of the water collapsing on me again. The water threatened to drown me, to press me into its grasp, but it no longer had that power over me. My chest hurt, but I was finally able to breathe normally. It was as if I'd been running for miles, and I'd finally caught that second wind.

The full moon flashed in my mind like a broken motion picture as heat filled my body. My muscles swelled as I took a deep breath, a breeze suddenly rushing through my hair as all the water around me vanished.

What the hell? I frowned, looking around.

Glancing down at my body, tiny little beads of water covered me as if I was sweating. My skin turned pale as the water flowed within me, and this time, I embraced it.

Eyeing the nearly eighteen-foot wall of the pool, I wondered how I was going to get out of there. That is until my instincts kicked in, and I sprinted for the wall. The wind flew past my skin, feeling warm in comparison to my body. I was unstoppable. I leaped into the air, the palm of my hand grabbing the side of the pool.

"Whoa!" I gasped, not even feeling a strain as I held my enormous body with one arm. Swinging my body over the ledge, I landed on my feet by the side of the pool next to a stunned Choyce.

He applauded me. "That was impressive."

I took a deep, satisfying breath of fresh air as I proudly eyed the drained pool. "There isn't supposed to be water in there this time of year anyway, right?"

Choyce smirked. "I think a school employee is bound to notice."

"I'll put it back, don't worry." I sighed, extending my

arms, and took a deep breath.

My heart suddenly raced as I thought of the full moon, exhaling. The roar of the water gushing from my palms back into the pool was like a waterfall. The hairs on my arms stood up as it rushed from my body, the power surging through my veins as the flood drained from me, and I knew that this was just the beginning.

28
S.O.B.

- Detective Shane Walker -

"Talk to me." Shane entered the station with his usual cup of black coffee, greeting the officers.

He hadn't slept very well in months and needed a distraction from his constant obsession with the recent murders that'd been going on.

"Well," Officer Ramon began, taking a bit of his poppy-seed muffin. "The Ardmoreite's got a name for your perp."

"A name?" Shane snatched the newspaper from his thick fingers. "Great."

"The Sooner Heart Ripper." Ramon grinned. "It's

kinda got a ring to it, don't it?"

Glancing at the front page, sweat formed at his brow as he read the headline: *Ardmore Little Theatre murders linked to Oklahoma City killing.*

Shane threw the newspaper back onto Officer Ramon's cluttered desk. "How the hell did they get this intel? That scene was supposed to be locked down."

Ramon shrugged, smacking his lips mid-chew.

"Detective Walker!" Another officer called interrupting them. "We've got another S.O.B. sighting at Fullerton Park."

"Gah, would you all stop calling it that?" Shane sighed, not in the mood for the officer's acronym for anything weird or unusual that got called in.

"Sorry." She half-smiled. "We just got another strange obstruction call. It was sighted near Fullerton Park. The tech thinks it's something you should definitely take a look at."

He placed his unfinished coffee on the desk. "Alright, I'm right behind you. Coming Ramon?"

Wiping his hands, Officer Ramon dropped his feet from the top of the desk and grabbed his jacket. "Absolutely."

Once they hopped in the squad car, they headed east down Main Street towards the Sooner Foods grocery.

"So, did they get anything from the blood samples y'all sent?" Ramon asked as he drove.

"It never made it." Shane licked his lips, suddenly getting a bad taste in his mouth. Something was fishy about this whole thing. "It all disappeared before they could test it."

"How did that happen?"

"Not a clue." He shook his head.

No one was more upset about the security breach than he was. He could've been a step ahead in finding out who was doing all of this if only they'd kept a closer eye on that blood sample. Knowing this just drove him crazy each night as he studied his board at home. He'd linked four occurrences to the same mystery perp, even though this last one presented some complications. Aside from that, he knew he was on to something.

Pulling up behind the beige and red building, they made their way to where the other officers had already tacked up yellow tape. Mothers coaxed their children away from the playground as others stood at the back of the grocery store, curiosity getting the better of them. Shane wished they'd all just go back to their own business. The only reporter in Davis stood among them, and he prayed he wouldn't have to answer any of their questions.

"Remember that room filled with feathers?" The technician from before asked when he arrived on the scene.

"Yeah, what about it?"

She motioned for him to follow. "We may have just found the source."

They walked to the center of a group of trees within the yellow tape. There, lying as if a prop in a movie, lay two large, black wings, its feathers fluttering in the brisk morning breeze.

"What is this, some sort of prank?" Shane asked.

"I wish," the tech replied, pointing to the dried blood caking the top where it would've attached to whatever a pair of wings that size would go to. "That's blood."

"And it's *real*?" Ramon gawked.

"From what I can tell." The tech shrugged.

Ramon's complexion paled, covering his mouth at the sight of the giant mangled wings.

"We've measured the wingspan at twenty-five feet," the tech concluded.

"Well, that's no scissor-tailed flycatcher," Shane scoffed. "What could these wings possibly belong to?"

Ramon shrugged. "Your guess is as good as mine. Nothin' natural that size lives around here, that's for sure."

"Where's the rest of it?" Shane asked, looking around, but the wings were the only thing in sight.

"This is all there is," the tech replied.

Shane scratched his head, not knowing what he thought about all of this.

"Alright, pack it up." He sighed, his stress levels on the rise. "But this time, you folks better not lose it. And get me all of those photos ASAP."

"You got it, sir." The tech nodded.

"What do you make of this?" Ramon asked as they headed back to the car.

Shane scratched his head. "Not a clue."

***

- Izara -

"Again!" Chuck ordered as he waved his clipboard for the hundredth time.

We'd been going over scene sixteen on loop, and I was getting sick and tired of hearing the Birdsong. Choyce and I had to act all lovey-dovey towards one another while spouting our lines in sing-songy voices.

"Cue nurse," Chuck called over the loudspeaker.

"Madam!" Tiffany cried as she rushed onto the stage. "Your Lady mother is coming to your chamber."

"The window! Let day in and let life out," I replied.

"Farewell." Choyce took my hand in his.

The script doesn't say to hold my hand. I rolled my eyes.

I'm improvising. Choyce winked as he continued his lines aloud. "One kiss and I'll descend."

I glared at him.

"Romeo!" Chuck was a broken record as he interrupted us for the umpteenth time. "You're supposed to be gone by now, so move it."

I hate you. I fumed.

"I doubt it not," Choyce replied, annoyingly sticking to

his lines.

Kia entered as Choyce disappeared.

"Why, how now, Juliet?" Kia asked, coming to my side.

"Madam, I am not well." I sighed, resting the back of my hand against my forehead.

"CUT!"

"What is it now?" I asked, turning to Chuck as his Converse squealed against the front stage steps.

"You're not believable."

I tried not to cough as his rotten egg perfume neared.

"It's too much. Just tone it down a bit. Alright, *dearie*? AGAIN!"

And so, it continued. I wondered if we'd ever get past scene sixteen. By the end of rehearsals, I was beginning to hate my character. How could anyone be so broken-hearted about someone that they'd take their own life? Oh, and don't even ask how many times we had to redo the death scene. I was pretty sure Chuck just enjoyed watching me die on loop.

"I think that went well," Choyce commented as we left the auditorium.

We'd been practicing for nearly five hours, and it was already sunset.

"Yeah, but could you be less handsy next time? That'd be great."

"Touchy!" He chuckled. "You do realize that we'll

eventually have to get much closer?"

"Not even in your dreams." I rolled my eyes. "They'll fade the lights, of course."

"Oh, to set the mood. Good thinking." He leaned in close, making smoochy faces at me.

I shoved him away. "You know what I mean."

"Wait up!" Kia called behind us. "Are you heading to grab something to eat?"

"Yeah," I said as she caught up.

"You're more than welcome to join us." Choyce grinned, knowing full well that I hadn't asked him to come.

"Cool, let's go." Kia led the way to the cafeteria as we chatted about everything that had to be done before the fall production.

It was just around the corner, and we hadn't even had a chance to rehearse the entire script. Not at the rate was Chuck interrupting us. No wonder he expected us to rehearse on our own. We were going to need to if we were going to be ready.

After grabbing food, I followed Kia and Choyce through the rows of tables, a feeling like I was being watched, sending goosebumps down my arm. Though no one was explicitly staring, I knew I was surrounded by nightwalkers. I would need to be careful with my words. I knew they'd be looking for any reason to bury me six feet under.

"Hey, guys?" I stopped, deciding then I couldn't be in the same room as them right now. I'd had enough of their drama. "I think I'm going to get this to go. I'm not feeling well."

"Oh, sure. No problem." Kia shrugged. "I'll catch up with you later?"

"Yeah, sounds good." I turned to the rest of the drama crew and waved my goodbye before leaving.

Finally, out into the fresh air, I sighed with relief. I was free from their scrutiny for now. How did they expect me to live like this? Always being watched? I shivered when I realized they probably didn't expect me to live at all. Finally making it back to my room, I crashed on the bed and fell right to sleep. I hoped that I could just forget about all of it, but deep down, I knew that was probably just wishful thinking.

***

I was dreaming, but I knew it was more than just a dream. It was a vision of the past, one that I'd experienced many times before. My feet were those of a man, long and stuffed into work boots.

"When will it come to pass?" A man's voice escaped me as if it were mine, but I knew it wasn't.

When all have partaken— A cold voice I recognized replied.

It was Credan. It had to be.

—And when all are united in strength. You will know

the time, and I will reward you for your patience.

"But we've all partaken," The man replied. *"We're all strong and united."*

Do you think me a fool? *Credan bellowed.* I know you left out one. The one who will fulfill the prophecy. The promise I made.

"How could he fulfill the promise? He tricked us, deserted us. He's a traitor."

I wondered who they were talking about. Whoever it was, I was pretty sure would be the one to bring back Credan. The prophecy was about him, right? And the Assembly would do everything to keep him from coming back. If it wasn't Choyce they were after, then whoever they were talking about would definitely be it. I just hoped they would say a name or give me a hint.

"We must do this now." The man argued.

Until the twins have drunk. Until the past and future are entwined, you cannot unite. Only then will I be able to return. Otherwise, your efforts will be for not.

"I don't understand," the man cried, but Credan didn't speak to him again.

I frowned. Credan was talking about us! But who was he talking to? Who was this who knew we had these powers? Since we all had drunk blood now, did that mean we were one step closer to releasing him? A chill ran down my spine at the thought as the world shimmered around me, dissolving into another time and place.

Standing in the middle of an old hotel room, Kain suddenly appeared next to me.

Did you hear? *I asked him.* Someone's helping Credan return. He knows about us.

Who? *Kain wondered.*

It was weird. Even though I knew I was dreaming, it was as if he was really there with me.

I shrugged just as a man in a suit entered the room. We darted out of the way as he took a seat near the bed. It didn't seem like he could see us.

"Tonight is the night." The man's nasally voice made me freeze. That was him—the man who was helping Credan.

Emma waltzed out of the bathroom, a blue silk dress clinging to her. "Didn't he warn us to wait?" She asked, securing her earrings.

The man in the suit took a long draw of his cigar. A sly grin spread across his face as he let out a puff of smoke. "Why, don't you look dashing."

It's the strange human that was with Emma and the wolfman in the basement, *I thought.* Kain and I both recognized him. It was also the man we now knew was assisting Credan, but I hadn't seen anyone like that at the school.

A growl came from the other corner of the room. Abram flashed his fangs territorially.

"Oh, calm down, there, Abram." The man chuckled. "She's not exactly my type."

The tension rose as the wolf stood from his seat.

"Darling, please." Emma gave him a warning look.

"You heard what she said," the man taunted.

"If he says we shouldn't proceed, who are you to question his authority?" the wolf hissed.

"I beg your pardon?" The man arched his eyebrow.

"If he warned us to wait, then we must."

"How dare you question me!" The man bellowed. "You may hear his echo, but he speaks directly to me. Through me. We are the same."

"You're a lost soul." Abram shook his head. "Scrambling to get back to a time that has long since passed."

The man drew in another long puff of smoke and looked away. "We continue as planned."

"Come, Abram." Emma reached for his hand. "Let's go enjoy the party before the full moon."

Abram hesitated but finally took Emma's slender hand as he let her lead the way.

"Yes, do enjoy the party." The man snickered after them. "While it lasts."

29
TOO CLOSE FOR COMFORT

- Lee Walker -

Lee chose a secluded part of the library to pull up his photo he'd taken of the Halloween festival. He regretted sharing the picture, but he had to know who was in it. He knew that there was a risk in the entire school seeing it, but if anyone could recognize the blurry faces in the photo, it would've been Raquel. She'd lived in Oklahoma her whole life, and her advantage was that she was the school's biggest gossip. That was also her disadvantage. But she hadn't been much help.

He was glad he'd kept the photo he'd taken with Duran in it to himself. He couldn't stop staring at it. Who were they? What were they? And why did Duran look dead in this photo?

Darkness covered the left side of the image, but he could just make out a person's shape as if they were hunched over Duran's body. On the other side were two figures with enormous wings. One had blondish hair, and the other had black. The photo was just out of focus enough that he couldn't determine who they were.

Clicking open his copies of his dad's files, he finally came up to the one he wanted. He knew he shouldn't have done it, not to mention his dad would be mad at him if he found out, but he didn't have any other choice. No one seemed to be telling him the truth, and he had the feeling that he was missing something.

"Who are you?" He studied the image of his dad's tackboard for any clues.

It was unsettling to stare at the photos so closely, but he mostly kept his eyes on the sticky notes below the images. He skipped over the one of his mother, knowing he hadn't missed anything there, and went straight to the murders that had taken place at the Ardmore Little Theatre. The note below it read the date *September twelfth* of this year along with a scribbled message he couldn't quite make out. He zoomed in closer, trying to make out his dad's terrible handwriting.

"What were you thinking, dad?" he wondered aloud.

The more he stared at the image, the clearer it became. He zeroed in on one letter at a time, writing them down in his notebook. When he finished, he looked down at his chicken scratch.

Poss. 3 perps.

Three perpetrators? Was this possible? Everything before this suggested that his dad only found proof of one. Now he was thinking that two others were working with him?

Lee pulled up the image from the haunted trail yet again, eyeing everything closely. He then had an idea and started jotting down all the dates he saw from the sticky notes.

"September twenty-three of last year," Lee muttered to himself as he wrote. "February eighteen of this year, August thirteen, September twelfth..."

And just for kicks, he added the date of the haunted trail, *October twelfth.*

"What's the connection?" He turned back to his laptop and pulled up a calendar for this year and last. Checking each of the dates, they weren't the same day of the month. Were they on particular holidays? He searched for a more detailed calendar that had all the holidays on it.

Nothing.

Then he glanced at the bottom of the little box for October twelfth and saw the full moon icon. He checked out all of the dates and gasped.

"All happened on the full moon." Goosebumps covered his arms.

He didn't really believe in all the hocus pocus some bought into the full moon but was it possible that this wasn't just some serial killer? Was it a cult ritual? Or was there something darker going on?

He gazed at the image of the figures with large, black wings for the hundredth time. Was the blond-haired one in the back Choyce? And, if so, who were the other two?

***

- *Kain* -

"That was rough," Lee exclaimed, taking a drink of water.

Coach had us running sprints for so long we were all dying except for me. I had to pretend to be exhausted, even though my body could've kept going. It turned out having enhanced strength also boosted my endurance.

"Yeah." I tossed a towel over my shoulder as I sat down on the courtside bench.

Taking a tiny sip of water, I inhaled as the liquid rippled through my body. I learned not to chug as that would overload my absorption, but little sips went a long way. A shiver ran down my spine as small beads popped up all over my arm. Glancing around, I made sure no one was watching before opening the palm of my hand. Focusing on the energy, I flexed my fingers, forcing the droplets to spin in circles forming a mini whirlpool.

"Hey—"

I shut my palm immediately as Lee sat down next to me.

"—I've been meaning to ask you something."

"What's up?" I asked.

He hesitated, rubbing the back of his neck. "Eh, well, have you noticed anything strange about Choyce?"

I laughed internally. I was pretty sure encouraging Izzy and me to drink blood and spending the last few weeks drowning me in the school's pool was strange. Not that I could tell him that.

"What do you mean?"

"I don't know." He grimaced. "I just saw something weird at the haunted trail that—you know what? Never mind. It's nothing."

My heart skipped a beat. "What is it?"

He fidgeted with the cap of his water bottle. "If I show you something, will you promise not to think I'm crazy?"

"Sure…" Not knowing what he was getting at, I was a little apprehensive.

"And you can't tell anyone."

"Okay, what is it?"

Lee sighed, turning towards me. "You know that photo Duran's been showing everyone?"

"Yeah."

He reached for his cellphone. "Well, there's another version of it."

"What do you mean?"

"I took the photo," he confessed. "But I didn't mean to. I was trying to take a photo of one of the zombies. It wasn't until later that I noticed the winged people in the background. I showed a friend of mine if she remembered seeing them on the trail and if she recognized them, but didn't want to show her the rest of it out of fear of it getting leaked out. Which is exactly what happened."

He tossed me his phone. "Here. See for yourself."

Glancing down at the phone, I shook as my worst nightmare displayed on the screen before me. Duran was lying on the ground, and a shadow hovered over him. It was a blur, but I knew it was me. It was taken just after I'd killed Duran, but before bringing him back to life. After a closer look, I noticed what had to be Choyce and Izara standing in the background. Luckily the quality was really low.

"That's Duran, but he doesn't remember anything about it—"

"You showed him this?" I asked.

"No, but I asked what happened to him when he disappeared, and he doesn't remember that whole part of the haunted trail."

My heart thumped loudly, and I cleared my throat, hoping Lee didn't notice.

"Do you see those two figures in the background?" Lee asked.

I hesitated. "Sort of... maybe?"

"Look!" He pointed towards the shapes in the background. "Doesn't that look like Choyce?"

"I don't know." I shrugged. "It's too blurry. I can't really tell."

"I'm telling you, this guy is into some messed up stuff." Lee took the phone from me.

"What do you mean? Wasn't this Halloween? I mean, it could just be related to the festival."

Lee shook his head. "I don't think so. Tiffany saw something with giant black wings snatch Duran up, and he disappeared until the end. Davis couldn't pull off anything that elaborate. Plus, he looks like he's dead in this photo."

I didn't know what to say. I hoped Lee would just drop this.

"It's Choyce." He pressed. "It has to be. It's his face. The only thing I can't figure out is who this other person is."

"I think you want it to be him."

"Believe me or not. I swear this is Choyce. I'm going to prove it."

Lee's going to be a problem. I made a connection with Choyce sending him the information telepathically. I hoped he got it as I was sure they were at the auditorium going over last-minute rehearsals.

"Are you going to the play tonight?" I asked as we made our way out of the gym.

"Yeah, I promised Izzy I'd go. You?"

I nodded. "If I don't, she'd kill me."

Lee laughed as we crossed the quad. "Heading to the dorms?"

"Nah, I'll catch up with you later." I waved as he headed for the bridge.

Did you hear me? I asked Choyce.

Yeah. Choyce finally replied. *I wouldn't worry about it. He's not going to figure it out.*

What if he turns the photo over to the school?

Izzy's heart thumped within my own, and I could sense her fear.

Well, Choyce replied calmly. *You'll just have to stop him, won't you?*

Easier said than done. I rolled my eyes as I marched for the cafeteria for a snack.

We can't risk Chuck getting his hands on that photo. Izzy pointed out.

It's not like he's got any concrete evidence. Choyce responded. *I highly doubt this will be as much of a problem as you're making this out to be.*

Don't downplay the situation. The photo clearly shows Duran dead. I growled.

I know that this is a big deal. Choyce agreed. *I'm simply suggesting we don't worry about it for the time being. The play is in a few hours. We need to focus on this. Let's take care of the image later.*

Sighing, I supposed he was right. But first thing in the morning, I was going to delete the image Lee had on us. It was a huge risk letting Lee walk around with the photo. If Chuck got this photo, he'd have proof to pass along to his uncle to have us killed. But they wanted to wait, so I'd give them until tomorrow. The photo would be gone. I would make sure of it.

Garlic and basil hit my nostrils as the kitchen staff preparing for the reception after the play echoed throughout the cafeteria. I grabbed a leftover sack lunch and found a seat in the corner.

It will happen tonight. The dead voice I recognized as Credan's surrounded me. *You will have to reveal yourself to them soon.*

I frowned. Them? Was he talking to me?

I will await your command. Amadeus replied.

The hairs on the back of my neck stood up as I heard Amadeus. He was helping Credan. But how? Why?

Call for the others. Credan continued.

Yes, father. Amadeus's voice faded away, and I glanced around the empty cafeteria.

Where was he? Who was he going to call for? And why was Credan acting now? Suddenly I wasn't hungry anymore as the questions kept bombarding me. I had a feeling that things were only going to get worse before they got better.

30
CALL TIME

- Izara -

Butterflies fluttered as my heart raced. I was more nervous than I'd ever been before. I'd performed over a hundred times in other productions, but for some reason, I couldn't stop my hands from shaking now. I tried to take long, calming breaths, but the backstage buzzed with the stage crew racing around like chickens with their heads cut off, making relaxation impossible.

I looked in the mirror, I fidgeted in my empire waist bodice, and I knew I wasn't pulling this character off. I didn't feel like Juliet at all. She was madly in love with Romeo. So much so that she would rather die than be apart from him. This was a feeling so foreign to me that I couldn't even fathom being that much in love. But I had to conjure the feelings. To become Juliet. My stomach churned as I dreaded what I was about to do. We'd rehearsed many times, but I was just going through the motions. I hadn't truly allowed the character to take over me. To do that would require me to tear down the wall I'd so meticulously built between Choyce and myself.

Quiet murmurs from the audience echoed from underneath the heavy red curtain as the school's orchestra did a quick soundcheck.

"We start in five!" The stage manager called, signaling the stagehand to hurry up.

Instruments began to play as the murmuring audience quieted and the lights dimmed. The backstage floor groaned as we made our way to the sidelines, awaiting curtain call.

"Are you ready?" Kia asked, coming to stand next to me.

"As ready as ever."

Kia sighed. "Why aren't you more excited? Are you still worried about actually having to kiss him?"

I shrugged.

"Have you told Lee?"

What was with the third degree? I didn't respond as I peeked out at the crowd through an opening in the curtain. Spotting Lee in the audience, my stomach fell. The truth was I hadn't figured out a way to tell him. He deserved a heads-up, but how could I deliver this news without sending him over the edge? A part of me wished he hadn't come, but it was too late now.

My vision suddenly faltered. A throbbing, lip numbing explosion erupted at my temples as a skull flashed before my eyes, only to be replaced by a man in a black hat and suit, Emma and the wolfman by his side. I squeezed my eyes shut, tears forming at the corners as the collage sped up, ending with Credan, his body sprawled at odd angles within a rose field. Blood dripped from his lip as his eyes locked on mine.

I blinked several times, the auditorium reappeared as Amadeus sat next to Lee. What was he doing here?

He leaned in to whisper something to Lee, and I focused on finding Kain.

Are you here? I asked, sending my question out in an attempt to make a connection.

Kain's heartbeat thumped once inside my chest, receiving my message. *Just entered.*

Middle section, center row. Amadeus is up to something. He said something to Lee, and now he looks mad.

Nothing much I can do about it right now. He pointed out. *There are only a few seats left. Plus, the show is about to start.*

I huffed. *Just try to find out what he said.*

"Izzy!" Kia hissed, an edge to her voice like she'd been

trying to get my attention for a while.

"Yeah?"

"Whoa, you really zoned out there. Are you sure you're okay?"

"I'm fine," I replied. "Just a bit nervous."

"I'd be so too if I were in your shoes."

"What am I going to do, Kia?" I sighed. "Lee's going to see everything, and I totally didn't tell him about... you know."

"Turn your face?"

I rolled my eyes. "That would be too obvious. Why couldn't you be Romeo? I'm sure Lee wouldn't mind watching us kiss."

Kia laughed so hard she snorted, winning her a glare from the stage manager as we waited for the announcer to finish.

After the chorus, the fight between the Montagues and the Capulets began. Kia, acting as Lady Capulet, stood by her husband and entered center stage.

"What noise is this?" Capulet exclaimed. "Give me my longsword, ho! Old Montague is come!"

Kia didn't skip a beat. "Thou shalt not stir one foot to seek a foe."

She was always a remarkable actress, and I was happy she got a front running part. She should've gotten my character instead. I grinned as Kia tried to hold back Mr. Capulet from pretending to beat the other guy up.

Then Choyce entered, and I was almost embarrassed for him for having to wear that ridiculous costume. His tights left absolutely nothing to the imagination, but he didn't seem to care. He walked around without shame.

"Good morrow, cousin," an actor greeted him.

"Is the day so young?" Choyce replied. "Ay, sad hours seem so long."

His dramatism made me roll my eyes.

"What sadness lengthens your hours?" the other actor asked.

"Not having that which having, oh, makes them short." Choyce's gaze fell to the ground.

"In love?"

"Out," Choyce cried. "Out of her favor, where I am in love!"

I couldn't watch anymore of this nonsense and marched past the rows of costumes and props to where I could sit at one of the vanities.

Why did he have to join the drama club? Why couldn't he just stay away from me? His attempts at strengthening us and helping me time travel had backfired. We weren't even close to being able to go back in time to save his brother, anyway. Yes, we were untied from the full moon and definitely stronger, but all of it was at a cost. I wanted to stop transforming altogether. I wanted to stop hurting innocent people. I couldn't live with myself this way. I despised every part of me for what I'd become.

Closing my eyes, I fell into a deep sleep. *Suddenly no longer backstage, I found myself surrounded by the nightwalkers, their pitchforks reflecting from their lanterns. Directly in front of me, a scrawny guy glared down the barrel of an M520 at me, and I shivered. I was going to die. Would I feel Edwin's pain this time? Would I wake up back in the auditorium? Or would I be trapped in this dream?*

"I'm not strong enough!" Choyce's desperate voice shouted through the forest that surrounded us.

Looking through the trees around me, he was nowhere to be seen. It was just me and the nightwalkers before me.

"Shoot it in the heart!" Sarge bellowed.

Hate flickered in the guy's eyes as he took several steps back, aiming his gun. The trigger snapped, and I froze. The breath was knocked out of me. Seconds seemed to pass like an eternity before the pain spread through me. Numbness crawled through my limbs as I teetered forward. Hitting the uneven ground, everything went dark as I took my last breath.

***

Luckily, I hadn't fallen asleep for long, but the dream kept tugging at my thoughts throughout the play. What caused me to witness Edwin being shot? Was it a clue?

These questions hung in the air as I spun around the room. The stage was transformed into a ballroom, and everyone was dancing and drinking merrily. I soon was swept up into Choyce's arms, who winked at me. Making a face, I hoped no one in the audience noticed.

The actor playing Paris pulled me away as the dance continued. I could feel Choyce's eyes still on me as he followed my every move. When the dance finally came to an end, Choyce was immediately at my side, taking my hand in his.

"If I profane with my unworthiest hand." His brown leather eyes locked onto mine. The intensity in them made my heart skip a beat. "This shrine, the gentle fine is this. To smooth that rough touch with a tender kiss."

For a moment, I was swept up into the moment, the thought of us kissing making my heart soar. As quickly as the idea entered my mind, I shook the thought away and scolded myself. How could I think something like that? I should've flung myself off the stage, but the show had to go on.

"Good pilgrim"—I hoped no one could hear my elevated heart rate through the microphone—"You do wrong your hand too much, which mannerly devotion shows in this. For saints have hands that pilgrims' hands do touch, and palm to palm is holy palmers' kiss."

Choyce took a step closer, his face inches from my own, and my breathing stopped. It took my entire might not to take a step back.

"Have not saint's lips?" He asked, his honey breath hitting my cheek.

"Ay." I gasped. "Lips that one must use in prayer."

"Then, dear saint, let lips do what hands do," Choyce whispered, his fingers caressing my cheek. "They prey."

The room disappeared as his lips lowered to mine—every fiber of my being shivered. My heart threatened to burst through my chest as our lips moved together. Despite the little voice inside my head telling me that I loathed him, my body deceived me. His hands slipped around my waist, pulling me closer. My hands rebelled against my better judgment and wrapped around his neck. The whole world blurred around us, vanishing as if we were the only two shifters left on the planet. Wind billowed around us, tangling his long, blond hair and pulling at the seams of my dress.

When the ground stopped spinning, I finally pulled away, opening my eyes. "What was that?"

"I—I don't know." He couldn't seem to find the words as he licked his lips.

I frowned. Everything around us had gone dark. Where was the stage? Where was the audience? A strange honk echoed in the distance, and I ran blindly towards it, Choyce at my heels. Emerging around a corner, my jaw fell open at the sight of a dark street lined with old cars straight out of the roaring twenties.

Choyce pulled me out of the way as a Cruella looking car buzzed past us.

"What the heck? Where are we?" But my question was soon answered by the four-story Artesian hotel standing before us, welcoming a very dapper Bart Bessler. His long, blond hair was slicked back and had the uncanny resemblance of Choyce.

"We are in 1919," Choyce gasped.

31
CATGROOVE

- Izara -

Realizing that we stuck out like a sore thumb in our medieval clothes, we darted around the back of the hotel just out of sight.

"We did it!" Choyce exclaimed, his eyebrows rising in disbelief. "We really time traveled!"

"Yeah, I think we did," I mumbled, a bit disoriented.

"Maybe we can do it again and actually get to my brother's time—" Before I knew what was happening, his lips were on mine again.

I shoved him away. "Stop it! That's definitely not how this works."

"Well, not with that attitude." He winked, giving me a crooked smile.

"Wait!" I gasped, suddenly realizing the significance of where we were. "This is when you followed that redhead and the guy who can control wolves down to the cellar, right?"

"Eh, yeah. Maybe?" He shrugged, leaning against the dark brick building, the lively beat of jazz echoing in the distance.

"We need to get inside," I said, scanning for a back entrance.

I squinted, but it was way too dark to see anything. Preparing to march along the entire length of the hotel to find a door, Choyce grabbed my arm.

"You don't want to go in there," he said huskily. His usual leather brown eyes flashed black for a second.

"Why?" I snapped.

He quickly let go of me, trying to act nonchalant. "I just don't think it's a good idea, that's all."

I frowned. "What don't you want me to see?"

"Nothing." He tucked his long, tangled hair behind an ear. "You know the story; I saw a strange woman—"

"The redhead."

"Yeah, and I got trapped in the cellar, then they got away before I could get any answers out of them."

Remembering my dream of the wolf accusing Choyce of doing something to ruin whatever they were trying to do down in the cellar, I arched my eyebrow. "That's not all that happened."

"I—I don't know what you're talking about. Nothing happened."

"Well, let's go find out," I said as I marched off in search of a backdoor before he could stop me. We needed to find less conspicuous clothes.

"What?" he cried, hurrying to match my pace. "You're crazy. We can't go in there."

"Why not?" I asked. "You clearly have something to hide, and I want to know what it is."

"I'm not hiding anything."

"And I don't believe you. Ah!" I smiled when my hand found a doorknob. I hoped it was unlocked, but no such luck.

"See? It's locked. It's a sign we need to get out of here."

I grinned, my heart fluttering as an idea dawned on me. Stepping back, I pictured the full moon in my mind's eye. Taking a deep breath, I stretched my hand forward and flexed. With a snap, the knob turned, and the door swung open. "Come on, let's see what that wolf guy was accusing you of doing."

"This is beyond insane," he muttered, following me through the backdoor.

Entering a long hallway, a light flickered ahead of us, so I carefully crept towards it.

"Izzy, we can't just—" he hissed, but I turned and

covered his mouth with the palm of my hand.

We're going to get caught if you keep talking out loud, I warned. *We need some new clothes, right?*

What we need is to go back outside and find a way to get to 1911.

I rolled my eyes, turning back towards the light. Bumping into a small staircase, I took the steps two at a time, the light seeping under the cracks of a closed door. Reaching for the handle, I flexed again, and the door flew open, crashing against the wall.

"And you said *I* was going to get us caught?" he snickered.

"Shut up." I checked the bright, maroon carpeted hall the door lead into to make sure no one was there. The laughter of hotel guests echoed from a distance as I carefully walked down the aisle.

The floor creaked behind us, and Choyce pulled me around the corner, my arms pinned against his frilly jacket.

"What are you doing?" I hissed, spitting at the lace that stuck to me.

"Shh." He pointed to his ear as the giggling women got closer.

I peeked around the corner in time to see two women disappearing into their room. Pushing away from Choyce, I ran towards the door before it could close.

Are you crazy? Choyce ran up behind me.

I waited until I heard the bathroom door closed and crept into the room. *If they're guests, they'll have clothes I can borrow.*

"I hope you ladies aren't starting without me!" A man's voice hollered just outside the room.

We ducked behind the door just as it swung open. A man waltzed in, a cigar hanging from his mouth as he pulled off his suspenders. Joining the girls in the bathroom, I rammed my elbow into his side.

"Ow!" He protested.

I brought my index finger to my lips. *Come on, let's find some clothes.*

I pulled the wardrobe near us open and grabbed the nearest hangers. Throwing him the one that looked like a suit, I unhooked the rose-colored chemise from the hanger. The image of a drunk woman stumbling down the cellar steps flashed before my eyes. I recognized this dress. It belonged to one of the women that interrupted the group that had chained Choyce. Perfect.

Oh, hello. Choyce's eyes widened just as I was pulling off my medieval garb.

Turn around! I ordered as I quickly covered myself up again.

He chuckled, turning his back to me as he changed.

I don't think you've quite thought this whole thing out. If Choyce's mind didn't stop racing, I knew I was going to get a headache.

Maybe I haven't, I replied as the last button snapped into place. *But there has to be a reason we're here and not there. It's only fair we see why we were brought here, right?*

Glancing at my reflection in the full-length mirror, the flattering cut of the vintage dress sparkled back at me as I spun around. Catching Choyce checking me out and his mind wandering to thoughts I wish I could unsee, I stopped.

Smirking, he added, *but what happens if my past self sees me?*

I shrugged. *Just stay out of the way while I follow Lawrence—I mean you.*

Eyeing Choyce as he tied a perfect bow tie, I realized it would be a little confusing keeping track of which Choyce was which.

Placing a matching rose gold headband over my hair, I took one last glance at my reflection and determined that I was ready.

Ready? I asked, turning towards the door.

Choyce grabbed my arm before I could leave. "You can't go down there," he whispered urgently. "Those people are dangerous."

"Aww, that's cute. You're worried about me." I brushed his arm away, disappearing through the door and out into the hallway.

Looking both ways, I marched down the corridor

towards the jazz.

"Wait up!" Choyce called.

I glanced over my shoulder just as he placed a top hat on his head. Strangely enough, it suited him. Coming to a long staircase, I gripped the mahogany handrail and made my way down. My heart pounded with excitement as I realized the significance of what I was about to do. I was about to interact with the past, and the prospect of this thrilled me.

The trumpets blared, as a raspy voice sang a lively tune. My jaw dropped at the sight of couples dancing the Charleston before me. I could hardly believe it.

"May I?" Choyce offered his arm to escort me into the ballroom.

"I guess. When in Rome, and all." I laughed, taking his hand as we entered.

"Want a drink?" he asked, leading me to the bar.

"What about that thing you said in history class?" I asked.

"About the poison? This stuff's fine. That doesn't start for a couple more years." He leaned against the bar, lifting two fingers up for the bartender.

I gave a reluctant shrug. "Might as well."

He handed me a coupe glass filled with bubbling champagne. Nearly choking on the brut, Choyce gave me a crooked smile.

"What?" I asked.

"It's nice to see you cut loose."

I rolled my eyes. *Don't get used to it.*

Taking another sip, I gazed about the room. The sparkling flapper dresses shimmered around as couples danced. I still couldn't believe I was actually here.

When the wolfman will arrive? I wondered.

Very soon. Choyce nodded towards the doors we'd entered from the hotel's lobby.

Emma sauntered into the room, catching the eye of the nearby gentlemen as the sheen of her blue silk dress caught the light. A smile tugged at her lips as she slipped her arm through Abram's. His suit fit snuggly on his robust build. He seemed so much taller and foreboding in person.

My heart thumped four times more per minute than the usual two when I was in Choyce's presence. I reached for my chest, grimacing at the discomfort.

You feel it, too? Choyce asked.

Yes.

Emma's golden eyes suddenly met ours, and she frowned.

Is she looking at us? I asked.

Choyce nodded.

She turned to whisper something in Abram's ear, and he looked directly at Choyce.

"Crap!" He lowered his gaze, turning away from them.

I reached for his arm. "What is it? Have they seen you

329

before?"

"Look behind you."

I glanced over my shoulder, careful not to face the couple nearby, and spotted a near duplicate of Choyce entering the ballroom.

"Bart!" A man next to us waved the other Choyce towards us.

I think we need to get out of here. Choyce placed our half-empty glasses on the bar and, taking my hand, pulled me towards the lobby.

You're not the only one who thinks so. I spotted Abram and Emma heading towards the back staircase leading downward.

Quick, watch my back. I need to stall yourself before he tries to follow them. I yanked my hand from his.

"What? No way!" He cried aloud.

"I want to see what those shifters were doing down in the cellar, and I can't do that if your past self intervenes, okay?"

"But that will change *everything*." He warned.

"We don't have any other options." Not waiting for a response, I rushed back towards the party before he could stop me.

Choyce's past self wasn't watching where he was going, he was obviously too distracted in his search for the redhead, so I took that opportunity to cut him off.

His shoulder bumped into me, causing me to stumble. "Oof!" I gasped as I nearly fell to the ground.

Bart stopped. "My lady, are you alright? I didn't see you there. I'm terribly sorry."

"It's quite alright," I replied, taking the gloved hand he offered.

Brushing my crumpled dress with the other hand, I blushed as his eyes locked on mine. For a second, his brown leather eyes flashed pure onyx, and the man I saw was no longer Bart or Choyce, but Lawrence Bartholomew. The man from my dreams. Goosebumps covered my arm as he continued to hold my hand in his.

"Do"—he furrowed his eyebrows, stepping closer, and I held my breath, hoping he wouldn't recognize me—"do I know you?"

"Me?" My voice faltered. "I don't think so."

His head leaned to one side as he continued to study me, and I pulled my hand away. "I'm sorry for my clumsiness."

"It's alright." He shook his head, once again eyeing the doors the couple had disappeared through. "I'm glad you're uninjured. Please, do excuse me."

He pushed past me as he made his way towards the exit.

He's on his way out. I warned Choyce.

Don't worry, he won't find them. Choyce replied. *The two have already disappeared to the lower level.*

Pushing my way through the crowd, I entered the lobby just as the Choyce from the past headed up the staircase on the far side of the entrance.

"Why did you let him go up there?" I asked.

"You think I was going to let myself see me?" Choyce hissed. "Besides, the couple went downstairs, not up."

"But"—I shook my head—"that's not how it happened."

"Exactly." He laughed angrily. "Thanks for changing my entire life. Now I'll probably never meet you or be *this* close to being able to save my brother."

He ran a hand through his long hair, taking a deep breath.

"Choyce." I rested both my hands on his shoulders. "There's a reason we traveled to this time. I believe that. Otherwise, why would every bone in my body be telling me we need to be down in that cellar?"

Choyce had no response.

"So get a grip and let's see what this is all about, okay?" I removed my hands as Choyce's shoulders slumped, giving in.

"Fine," he muttered as we made our way to the staircase.

I had no idea what lay ahead of us, but I really hoped I was right about changing the past. Otherwise, I was really uncertain what would happen when we went back to our own timeline. Would Kain and I still be at the school? Would Choyce have come back to find us? How much did this one event affect the future? Or, was this exactly how it should've been? I hoped and prayed it was the latter.

32
UP IN FLAMES

- Izara -

It's got to be around here somewhere. I thought as we searched the basement of the hotel for the cellar entrance.

Trying to remember how Choyce got to the cellar in my dreams was like trying to catch a bubble without bursting it. Each time I got close enough to the answer, it vanished from my mind.

This way. Choyce walked ahead of me, motioning towards the old wooden door at the end.

I reached for the door handle when he stopped me. *Are you sure you want to do this?*

Taking a deep breath, I nodded. We were this close to finding out what these shifters and their human companion were doing, and I wasn't about to back down now.

The door creaked as I slowly opened it. A bright light shot out from deep down in the cellar, causing us to cover our eyes.

"The destiny of shifters is about to come to fruition!" A man exclaimed from somewhere down below, and I recognized it as the human. "Do it now, Emma!"

The light suddenly imploded, and we crept to the top of the rotting staircase. Emma stood on the edge of a large circle drawn on the floorboards, her body glowing as she held the energy within her. She lowered her hands to the interlocking symbols at the center as light exploded from her palms through the center of it.

What are they doing? I wondered.

Nothing good, Choyce replied.

My jaw dropped as the light engulfed Emma, spinning around in a tornado storm of fire. The symbols lit up, and a dead cry echoed from deep under the ground. The full moon flashed before our eyes, followed by the face of Credan and his white, glaring eyes. The ground shook underneath us, swinging the door shut behind us, and suddenly the vision dissipated.

"Who's there?" Abram growled, flashing his wolf-like teeth.

The human companion looked up, our eyes meeting, and a sneer appeared across his face. "Good, you're here." He laughed darkly as he motioned towards Abram. "Grab them before they get away!"

Let's get out of here. Choyce pulled me back towards the door, but the world began to spin as the light filled the room once again, dissolving everything within its flames.

My heart leaped up into my throat as I fell through the abyss, and my arms and legs were pulled in every direction.

"WHAT HAVE YOU DONE?" The human's voice echoed in the distance as everything vanished.

I closed my eyes as I continued to fall. Suddenly everything stopped spinning, and I slammed against something rough and solid. Peeking out from under an eyelid, I was surprised to find the sunlight shining down on a paved road next to me.

"Where are we?" I asked, picking my aching body up off of the concrete.

Choyce coughed. "No idea."

We were standing once again on the sidewalk in front of The Artesian Hotel. A sense of déjà vu washed over me as an Oldsmobile with a woman looking like Audrey Hepburn in the passenger seat passed us by, and then it dawned on me. I was reliving the dream I'd had from Choyce's perspective when he'd followed Abram and Emma into the park.

"This is it, isn't it?" I asked Choyce. "This is what happened."

"What are you talking about?"

"I had a dream of you standing here, watching the fire

and then—"

"Iz, none of this happened to me. I've never been here before. I mean, we're in 1962." Choyce threw me a used newspaper he'd picked up off of the ground. "I wasn't anywhere near Oklahoma then."

"But then, why are we here? And how could I have a dream of a past event that never happened?"

Choyce shrugged.

"And how did we travel to the future?" I asked. "I thought your power didn't work unless you were with your brother.

"Maybe it's you." Choyce shrugged. "I mean, our powers are connected. Maybe whatever that light was in the basement triggered—"

Choyce was unable to finish that sentence as the ground shook once again, and suddenly, an explosion came from deep within the hotel, causing the four-story building to erupt in flames. People flooded the streets as they emerged from the burning building. Among the crowd, I spotted Emma and Abram running across the street.

"Come on!" I motioned for him to follow me.

Racing across the busy streets, sirens blaring in the distance, we reached the park when a growl behind us made us freeze.

Slowly turning around, we were welcomed by a pack of wolves, their heads lowered and eyes glaring as they crept through the dead grass towards us. I determined that I liked time-traveling better when it was just a dream, and I didn't have to actually fear for my life.

Out of the corner of my eye, I saw a dark hand wrap around Choyce's neck, and before I could warn him, Abram had him pinned against a nearby tree trunk.

"How did we get here?"

"I don't know," he gasped.

"Who's she?" Abram nodded towards me as his wolves surrounded me.

She's one of us. Emma's melodic voice surrounded us as she emerged from behind the tree.

Her golden eyes locked on mine, and suddenly I couldn't look away. It was as if she had me under some sort of spell. *She's the past. He's the future.*

"What do you mean?" Abram asked.

She placed her hand on his, ushering him to loosen his grip on Choyce. "Time is now entwined. Our friend was wrong. This is how it should have always been."

"Until the past and future are entwined," I whispered, remembering Credan's voice from my dreams.

Choyce fell as Abram let go of his neck, but I still couldn't move. Emma weaved her way through Abram's wolves to my side, resting a slender hand on my cheek. *It's time for you to return to your timeline. We will join you for the return.*

"The return of who? Credan?" I asked.

"Yes."

"But why? He's a monster!"

"He is our maker. You will understand soon enough," she replied as a sudden warmth emanated from her hand onto my cheek.

A shimmering light enveloped me as the falling sensation returned. The world blurred around me as the park vanished. Images flashed around us of the past and of the future.

"He's using his magic!" a man cried from the night Edwin was murdered, followed by a gunshot before everything suddenly went black.

Falling in a heap, light from the bottom of a doorway illuminated the floor below me.

"Izzy, are you there?" Choyce asked from somewhere in the darkness.

"Yeah."

"Did you hear that gunshot? I think we traveled to the past." Hope emanated from his voice.

Picking myself up once again, I hoped that I'd at least land on my feet next time we time traveled. "Well, there's only one way to find out."

I reached for where the door handle typically was and pushed through.

"Izzy? Choyce? What are you two doing in the closet?"

We nearly ran into Tiffany as she packed up her makeup supplies from the play.

Choyce groaned, and I knew he was disappointed that we were backstage in our own timeline.

"Uh." I blushed, realizing how awkward this must've looked. I obviously couldn't tell her the truth. "I lost something."

Tiffany eyed us suspiciously, and I worried that she might already know where we actually were. She was prophetic, right?

"The after party's about to start in the cafeteria if you'd like to join us." She shrugged. "Nice dress."

"Thanks," I said as she walked off.

Choyce turned to me once Tiffany was out of earshot. "We need to go back."

"What, are you crazy? We can't time travel again. We've already lost too much time in our current time. Like, what happened to the rest of the play?"

"We have to! We're *this* close to being able to save my brother from the demons that run this place."

"Didn't you hear what Emma said?" I asked. "She said it was time for us to be in our timeline. She somehow used her energy to force us back here."

Choyce groaned. "She can't see the future, can she? How would she know? We changed the timeline!"

"And how would you know? You've even admitted

your power is useless since..." I stopped before I could finish that sentence.

He glared. "I'm out of here."

"Choyce, I didn't mean—" He waved me off as he stormed through the back exit of the auditorium.

I wanted to help him save his brother, I really did, but traveling back in time wasn't working. I couldn't guarantee we'd wind up in the right time, and we'd probably end up wrecking our own timeline too much in the process. Couldn't he understand that? Was he too blinded by his goal to see the big picture?

It's time. A cold voice filled my head, sending knife-like jabs into the cartilage of my skull. I doubled over in pain. I was sure my head was going to crack.

Come for me. The voice continued. *Your destiny awaits. Come, and we will be united.*

Tears blurred, my vision went dark. *Suddenly I was back in the forest where Edwin stood, facing a man with a gun pointed towards him.*

"Shoot!" The pudgy man named Sarge bellowed.

Standing among the nightwalkers, jeering as the rifle sounded, I watched in horror as the bullet hit Edwin's chest. I flinched. The memory of reliving this in my dream through his eyes reminded me of what it felt like to die.

But this time, I saw it. As Edwin's body fell to the ground, a ghostly figure remained. Like black smoke, it

341

shimmered where Edwin's body once stood. For a brief moment, the smoke formed into an image of his oval face, his perfectly trimmed hair slicked to one side. Then it lunged for the boy holding the rifle. The boy's eyes flashed black as the smoke entered him, and suddenly, he dropped the gun, scooting away from it as if he'd never held a gun in his life.

"What do you think you're doing?" Sarge growled at him. "Pick that up, and let's get this thing buried."

I blinked, and suddenly I was back in the cellar, standing at the center of the strange circle the couple had drawn on the floor. The human companion stood before me, his piercing brown eyes never leaving mine.

I'm Edwin. *The human's thoughts entered my own before everything went dark once more.*

Blinking, my vision returned as I stood there, still backstage. I gasped. I couldn't believe it. Edwin was alive. And if he was still alive in 1919, then that meant he was still alive today. I had to find Choyce.

Running for the back exit, I scanned the sidewalk, stretching the length of the auditorium. The street lamps provided just enough light to spot Choyce's blond hair disappearing around the corner.

"Choyce!" I called racing after him.

I turned the corner in time to find Lee punching him square in the jaw.

"That's for everything you've done," Lee hissed.

"Lee!" I couldn't believe what I'd just witnessed.

"Enjoy life with your murdering new boyfriend." He glared before walking away.

33
ANGELS WILL RISE

- Kain -

"What happened?" I asked, meeting Izzy and Choyce as they entered the cafeteria.

His jaw was swelling around a giant black bruise.

"Lee just became a problem, that's what." Choyce snapped.

"We shouldn't talk here." Izzy nodded towards the back door.

Following them back outside, I closed the door to ensure no one would overhear us. "What's going on? What happened to your face?"

"Ask your sister." Choyce spit bits of blood on the ground.

"Shut up." Izzy rolled her eyes.

"And apparently, my brother is still alive." A sinister laugh escaped him.

"Why is that so hard for you to believe?" Izzy cried. "We both can time travel. Kain absorbs crap and brings people back from the dead. Oh, and thanks so much for ruining my relationship with Lee."

"Ruining your relationship?" He scoffed. "I didn't ruin anything. You did that all on your own."

I raised my hand. "Hold on. Edwin's alive? But *how*?"

"Apparently, he's the very man who shot him, according to your sister." Choyce snarled.

"No, that's who he possessed first." She protested. "Then he became the human we saw with Emma and Abram. His spirit has been possessing other people's bodies to stay alive."

"She's nuts!" Choyce laughed. "Utterly, and completely—"

"Hello, brother." A familiar voice came from behind us.

We turned to face none other than Amadeus just as his hand stretched out towards us, causing the most excruciating pain to burn through our skulls. I grabbed my temples, crying out as I fell to my knees.

"Surprised to see me? I thought you might be." A smile spread across his olive skin, his green eyes glaring down at us.

"How—?" Choyce managed to ask just as another wave of pain tormented us.

"How am I alive?" Amadeus raised a brow. "Well, it's been a long, calculated, and trying journey. Leaving a body after it dies to possess another is... Well, put simply, exhausting."

He's lying! Choyce cried.

"I'm not," Amadeus replied. "As you may already know, since I'm not in my original form, I'm unable to shift on the full moon or speak to you telepathically, but I can use some of my powers. It's what's allowed me to survive."

"What have you been doing all this time?" Tears spilled down Choyce's cheek. "Why didn't you come to me sooner?"

"Come to you?" He laughed, a wicked glint in his eye. "You left me behind! And when the nightwalkers captured me, you didn't even *try* to save me. You stood by and watched them shoot me."

"I *did* try." Choyce shook his head, his shoulders sagging in defeat. "I just wasn't strong enough then, and my entire life, I've tried to be stronger. To find a way back there and save you."

"LIES!" Amadeus flexed his fingers, sending another

346

wave of pain through us all. "You're as good as the scum who shot me, and I wish I didn't even have to see you now, but he won't let me do this without you. After everything, you're still a part of his plan."

His body shook with rage as he tried to gain control over his emotions. Cracking his neck, he eyed us once again. "As for what I've been doing all these years, I've been doing everything I can to ensure I return to my own body. To my full power. You see, I can only move into a living body, but our maker can change that."

"So, what do you need us for?" I asked, the pain subsiding as my body fought against the energy tormenting me.

The full moon flashed before my eyes, and suddenly, my muscles grew to hulking proportions.

He eyed my newly acquired strength curiously. "You're here because our maker needs us to return."

A movement behind him caught my attention as the redheaded Emma emerged, her yellow eyes nearly blinding me. She was followed by Abram, their black wings fluttering behind them in the night's breeze.

"It is our destiny to bring Credan back." He said, simply.

I will return. The dead voice whispered around us, filling our thoughts.

"He is why we have these powers; they belong to him." Amadeus continued. "And he's the only one who can save us."

My heart skipped a beat. Was he crazy? Credan couldn't save us. I was sure the only thing he could do was curse us and force us to murder innocent lives.

"We can't bring him back," I shouted. "He's evil. We can't do this."

"You don't have a choice." Amadeus smiled. "Your heart belongs to him. Why else do you think we can feel each other's heartbeats?"

I opened my mouth to reply but stopped. This couldn't be happening.

"You can't control the monster within you because, from birth, his power has lived inside of you. He controls us all."

I frowned. Amadeus didn't seem one bit bothered by being controlled by some unknown power, but it definitely got to me. I wouldn't be manipulated.

Count me out. I thought. *I won't be a part of this.*

Amadeus shrugged. "You can try to stay out of it, but you won't succeed. He is returning. It's already been foretold."

My vision blurred as I looked into the white eyes of a black-winged shifter facing the Assembly.

Surrounded by a field of roses, it was a dream I knew all too well.

"This is your end, Credan." Principal Chomsky's shrill voice rang out.

Credan chuckled, a brilliant smile spreading across the

kindest face I'd ever seen. "This is not the end."

Blood dripped from his lip, his wings quivering as they lay at odd angles around him. The Assembly stood before him, crouched and ready to attack him yet again.

"Shifters, like I am, will rise." His legs shook as he stood. "Both of the light and dark. And I promise you, we will fight you. We will devour you. And we will triumph over you."

I stumbled back as the vision left me. My heart fell as a realization sunk in. There were many things I didn't understand, but two things had become apparent to me. A war was coming, and we would not be able to stop it.

EPILOGUE

- Lee Walker -

"I'm ready," Lee said, seated in a dark office.

The drapes were pulled shut, the room illuminated by a single lamp placed so far from the desk he could barely see the man seated across from him.

"What's changed?" the man asked.

"Everything," he replied. "I didn't understand before, but now I do. I'm ready to join your army."

"And you're willing to do whatever it takes?"

"I am." Lee nodded.

The man leaned forward, resting his knobby elbows on the desk. Chuck tilted his head to the side, a smug glint in his eye. "Good, because our targets are a few of your friends."

"Let me guess, the Torviks and Choyce?"

"You're quick."

Lee folded his arms. "I wouldn't call them my friends."

Chuck lifted his eyebrows in surprise. "Well, then I guess it won't be any trouble for you to give us all the information you have on them. No second thoughts?"

"None at all."

"The nightwalkers can't afford any hesitation," Chuck said. "These students must be eliminated. Principal Chomsky is going to want three body bags as soon as possible."

"Not a problem." Lee stood, shaking hands with Chuck. "I'm at your service."

Chuck leaned back in his chair, pushing his glasses back up his nose. "Then welcome to the team."

CONTINUE THE SERIES

For more information visit www.TabiSlick.com/books

DISCOVER YOUR POWERS

Are you a Philosopher? Warrior? Patriot?
Or something else entirely?

Discover this and more when you take the quiz to
reveal which of the 7 Keys of the Transitioned World
you wield!

Begin the quiz here:
www.TabiSlick.com/quiz

CONNECT WITH THE AUTHOR

Join my monthly reader's group for a FREE copy of my award-winning novella 'Unforgivables'!

www.TabiSlick.com/subscribe

Follow on Social Media:

www.Facebook.com/TabiSlick

www.Twitter.com/TabiSlick

www.Instagram.com/TabiSlick

If you enjoyed Tompkin's School (A Supernatural Trilogy Book 2), don't forget to leave a review on BookBub, Amazon, and Goodreads!

ABOUT TABI SLICK

TABI SLICK is an award-winning author of paranormal and historical fantasy. Her younger years were spent living in the countryside of Oklahoma until she started her college studies in Puerto Rico. After several years abroad, she finally settled down in the Dallas-Fort Worth area of Texas.

With a background in Linguistics, she's often found either researching or with her nose stuck in a book. She's not only the wife of a systems engineer, and mother to a beautiful German Shepherd and Rhodesian Ridgeback pup, but she's also a blogger and book ninja.

Learn more about Tabi and her books at:
www.TabiSlick.com

ACKNOWLEDGMENTS

I would like to thank my parents for raising me and instilling in me a thirst for literature. I know I didn't make it easy for you at times, but I'm so thankful that you didn't give up on me. I now understand the struggle of persevering and the delight in overcoming obstacles.

Thank you to my older sister, Elesha, for all of your advice throughout this novel and also for inspiring me to write. You were the first to pave this path for me and your writings influenced me to write my own at a young age.

To my husband, Devin, I thank you for your continued support during this writing process. It has been fundamental in making this possible and I hope you enjoyed this adventure as much as I did.

To Gabe, my brother, for all of your hard work you put into researching and brainstorming ideas. I'm so thankful for the time you took out of your own schedule to listen to my shenanigans and for helping me out when I didn't know which way to take the story. This novel wouldn't exist without you.

A thank you also goes out to my ARC team who kindly took the time to read this novel. I appreciate all of your feedback!

Last, but not least, I want to thank you for making my dream possible. For without amazing readers, like yourself, my story would remain unheard.

CPSIA information can be obtained
at www.ICGtesting.com
Printed in the USA
LVHW051944260421
685589LV00004B/140